About the author

Pamela Hansford Johnson was born in 1912. Brought up in Clapham, her novels often portrayed life in postwar London. *The Unspeakable Skipton* is part of a trilogy of novels satirising the literary ego, and these are the books for which she is best known. In 1950 she married the novelist CP Snow. She died in 1981.

Prion Humour Classics

* For copyright reasons these titles are not available in the USA or Canada in the Prion edition.

The Unspeakable Skipton

PAMELA HANSFORD JOHNSON

New introduction by
RUTH RENDELL

This edition published in 2002 by
Prion Books Limited,
Imperial Works,
Perren Street,
London NW5 3ED
www.prionbooks.com

First published in 1959
Copyright © Pamela Hansford Johnson 1959
Introduction © Ruth Rendell 2002

A catalogue record for this book is available from the
British Library

ISBN 1-85375-471 4

Jacket design and illustration by Ian Heath
Printed and bound in Great Britain
by Creative Print & Design, Wales

To

DAN WICKENDEN
Fellow-writer

NOTE

I have always wanted to write a study of an artist's paranoia. This is a state which is, of course, not true of all artists, and very rarely of the greatest: but it is true of a certain number. Anyone familiar with the life of Frederick Rolfe will detect some of my sources: but in Daniel Skipton I have tried to include a good deal more and make a living figure out of what I have learned and can imagine of this special sub-branch of the artistic life.

P.H.J.

INTRODUCTION

by RUTH RENDELL

Novelists like to put writers into their fiction, often as protagonists. After all, their own is very likely the only profession they know anything about, and they will know a lot about it, the technicalities among other things, the role of an agent, the duties and obligations of a publisher, the royalties system. Pamela Hansford Johnson was not a serious offender in this respect – her characters have a diversity of jobs – but in one short novel she created a writer whose absolute rightness for his type has seldom been bettered in any fiction.

She was born in 1912 and brought up in Clapham. Her first novel *This Bed Thy Centre* was published in 1935 and her last *The Bonfire* in 1981, the year of her death. Hansford Johnson is undeservedly almost forgotten today just as, in her lifetime she was undeservedly overshadowed by her husband C. P. Snow, but his 'corridors of power' fiction, political novels mystifyingly compared by some to Anthony Trollope, have gone out of print almost faster than hers. Revival for his work is unlikely while hers is overdue. She possessed the imagination and the ability he lacked to write lyrical but never 'purple' prose, and there is no finer example in her canon than *The Unspeakable Skipton*.

It is a short book, economical and spare, with not a line of description that does not contribute to a portrait of the town in which it is set, nor superfluous word of dialogue. Every character is clear-cut and separate and all but one have recognisable personalities, subtle and strong. Daniel Skipton is a novelist. He lives in Belgium, in an attic in Bruges, and has lived there for many years. The date is sometime in the 1950s. Skipton is poverty-stricken, pompous, appallingly rude to everyone, a master of language, a passionate lover of words and a raging paranoiac. This last is the word we would use for him today, though Johnson uses it only in her prefatory author's note where she admits to basing her anti-hero on Frederick Rolfe. She writes from inside, from Skipton's viewpoint, so that we see him as he sees himself as grossly put upon, a repeatedly injured victim, a genius exploited by his publishers and misused by the parsimonious relative on whose largesse he must rely.

For Skipton is a remittance man, one who is paid to stay away, though this is never explicit. It is with consummate skill that Hansford Johnson reveals to us, while writing always from Skipton's point of view but allowing us to read between the lines, that his cousin 'Flabby Anne' is in fact a kind and generous woman and his publisher William Utterson tolerant and forbearing under a campaign of flagrant insult. Skipton has no friends. His bile, his vindictiveness and his overweening vanity have driven away any there might once have been, and no one is sensitive enough to recognise the vulnerable creature beneath the carapace.

Such a character may often embitter the fiction in

which he appears; he will be too unattractive to interest the reader. This is not true of Skipton. Hansford Johnson is accomplished enough to endow him with traits that endear – his love of beauty, his pathetic and long protracted virginity – his perpetual shame, and shrewd enough to make the other personalities in the novel, if not nastier than he, possessed of inferior mental calibre. Everything Skipton says is pithy or witty or otherwise inspired. His is clearly a towering intellect. But unspeakable he is. His rudeness is breathtaking, much of it directed at the other writer in this novel, Dorothy Merlin. Hansford Johnson must have revelled in this dreadful mother of seven sons for she appears in the two other books in the 'Merlin' trilogy of which *The Unspeakable Skipton* is the first, and it is easy to see why. Yet if there are flaws in this novel Dorothy Merlin must be one of them. She is too Freudian, too much the earth mother. Her poems *Should Seven in the Womb be Made* and *Joyful Matrix*, were over-the-top when *The Unspeakable Skipton* was written and are frankly unbelievable now. She is the novel's weakness. To swallow her we must make a purposeful effort to suspend disbelief, something quite unnecessary in the case of the very nearly as bizarre Querini, waiter, charming con-man, and 'third-rate tenor from the back row at the Scala' or that of Mrs Jones, down-to-earth and forthright daughter of a duke's second son.

The narrative hangs on a series of set-pieces, Querini's recital in the countess's dusty drawing room, meals with Dorothy and her husband Cosmo Hines and their hangers-on, Dorothy's poetry reading. Perhaps the funniest and most memorable of these, and curiously the most moving, is the sex show to which Daniel, for his cut from the proprietor, conducts the Hines party. It is a Flemish rendering of Leda and Swan, grotesque and ludicrous, the god played by a coke-washer, the swan by a boot repairer's assistant; erotic to none but Daniel himself to whom it brings, '...the only joy he knew, the satisfaction of the spirit that was denied to his flesh: a satisfaction so supreme that it almost played puppet-master to his body, bringing it alive, flushing into his veins those jets of joy that more fortunate men possessed as a birthright. It was not so much the excitement of the classic union as the heart-taking beauty of it which moved him. He saw the billowy god sinking down upon the helpless breast of the daughter of Thestius, the wife of Tyndarus, making her one with whiteness as a cloud obliterates into itself the peak of a mountain.'

His pleasure, 'denied him by the injustice of all earthly things' is ruined by Dorothy's scorn and the uncontrollable laughter of one of her friends. All that is left to him, all that is ever left to him, is the meagre monetary reward he has collected prior to the performance. And, as always, he is singularly unlucky in all his efforts to make a bare living. We can guess - if he can't quite - that his insults have exhausted the patience of his benefactress in England, that his novel *The Damask and the Blood* will never be published, that his rudeness to Dorothy has been too much for her husband to stomach and that Querini will eventually be exposed as a charlatan.

We guess too that Skipton's end will not merely be abandonment and poverty but the more serious business of illness and starvation. 'Death was written all over his face like graffiti on a wall...' And it is because of this that in the final pages we forgive him all his rudeness, his snobbery and his pride. He has made us laugh, and across the forty years and more since this book was written, retained the power to shock us in an unshockable age.

One

He knew everything there was to know about Belgium. He even knew Flemish. He knew a small printer in the street behind the Fishmarket who, for next to nothing, had made a die for him with his letter-heading in small script:

> 'Maison Bleue,
> Quai de l'Aube.'

Under this, when he had put the date in his own beautiful italic hand, he began to write.

> 'My dear Willy,
>
> Fellows of my kind are not two-a-penny. I say "fellows" because it is among them, I suppose, that you class me. All writers who do not bring you in a stupefying profit, sufficient to house you in East Grinstead and to enable you to stuff smoked salmon, are "fellows" to you. So I do not merely assume: so I know that it is. For if money talks, my dear Willy, so do your associates: Dickinson, for example, has a tongue like a tap with a withered washer, it never stops dripping. And it drips to some purpose when it repeats to others the things you say about them in your manifold clubs, because it spreads a useful awareness that treachery is your stock-in-trade. So I accept the word "fellow": I am such, as Villon was: but like him am not (I repeat, since I have noticed your inability to take in anything that is said to you until it has been patiently repeated three or four times) two-a-penny.'

At this point he stopped, for he saw that the sun had begun to set, and knowing that in a moment the quay would shine like a square opal in all the marvellous colours known to man, and better yet, with marvellous colours to which no man had yet fitted a name, he went to his attic window and looked out.

The water was dead still, the reflections of houses and trees dropped down in it without a ripple. As he watched, it slowly filled with light; at first with aquamarine, then with topaz and then with thin, tremulous rose. The bells began to ring in their sweet mournfulness, each note rounded as an O. They were playing *Dixie*, an air so foreign to the tongue of the carillon that it took on all the gnomic charm of a language still undeciphered, like Etruscan or Minoan. It was an evening in spring.

The house in which he lived was one of the last of the patrician houses. The basement was now almost below the water line, and access had been given to the storage rooms on the ground floor by a stone step greened over with weed. By craning out across the sill he could see the step-gables, like two staircases of russet brick joined together at the top, falling steeply away into the water. He could just see his own white face with its dark and Christian rim of beard. The noise of the traffic came to him faintly through the bells. This was a peaceful quay, little frequented by trippers or by tourist motor-boats, but the Lange Straat was not two hundred yards away over the wooden bridge and round the corner.

The tune had changed. Geert-gen tot Sint Jans, said the bells to him charmingly, Tot Sint Jans, Tot Sint Jans. He had words of his own for all the wordless tunes. And then the big bell tolling: Jan van Eyck, Jan van Eyck, Jan, Jan, Jan.

A miraculous evening. The sky broke like an egg into full sunset and the water caught fire. He held his breath: an angel could appear in full dress with insignia, he would not be surprised. It was a wretched thing that, on an evening like this, he had to turn away from such majestic sweetness to write to such a swine as Willy.

Still, these things had to be done. As he turned back into the room he noticed that he had ink on his forefinger. He poured a little water into the washbasin (not too much, since Lotte insisted that a jugful must last a whole day because of all those stairs) and scrubbed himself clean, carefully poking beneath the nails. He threw the water out of the window; it broke the reflection of the house, which rocked and crumbled as if it were really tumbling down, then slowly reformed and hung steady. Good. Now he could get to work again. But as he sat down he saw that one of his socks had fallen from the line, and he had to get up to repeg it. He inspected it carefully. Not a bad job; like most of these Flemish mares, Lotte could knit. She had made a fuss about the pattern at first, had laughed like an ape; they weren't socks, she said, they were gloves for a man whose fingers had been cut off at the knuckle bones. He had explained to her patiently that they were the only type to keep the feet in perfect health and cleanliness, that it was disgusting to have the naked toes rubbing together, the sweat rolling between into grey crumbs: but even though she now made the socks herself she always had to laugh when she saw them on the line, she just couldn't help it; they took her (she explained) like that.

He looked about him again. Something wasn't there. Still something he should have done but hadn't. Now then, what? Bed made, supper tray ready to receive whatever it pleased them to bring him, knife and fork crossed – a small symbol, but it must give pleasure to Him, if only pleasure of a minor order. Chamberpot out of sight, slippers side by side. So much for that. On the chair, his book, his pill bottles, all three, in order of height – no tumbler. That was it. No tumbler.

He found one in the cupboard, took from the table drawer a packet of raisins, poured a quarter of them into the glass and just covered them with water. Excellent. Seven o'clock now, twelve hours for soaking. He could go on with his letter.

'Do not think that I am such a fool as to be unaware of your plans. You refuse to take up your option on my book, though my two previous works must have made for you very much more than the royalty pittance received by me would appear to represent. I, too, exiled though I am, have my informants; they tell me how I am regarded in England, to how many persons of superior intelligence I am prophet, preacher and poet. No! I am wise to you. You will not publish my book: but in a year from now you will publish another, under the name of some puppet or frontman, in which all the guts of my book, all the gold, all the gleam, will have been garbled to make a popular success. You will be clever, Willy, you will watch your step, you will set your shyster lawyers to work; you may escape me. But I shall know; and you will not spend an hour waking or sleeping without feeling my hot breath (the hot breath of starvation) on the pig's bristles at the back of your repulsive neck.'

He was not altogether pleased with this paragraph, feeling it lacked polish: but he went on.

'I observe that you have the impertinence to offer me a small loan of money. I will, you calculate, be too proud to refuse it, for like most of the mean-minded it is only money which you associate with pride. But I shall not give you the satisfaction of a refusal. I am fifty years old today, on this feast of St Mark, the Beloved Evangelist with whose lion heart my own, even in this sickly frame, beats like a drum; and if you think that I am going to starve for your benefit, so that you may pirate my work after my death, you are a sillier man even than your pug-dog's eyes and slopping lips would indicate. I will take your money without a pang; my pride has nothing to do with you. I await your cheque, which should be made out to

'Daniel Skipton
Knight of the Most Noble Order of
SS. Cyril and Methodius,
Banque de Flandres, Bruges.'

That was enough: no need for signature. Anyhow it was getting too dark to write without a light, and he was not going to switch it on yet awhile.

He addressed the envelope,

'William Utterson (Publisher),
of Uttersons,
241, Audley Square, London, W1, Angleterre.

'For the eyes of Utterson alone.'

4

Stamps; he had only one, and it was not enough. Still, it would do. Willy could pay the excess, the fat profits of his swindling firm could cope with that. It occurred to him to ask Madame la Botte if she had another, but he decided against it.

As he looked at the envelope in his hand another idea struck him, a bright one, extremely amusing. He scored through the first 'Utterson' and wrote 'Unutterable', scratching that out in its turn, though leaving it easily readable, and then printed the correct name in again above it. It looked, he thought, most striking. He could imagine the clerks laughing when the mail came in.

Two

There was no need for him to go furtively down the dark stairs, since he had paid Madame la Botte something towards her rent only that morning, and she had seemed grateful for the small relief. He went down from his attic, past the old mother and daughter on the third floor, the La Bottes on the second, and the prosperous dentist on the first. There was nothing except the smell to indicate the various income levels through which he passed, since the whole staircase was shabby; but the third floor smelled of dust and biscuits, the second of stewing steak and cheese, and the first of ether and flowers. He went out at the side door into the little square, and over the bridge on to the Quai Vert.

He dropped his letter in the nearest posting box and then sat down on the parapet to roll a cigarette. The morning's breeze had tumbled the pear-blossoms into the canal; some were still floating down like confetti, some, like surf, had piled up along the wall. He heard the man with the megaphone shouting to his boat-load, the roar and chug coming nearer.

Jan van Eyck, the big bells called; gruut Jan, gruut Jan.

The sky was greening over above the roofs, peridot

where the sun had been, apple above that, and then a strip of olive. The lights were beginning to sparkle up all over the quay, only to be doused again as the curtains were drawn, giving privacy to comfortable householders, Docteur Joos, Madame Poupin.

Yes, he thought, this was the place for him and none other: he would die here. He had come to live in Bruges for cheapness at the end of the 1920s: had muddled through and out of the war by means of ill-health and broadcasting in Flemish for the BBC, and had come back not for cheapness, since the country was bloated with money and everything was dear, but because he could not bear to live anywhere else. And, so long as Flabby Anne kept up her payments, he could just about get along. He had the La Bottes (what a name!) in his pocket. He had his monthly reviewing of English books for a local paper. He could always earn a bit by painting a few more *bondieuseries*, and if the worst came to the worst, could start taking tourists around the sights again: or around just one of the sights, the special one. It might not, however, come to that. Flabby Anne had protested only for half a page this time, an improvement on protests covering three or four.

The canal smelt sweet, of rot and of the sea. He strolled along the Dyver, towards the Gruuthuse and into the paddock of Notre Dame, where the swans glimmered in the rustic dusk like washing left out all night; past the Cathedral, over the main road and into a side lane, narrow and high as a canyon, the rooftops clipping the sky into squares. There was a light in Wouvermans' rubbish shop: the old boy opened and shut up when it pleased him. Daniel felt in his pocket and touched the luxury of twenty francs. There might be something to buy. Perhaps he was to have the pleasure of buying.

Over the shop was a hanging board, announcing in gothic letters and something like the English language, 'Mine Olde Antiques of Flanders'. Wouvermans was inside, in the heat and smell of the oil lamp, squatting like an

6

octopus on the kind of stuff an octopus might regard as treasure. As Daniel came in he raised his loose-cheeked, pear-shaped face and pushed his gold-rimmed glasses on to his brow.

'Goeden avond, meneer! A rare visitor these days. How goes it?'

'What have you got?'

'Got?'

'I want to buy something.'

Wouvermans exploded into false enthusiasm, clapping his hands. 'Ah, that means meneer has cash! He has a little windfall, splendid. Because I don't give credit, as he knows.'

'I have cash, you old squid, so shut up and be grateful for a customer. You can't have many. How do you keep going? What do you really do for a living? That's what I want to know.'

The old man grinned. 'But I do what you see me do. I am a shopkeeper.'

He watched as Daniel routed around, poking into grimy corners, lifting rags and peering underneath, picking up bits and pieces, sniffing at them, replacing them.

'I have a little treasure; I would show it to no one but you. Not that you can buy it: but you might have a rich friend. It is a picture.'

'I don't want a picture.'

'A little Wouters.'

'Rik? You can keep it.'

'Not Rik. Johannes. Lovely as a song. Very dirty.'

'So are you. Bosh.'

'You don't want to see it, meneer?'

'No. This is what I want.'

Daniel came up from a pile of old clothing, clotted like the web of some mythological spider in the corner by the window, with a white dress tie, surprisingly clean, torn a little where it passed round the back of the neck. 'How much?'

'You sell the Wouters for me, you get that free. On the house.'

'I get it now. How much?'

'Twenty francs.'

'Bosh,' Daniel said again. They haggled. After a very long time, he got it for six.

'So you are going to a ball,' said the old man, 'you are out again with the Quality. Ah well, that's where you should be.'

Daniel walked out of the shop. He came back again.

'All right, let's look at the picture.'

It was a wood panel, split right down. Under the grime was a half-length of a woman weighing or counting gold coins at a table.

'Faked by an ass,' said Daniel, 'the original's in England. Belongs to Lee of Fareham, or did when I last heard of it. Pick on someone your own size, Wouvermans, someone very small.'

'Ah, but perhaps his is the fake!'

'No, it isn't. This is trash. And don't say "Ah" to me.'

He was at the door and half out of it when the old man said, 'Mimi is starting up again. Thought you might like to know.'

'I do,' said Daniel, and in his lordliest manner tossed him a five-franc piece.

'Better than nothing,' said Wouvermans. 'I'll tell Mimi.'

Daniel went back to his attic, just in time for supper. He was always punctual, for it was planked down on his table whether he were out or not, and if he was not in it got cold. Even Lotte refused to climb those stairs more than once.

She reached up over his shoulder with a plate of stewed steak and prunes. '*Als t'u blieft.*'

He squeezed her thick waist, not because he liked doing so, but because she needed the encouragement. She went into her usual jelly-dance of silent laughter, pushed at his head, flapped her apron up and down. He eyed her as he ate; she was the purest Fleming, the stuff of Teniers, a golden pig-girl, with her whole being concentrated about her healthy stomach.

He told her the food was good. 'Well,' she said, 'you give

8

Mamma little bits, steady, and it will go on being good. She don't want much, she's not greedy, it's just the idea of the rent, see?'

'I'll try to give her an idea of it. Go on, buzz off.'

It was a beautiful evening; it had turned warmer. All the stars were out in their full brilliance, shining without a single tremor between the lot of them. He washed up his plate and put it outside in the passage, to carry down later. Then he washed himself with his repetitive care, took out a clean sheet of paper, a bottle of brown ink and a fine brush. He sat down to work. Pinning the white tie over the paper with drawing pins, he painted little stars all over it, at quarter-inch intervals. That was better: now it didn't look like a dress tie, but the smartest thing in bow-ties for daytime wear. While it dried he washed himself again, shaved the bare parts of his cheeks, combed his hair back in its two thin sweeps, back from his temples and over his ears. He had to cut it himself, but with practice had learned to do so by no means badly. Anyway, he wore it rather long, smoothed down to a straight-cut line across the nape of the neck. He put the tie on, and made a careful bow. Now that had been an inspiration: the effect was just a little, but not too, bizarre. It was the tie of a rich man who did not care a damn for anyone's taste but his own, an aesthete's tie, but not a poor aesthete's. An American might wear it, or an English homosexual: but neither of them poor. It was perhaps the tie of a picture-buyer, or a dealer in rare books. He changed his socks for the clean ones, carefully pushing each separate toe into each separate little socket. Now he was ready, with nine francs left in his pocket, brisk, debonair, ready for an evening out.

Three

There was a band concert in the Grand' Place, and the cafés were nearly full. The belfry leaned its octagonal crown, floodlit, against the sky: one looked up and turned giddy. The visiting musicians were just rising to the high point of *Maritana* when Daniel crossed the square: the rigged-up lights sparkled on their brass and their braided caps. He found a free seat on the terrace of the café directly facing the Cloth Hall and ordered a coffee. He would have liked a beer but had not enough money for it.

Daniel was not one to peer round and about him. He sat proudly aloof, his profile raised, his mouth sternly set. He could see who was behind him in the pocket mirror concealed in his cupped hands.

Just behind him was a party of four people, English, one woman and three men. The woman was short and meagre, perhaps at the beginning of her forties. She was dark-skinned, and the hair wrenched back from her box-like forehead into a bun had a surface fuzz which the violence used upon it had been unable to repress. Her eyes were prominent, her nose was small and hooked. She looked like some distraught bird chained by one claw to a perch. She was obviously the dominating member of the group, not just because of her difference, that is, she was a woman, but because there was domination in her personality.

On her left was a very tall, fattish man, a little younger, who wore, despite the warmth of the evening, a pale grey duffle coat. He had a round porcine head, not unlike that of the Stratford Bust, with hair of a dark and lubricated chestnut, bright, jocund eyes, and a button nose. He seemed to Daniel like a person of many pleasures, seeking to enjoy, seeking to bathe in his blisses, who might be bad-tempered when blisses failed to materialise. Next to him was a slender man, fairish, with sharp features, who could have been any age between thirty-eight and fifty. He was conspicuously well-dressed. Unlike his fat friend, he looked not made for pleasure, but for disillusionments of an amusing nature. He had an air not of dominance, but of quiet authority: he looked as if he might have been a success in the world, as if, on the side, and not the side he was now showing to his friends, he might slip off for weekends at great houses.

The fourth member of the party, seated on the woman's right, was small, not much taller than Daniel, and was a good deal older than the other three; he might have been in his middle-sixties, despite his trim, straight, tight-buttoned look and his lineless cheeks. His hair was fair to white, very thick, and boyishly parted. He had rather bloodshot eyes of that pure Cambridge blue associated by Daniel with people who were a little mad, and he was looking from one to the other of the group like a kind father who likes to see the children happy.

The woman looked familiar: Daniel had seen that face before, in a newspaper photograph. He thought and thought. His visual memory was good, he could usually remember the minor detail of any painting which had interested him, even if he had seen it only once. All right. He knew who she was. She was Dorothy Merlin, Australian-born playwright, whose verse-dramas had given her a vogue in esoteric circles in London and were inevitably produced in reading editions with long, admiring prefaces by herself. He had not read any, since he never read English books at all except those sent to him for review, but he had gathered with repulsion that her plays were all about motherhood on some spiritual plane where the carnal and the mystical came clammily together. She was chattering on about what they should all do tomorrow. First of all, they must go to the Musée Communale to see Van Eyck's *Adoration of the Lamb* which was, she said, a tower among the six towers of art. It was the ultimate, it made one ache. Then she said, on a high falling whine, muted, but not muted enough, 'Why is that man like a carrion crow?'

If he had not had her in view in his mirror, he might have thought the reference was to somebody else; but she was looking straight at him. His spirits kindled. This was an introduction as good as another.

So he rose, and turning towards her, gave her his deep, courteous bow, allowing his gaze to rest as in veneration

11

upon her startled face. He bowed to the three men, then again to her.

'Madam,' he said, 'the difference between Cardinal Pietro Bembo, humanist and poet, friend of Lucrezia Borgia, and a carrion crow is simply one of the volume and distribution of extra flesh. I like to fancy that if I were a little fatter and had a few more inches, I should be more like him than I am like the bird. But I acknowledge the justice of the simile, and would be amply repaid for suffering it were I allowed to pay my formal respects to a great woman dramatist.'

All had their mouths open, except the man in the expensive suit, who was smiling in a kind of sad delight.

'Oh, I say,' wailed Dorothy Merlin, 'I honestly wasn't talking about you!'

He brushed this aside. 'It's of no consequence.'

'You can't be Mr Toots,' said the Stratford Bust, 'you really can't be.'

Daniel did not recognise this reference. 'My name is not Toots. My name is Daniel Skipton, Englishman, resident in Bruges. And, Miss Merlin, you will have to go to Ghent for the Van Eyck. You may be confusing it with the Floreins altarpiece of Memling, which is in the Memling Museum here, or with Van Eyck's Van der Paele Madonna. I will not offer to escort you, as I myself detest escorts: but if I can be of assistance to you at any time during your visit, here is my card. I should add that I am not a professional escort. So many people are.'

They passed it silently round from hand to hand.

> 'Daniel Skipton,
> Knight of the Most Noble Order of
> SS. Cyril and Methodius,
> Maison Bleue,
> Quai de l'Aube.'

The expensive man looked at the white tie with the hand-painted stars upon it.

Then Miss Merlin came to life, and the others with her.

'Oh, I say, do sit down, you'll think we're awfully rude.'

'Forgive me, but I don't think—'

'Please do.' She said shrilly, 'Cosmo, bring his chair here. We can all move up.'

Daniel waited, shrugging slightly, while this was done. 'My husband,' she said, patting the elderly man impatiently on the arm as if to bring him out of an amnesia, 'Cosmo Hines.'

She indicated the Stratford Bust with a broad wave of her hand, just catching his nose in the sweep. 'Duncan Moss.' (Daniel knew about him; he was a smart photographer.)

She smiled rather specially upon the expensive man. 'And Matthew Pryar. Not the poet, spelled differently: P-R-Y-A-R.'

'How extraordinarily pleasant to live here,' Pryar said. 'I do envy you.'

Daniel congratulated himself: he was right about the great houses. He had seen references to this one in the social columns of English newspapers.

'I am enviable,' he replied simply, 'in that way at least. Not in many others but, yes, in that.' He sat, reaching round to pull in his cooling coffee.

'Oh, but what are you drinking?' Miss Merlin cried, 'not that you can drink much here, it's practically dry, isn't it? We're drinking horrible Export. Let me buy you a horrible Export.'

At first he would accept nothing, but finally allowed himself to be persuaded into accepting a *gueuse*.

'I told you you were wrong about that Van Eyck,' Miss Merlin said fretfully to her husband, 'but you will pretend to know things. Why do you pretend you know things, when you know you don't?'

'*Hommages littéraires*,' Daniel said to her, raising his glass. He knew that Pryar was appraising him closely, his darned raggedness, the patina of green-bronze that had

13

settled upon his black suit. He could only hope, at this point, to be taken for a rich eccentric.

'Hell, Dotty,' said Moss, beaming, 'we can all go to Ghent. I want to see the Gravensteen, they have instruments of torture there. I have never quite grown out of them, though not to the extent of reading books on the subject.'

'Now I know something about you,' said Cosmo Hines, in a smiling, lazy fashion. He tipped back his chair, put his finger-tips together. 'And my wife might well return the compliment you have paid her.'

Daniel's heart lost a beat. Someone was going to recognise him at last, and for what he was: he had found an admirer. 'Oh, you mean–'

'A book. A most remarkable book. Published in 1946, in July, a deadish season, I know because I am a bookseller in a small way–'

The others made affectionate, jeering noises, to indicate that the way was not a small one.

'–and it was my grief that I could not make all my customers buy it. I tried, God knows I tried. It was called – now, don't tell me–'

Daniel had made no attempt to tell him.

'*The Damask and the Blood.*'

Daniel bowed his head. The others looked blank.

'A very odd book, if I may say so,' Cosmo continued, 'very remarkable. About Louis XV and the unfortunate Ravaillac. Most tactful treatment of the distressing conclusion. Ravaillac was a sort of saint in your view, I fancy—'

'Henry IV, not Louis XV, Cosmo,' said Pryar, 'quite a lot of years out.

— it was the mention of torture that put it into my mind,' Hines went on, untroubled. 'A queer choice for the Novel Society, I always thought, but much to their credit. Yes, an idiot saint. Always a happy conception, it cheers up the stupid, they feel there may be some point to their stupidity, after all.'

14

'Don't talk for effect, Cosmo,' said his wife, because she wanted to talk herself. 'Mr Skipton,' she said oratorically, 'I have not read your book because my reading nowadays is narrow. I read only theology and poetry. But I shall read it, I intend to, and I will.'

'I am a Roman,' said Daniel, 'and I know that your theology is not mine.' From what he had heard, it was nobody else's, either. 'All the same, I fancy you will find more of interest in my book than might a person who was unacquainted with the language of disputation.'

She bowed.

They bowed to each other.

This, he thought, is going very well.

He changed the subject, as if modesty impelled him, and began to talk about England. He had been away so long that his old ties were broken; he was now the true expatriate, trailing so many broken strings that he felt like Gulliver. Did they happen to know... He mentioned dead names. But, of course, Lady Ottoline was dead; so was Lady Auriol Mulcahy, with whom he had stayed so often in that extraordinary house in Donegal. And so was Howell Simpson, that best of friends, so childlike, so sweet, so untouched by his riches. He could not believe Howelly was dead, his spinning-wheel silent.

He saw Pryar brighten up at this. Pryar, it seemed, had known them all, though it was only as a schoolboy that he had been taken to Howelly's.

'I was no more than a child myself,' said Daniel sombrely. 'The years have dealt poorly with me; but I am only fifty now.' He asked whether they knew Lady Betty Hedingham, adding that, since it was all so long ago, she might not even remember him. (She would not; he had never met her. But he did not expect to see this crowd again after its holiday was over.)

'Dear old Betty!' Duncan Moss shone all over, smiles coming out not only from his eyes but from the pores of his skin, as if he had a hundred-watt bulb in his head. 'Dorothy, do you remember that photograph I took of her as a cactus, up to her neck in sand, all among a lot of other cactuses?'

'Scratchy old bitch,' said Dorothy, 'served her right.'

'No! I love Betty. I think she's an old sweety.'

'You will find, Mr Skipton,' she said, 'that I don't pose. I dislike few people, but when I dislike them, I make no pretence of doing otherwise. Lady Betty turns my stomach to cheese.'

He flinched at this disagreeable image and at Miss Merlin, but he merely inclined his head. He asked them how long they would be in Bruges, and learned that it was to be a week or ten days. They were using it as a centre. They might even stay over for the Procession of the Holy Blood.

'Why do people say it smells when they know it doesn't?' Dorothy Merlin demanded. 'It smells no worse than Chelsea Embankment, not as bad.'

'Would it be impertinent,' Pryar asked, 'if I enquired what is the Order of Saints Cyril and Methodius?'

Daniel put on a show of reluctance, before he launched upon his story. His father had been a minor official at the British Legation in Bulgaria prior to the First World War. Through a series of accidents, he had found himself in frequent contact with King Ferdinand, who had made a personal friend of him, and on one occasion had requested him to bring his wife and his small boy, at that time only two years of age, to the palace. The King had been so amused and delighted by the precocious child, who could already recite the days of the week and numbers up to ten in the Bulgarian language, that half in jest and half in earnest he had insisted upon conferring upon him, then and there, a Knighthood in the new Order only that year created.

'A trifle absurd,' Daniel said, 'or so I think. But if I did not use it – I would really prefer not to – I should be discourteous to the memory of His Majesty, a gentleman who showed infinite kindness to my poor father until the end.'

'Oh, I say,' cried Miss Merlin, 'that is prodigiously

16

romantic! One can hardly believe it.'

Daniel, never sure whether or not to believe it himself, since parts of it were true, was flicked on the raw.

'Forgive me,' he said, 'I have bored you.'

'I didn't say I didn't believe it!' Her voice rose to a sad yelp.

'Oh shut up, Dotty,' said Moss, 'you're such a tactless old silly. My dear Mr Skipton, this is a most attractive story. Thank you so much for telling us.'

Daniel smiled and bowed deeply.

He would not let them buy him another *gueuse*, he would not let them detain him, though by this time they were obviously quite eager to do so. He knew where to find them again all right, when he wanted them. There was no hurry. *Festina lente*, he said to himself.

He walked slowly across the square, feeling their eyes, like four pairs of prongs, upon his retreating form. The concert came to an end; he stood erect for the Brabançonne. Then he strolled back home, full of contentment, past the Hôtel de Ville, where the little stone kings glittered like Tenniel chessmen in the moonlight, down Stonecutters' Quay and along the Quai Vert. The floating pear-blossom was a galactic stream on the dark waters. The air was heavy with the smell of the limes, the smell of dew. At such times as these Daniel felt pure, a simple, good man whom misfortune had not soured. New prospects were opening out before him, doubtless as God's reward for his patience and gentleness.

And it was something to know about Mimi's, to know that the old cow was still in business. It might come in useful.

Four

Daniel had the knack, when entering Notre Dame for confession, of expunging from his mind all thought save the thought of God: and that expunging included all thoughts of what he had just been doing and what he was going to do next. The only sin he ever had to confess was the sin of Pride: and he laid it on thick. It seemed to him so grievous a sin, and so hard to overcome, that the more frequently he confessed it the better. He found it difficult to understand why Father Vinckeboons never made more of a fuss than he did.

It was Sunday morning and all the bells were rocking the bright sky about, boxing its ears with their glorious hands. The air smelled of apples. It was too early for many tourists to be about, though a few artists had set up easels in the usual hopeless attempt to make the quays look even prettier than they were, when the only hope was to make them look less. He despised them and the tripe they produced, but nevertheless liked to see them there. They were as much a part of his city as the cobbles under foot.

Then he saw, coming towards him along the Dyver, an extraordinary figure in a grey duffle coat, bouncing a child's yellow beach ball and staggering with every smack he gave it. Daniel stopped short. The figure came on. It hit the ball so hard that it bounced out of reach and trundled into the canal, where it started off briskly with the current and the breeze. The figure gave a shout, tore off its duffle coat, and flinging it on to a stone bench, swayed to the water's edge, arms flung up as if for a spectacular plunge.

'You cannot do that,' said Daniel, not laying a hand on him, since he hated to touch people, but speaking in his harshest and most penetrating rasp.

'I can swim,' said Duncan, dropping his arms and looking wounded.

'There would be no need to swim. The water is not deep and you would stand up in it to your waist. But it is full of mud.'

'Look, Mr Skipton, I must get my ball! A girl gave it to me, a lovely girl. Ahoy! Boatman!'

'There are no boatmen at this hour.'

18

Duncan's eyes opened wide, as if he had just awakened from the sleep of a hundred years behind briar-roses. He forgot about his ball. 'Why, how jolly to see you again! You must come and have breakfast with me. You see, I am not entirely sober, and breakfast is what I must have.'

'Forgive me,' said Daniel, 'I do not accept hospitality. I am too poor to repay it.'

'Oh God, that's silly! I'm not poor, so we don't have to worry. I mean, Mr Skipton, I don't want repaying, it wouldn't mean anything. I say, you mustn't be an old silly, Mr Skipton, you really mustn't.'

Duncan entwined his arm through Daniel's and shone down at him. 'Better soon,' he said, with a little lurch.

As they went towards the Grand' Place he explained himself. Dorothy and Cosmo had been flat out. They'd wanted to go back early to the hotel, but he and Matthew had still been full of life. They'd found out where they could get spirits: in a café somewhere, a long way off, not far from the railway station, in a downstairs room. You put your finger to the lobe of your left ear when you said '*gueuse*,' and you got not beer but whisky, about four doubles in the same glass. After a bit a girl had come and sung a song with a ball, it was a bubble song. She had given the ball to Duncan, he could not remember why, but she was a lovely girl, a generous one. Then Matthew had gone home, or he supposed he must have gone home: and Duncan had gone home later. He had woken at seven, feeling the worse for wear, so had taken a little whisky from his own bottle which he had bought on the boat. It had made him drunk again but most, most happy.

He swung Daniel to and fro, all over the pavement, till they came to the Cranenburg, where they ordered coffee and rolls. ' "A poet could not be but gay",' said Duncan, ' "in such a something company." Pity Dorothy isn't here, though, she is such a sweety.' He drained his coffee, steaming as it was, at a gulp. 'I remember she did go on a bender once, it was the year of should seven.'

19

'I beg your pardon?'

'Should seven. *You* know!'

'I'm sorry, I don't take your meaning.'

Duncan put down his cup. 'Look here, didn't you say you were mad keen on Dorothy's plays? I must say, I'm beginning to wonder. I mean, not knowing that, it's like not knowing *Sweeny Agonistes*.' His eyes beaded with a drunkard's suspicion, and lost a shade of colour.

'Ah!' Daniel exclaimed, his thoughts running round like mice on a treadmill. ' "Should seven…" I take you. I am afraid I suffer a little from deafness. Last year, I had an eruption of an abscess in the middle ear, it has left me somewhat maimed, for deafness is a maiming not only of the body but of the spirit.'

' "Should seven in the womb be made…" ' Duncan repeated gently. 'What a prologue, and to *what* a play! Marvellous. You know, she wrote it to commemorate their seventh, William, wasn't it, or was it Albert? I can't keep up with all the names. Queer, calling a child Albert in this day and age. But she's madly original, the duck. Whatever you expect, Dorothy won't do it.'

' "Should seven in the womb be made…" Yes,' said Daniel. 'At first I thought you said something quite different.

'There are other places where you can drink spirits,' he went on, thinking it as well to change the subject. 'Living here, one knows these things. But they are of small interest to me. I drink very little myself.'

This apparently failed to snag Duncan's attention. He said in sudden excitement, 'I say, you do know – or perhaps you don't, as you've been out of England – you do know Tony Purkess-Nidge produced Dotty's play just as Barrault did that Claudel thing, with actors muting on the stage, and a cinema screen behind? Dotty appeared on the screen herself, about a mile high, and recited Should Seven. I was there. I shall never forget it.' A critical shadow fell across a face essentially uncritical, acceptant. 'But mind you, it wasn't wholly successful. The verse was too austere in itself. Tony's chichi bitched it a bit. Or so I thought. They did the music by itself later, at the Wigmore Hall, but it didn't jell, it couldn't, without Dotty.'

At the next table was a young man, perhaps not so young, who looked like an Italian. He wore beautiful clothes. He had large fringed eyes, like windows reflecting brown velvet, and a long sad nose. There was a touch of Latin foxiness in the narrowness of temple and jaw. He looked, Daniel thought, like one of these travelling princes who married film stars and took them to work pig-farms on the Roman Campagna. He had a gold watch-bracelet an inch wide. Daniel would have liked to know him.

'I have little appreciation of modern stage-craft,' he said harshly.

Duncan's mind had wandered back to something said earlier. 'I expect there are some queer places here, though it is full of black beetles. Excuse me, I forgot you were Catholic.'

Daniel bowed.

'Even a town like this must have its knocking shops.'

Daniel allowed distaste to appear on his features. He drew in his nostrils. 'I believe so,' he said stiffly.

The Italian seemed about to speak. Then he consulted his watch, paid his bill and left, passing across the square with a long delicate step, one hand in his pocket, the other, long and white, dangling as if the nerves had been cut.

'I'm a crude fellow,' Duncan said remorsefully, 'I know I'm crude. But old Cosmo said your book was pretty warm.'

Daniel rose up. 'You will excuse me.'

'Look here, there's nothing wrong with being a bit warm! Nobody wants a book to be a bit cold, that is, nobody but Dotty.'

Daniel said, 'I accept your apology. And you will accept my assurance that I am too busy to stay with you any longer. If I can be of service to you and your friends you know where to find me. I could show them the more squalid side

21

of this city if I chose, but I hope they will not ask me. And that you will not. Because, if you did, I should have no option but to bid you good day.'

On his way home he saw the yellow ball lodged beneath a bridge. He called to a passing boatman and had it fished out. Later that day he delivered it, with his card, to Duncan's hotel, and did not stay for acknowledgement.

He received, as he had expected, a written invitation to dine, delivered by a page from the Memling Palace; but he refused it. There was plenty of time. And he had work to do.

Having had his lunch and rinsed out a pair of socks (he had only two pairs and kept one always in the wash) he took his manuscript from the table drawer, ranged before him his three pens, one with black ink, one with green and one with red, and sat down to the hypnotic delight of polishing. The first draft of this book had been completed a year ago. Since then he had worked upon it every day, using the black pen for the correction of simple verbal or grammatical slips, the green pen for the burnishing style, the red for marginal comment and suggestions for additional matter. He knew well enough that the cur Utterson would like to get his hands on it. It was not only a great book, it was the greatest novel in the English language, it would make his reputation all over the world and keep him in comfort, more than comfort, for the rest of his life. It would cause a rustle in the dovecotes, for in it he had pilloried, as Odysseus pilloried the wicked maid-servants on a line, like so many strangling birds, every one who had ever insulted or injured him. Cur Utterson was there: he wouldn't like it much, but he would put up with it, so long as he made enough money out of it. He would grin and bear it, pretend he was pleased to act as a model to so great an artist. But Utterson would have to wait. He was not going to get this manuscript until it was perfect, until every gem, from the greatest to the least, was gripped in every golden claw.

To work on this book was perhaps the greatest pleasure Daniel had ever known. When he did so he was not a man

22

but a god, improving not only upon a beautiful earthly creation, but upon a creation already divine. He wondered whether Utterson could not be persuaded to produce a first edition in colour-facsimile of the original manuscript, for it was like a marvel of jewellery itself, with its delicate glories of ruby, emerald and jet. It would cost him a pretty penny: but he would certainly get it all back through the cheaper editions.

Daniel polished for fifteen minutes only at a time, for the closeness of the work tired his eyes. After each spell he got up and leaned out of the window, resting his head against the painted frame, faded now to the greenish Nattier-blue which had given the house its name. Admiring breezes fell softly on his face, knowing him, paying him tribute. The sweet bells rang, the little ones. Geert-gen tot Sint Jans. Tot Sint Jans.

Turning back, blessed, he sat down to make a happy sentence even happier.

'Men like Billy Butterman are rarely recognised as parasites, since parasitism is associated with the minuscule; but if triple-visaged Dis gnawing the bloody heads in the bottom of hell were to have a louse in his armpit, that louse would be Butterman, sucking as much nourishment from Dis, in proportion to his size, as Dis from the arteries of Judas, Cassius and Brutus, for ever burrowing, for ever gorged, for ever content.'

He was fulfilled. All was going well. The day after tomorrow he should receive Utterson's cheque. He had a good dinner in store with his new acquaintances when he cared to stretch out his hand for it. He would almost certainly be able to take Duncan Moss to Mimi's, if he went about it slowly. That would be about nine-fifty francs in Mimi's pocket, fifty in Wouvermans', two hundred and fifty in his own. What about the others? Hines looked the sort who might be attracted. Pryar? Doubtful. Miss Merlin? Highly improbable. Though it was curious what the most strait-laced of women would tolerate if they thought they were going to be left out.

But apart from any of these things he was joyful, knowing genius in himself, burning tall and steady as a candle flame on a windless night.

Five

Next day the weather broke. Tantrums of rain burst across the Grand' Place, wild winds, stiffened by the sea, scolded the café blinds and slapped the skirts of the women over their legs. Priests, their cassocks turned into sails, found themselves blown into flight as they rounded the corners; and with the wind the gulls came inland, wet and screaming, to plop upon the roofs and bridges. The blossom was dashed from the trees.

Daniel ventured out as far as the Memling Museum to see if any of his acquaintances were about; but he saw nobody. The weather was as bad next day and his spirit, already maddened by it and by the coldness of his room, was driven to icy frenzy by a long letter from Utterson. When he read it, he knew that reality was upon him. And to Daniel, reality meant a cold, pure, steady insight into the swinishness of all mankind, and in particular of that portion of it in any relation whatsoever to himself. He had been living too long in the springtime dream. Now he was back again, eye to eye, breast to breast, with truth.

'My dear Dan,
'You will not, of course, admit that I am the most patient of men, but you damned well ought to. I have stood a great deal from you without complaint, but after your last ridiculous and offensive letter I am going to dig my toes in. I might have put up even with that, if it had not been for the fancy envelope in which you chose to send it. I am not going to have the juniors demoralised, as they were this morning, especially Miss Smith, who laughed until she began to scare herself and then treated me to a flood of hysterical tears.'

Daniel grinned, something like warmth touching his finger tips and his separated toes.

'But listen to me, now. I will implement my promise to send you twenty-five pounds, but not until you write to me in a proper civil strain. So don't watch the posts, Dan, there will be nothing in them for you. And your letter, by the by, was certainly actionable, so consider yourself lucky that all you get is a sharp rejoinder.'

Daniel smiled bitterly; he often smiled so, in order to repress a fury in which no smiling would be possible. If Utterson thought he could take that damned school-mistressy tone he was mistaken; and he would not receive any letter on terms more to his liking than the terms of the previous one.

'I feel that I must, however, in my own interests, make one or two things clear, even if the clarification upsets you. Let me enumerate them.. I am not taking up the option on your third book, because it is rotten. I am rejecting it both for my protection and for your own.'

At this point Daniel crushed the letter into a ball and hurled it in the direction of the chamberpot. He left it there for a few minutes, safe and bright, till he felt steady enough to retrieve it. He flattened it out again and read on:

'Two. You have received every penny of the royalties due to you, plus three substantial advances for books you have proposed in detail but have never written and which, I suggest, you never had the least intention of writing. *Blood and Damask*–'

He would get it wrong, the clown, thought Daniel, grinding his teeth.

'– earned the very minimum that could be expected, after the initial impetus of a Novel Society Choice. As I informed you at the time, it was a compromise choice, made in a dead season and in a moment of corporate weakness. Two of the members had influenza at the time. It earned you £1,157 17s 4d. Your next novel, *The Triple*

25

Tiara, earned you £396 11*s* 6*d*; since we paid you an advance of £500, this leaves a balance unearned of £103 8*s* 6*d*.

'The novel I am returning to you by registered post, at absurd expense (mine not yours), would not earn you four-pence halfpenny. It is thoroughly bad, both structurally and morally.

'What I want to see is that manuscript of which you write to me in such enticing terms. If it is one per cent as good as you intimate, I shall be glad to publish it. If not, not. So stop making a fool of yourself and pitch it along. 'Sorry to sound so cross–'

Ah, God, cross! Daniel shrieked within himself, and back the letter went across the room.

It was half an hour before he could bring himself to read the rest.

'–but you really are a trying chap.

'All well here. Had some hunting this season. Valerie sends her regards. As you know, she has always had a weak spot for you. So come off your high horse, and mend your manners, and send me something remotely publishable.

'As ever,

'W H UTTERSON.'

In the left hand corner was typed: 'WHU/CRB'.

The beast has had the hide, Daniel said to himself, to dictate that to a secretary; and it occurred to him that all persons who had secretaries were swine also. Probably, he thought, as he paced up and down, tearing the letter into smaller and smaller pieces as he went, that fat pig Moss, boasting about his money, had a secretary: Hines would have a secretary: Pryar – and here he swallowed bile – might have a social secretary to keep him abreast of his engagements at Holkham, Chatsworth, Blenheim and all the other gilded hell-holes where Privilege lapped its port, gorged its caviare and made a pretence of needing a half-a-crown a head on visiting days.

Rage tore at him like the fox in the cloak and he adored its fangs. A man without rage was no more than a jelly-baby, an artist a mere nothing. The rain banged on the windows as if asking to be let in. Sheets of it struck lightning from the water in the quay.

He looked at the tin clock standing on the mantelpiece before the picture of Pietro Bembo, which he had torn out of Madame Voerst-Verboeckhoeven's Burckhardt, when she wasn't looking. He would enjoy his rage for ten minutes more and then he would have to sit down and write to Flabby Anne. After that he must subdue his contempt for Dorothy Merlin and her circle, and consider how to get as many of them as possible round to Mimi's. He allowed fury to achieve its inevitable physical expression, which was at once a terror and a release.

Heat gave way to cold. The shudder started somewhere at the crown of his head, as if a finger had been placed there. It then divided into two streams, each one running down to his fingertips by way of his jaw, his collar-bone and his arm. From the same source a third stream sprang, trickling gloriously down his spine to his coccyx. Now he was shivering all over uncontrollably, like a foundation member of the Society of Friends.

Ten minutes up. Daniel stopped shaking and combed his hair. He wrote to Flabby Anne in a controlled and reasonable tone with an undercurrent of stringency, pointing out to her that though he was not unappreciative of her assistance in the past, he was becoming increasingly aware that it was of importance to them both for her to do considerably better. He would not emphasize the aspect of kinship, since he had never felt himself bound by its ties; but as his first cousin once removed, she might well feel that his artistic reputation reflected lustre upon herself. He was aware that the narrowness of her upbringing and her life of rusticity made it difficult for her to bring to his work that appreciation on all levels necessary to full understanding; he could assure her, nevertheless, that by the connoisseur he was regarded with a reverence upon which modesty forbade him to dilate.

'But,' he wrote, 'I am poor: as the pioneer in art is inevitably poor. I live as you would not choose, being my kinswoman, to see me; and in a manner the hundred pounds a year which you are so kind as to allow me does little to alleviate. Sometimes I am even hungry. You, with your broad acres, your watermeadows, your pleached walks, do not know what hunger is. There are, of course, *rentiers* who, even if they did know what hunger was, would not give up a penny of their rents to alleviate the hunger of others. I honour you, however, by my conviction that you are not of this kind, and that though your imagination is of no high order, you would respond instantly to the visual evidence of want.

'I have given much thought to our relative positions. I have a head for business: you may rely absolutely upon my calculations. It is obvious to me that you could increase your payments to myself by another fifty pounds per annum without noticing the difference by so much as a peach missing from your plate or a gewgaw from your wardrobe.'

He addressed this, and a good deal more, since Flabby Anne was thick in the head and took a lot of convincing, to:

'Miss Anne Wrigley,
The Mill House,
Steeple St Paul's,
Nr Colchester, Essex.'

He would post it without a stamp, to give her some idea of the genuineness of his poverty. He thought she could hardly fail to take the point.

When he had finished he was astonished to find himself in strong, cold sunshine. The rain had ceased, though the battering winds still knocked the water and the trees about.

An augury, he thought; he smiled and genuflected.

He put on the overcoat Madame la Botte had given him last winter (it was her late husband's and hung nearly to Daniel's heels) and pushed his way against the gale in the direction of Wouvermans' shop.

He found it shut, with no light in it, so he gave the door a good kick. If the old man were taking a nap upstairs, he could bloody well come down again. As there was no response he kicked it again, but this time too hard so that he stubbed his toe and had to hop around like Rumpelstiltzkin until it stopped hurting. He swore at some children who laughed at him, even chased them a little way, then returned to wait in the doorway, huddling himself out of the draught.

Luckily he did not have to wait long, for in another five minutes Wouvermans turned the corner in a gust of sallow sunshine and trotted up to Daniel, rubbing his hands together. All he wants, Daniel thought, is a ruff and a pearl on his forehead, and you could frame him. Only he smells.

'Well, well meneer! Come to buy something else? My word, if my patrons were all as faithful–'

'Shut up, Wouvermans, sarcasm doesn't suit you. And open up, because I'm not going to talk in the street on a day like this.'

They went into the hanging grime of the treasure house. The old man lit the lamp, the wick giving off a great reek and glare before it settled down.

'Tell Mimi she can give a show. I can get her an audience of one, maybe more.'

'When?'

'Thursday night at ten. If anything goes wrong, I'll let her know by midnight tomorrow.'

'How much?'

'Fifty for you – and don't haggle, Wouvermans. I've had enough to put up with today. Same as usual for Mimi. My commission according to the numbers I bring.'

'What will you want?'

'Leda,' said Daniel. 'That's usually a success, stinking

business though it is.'

'And it's nice for you when you can bring people, isn't it? Because otherwise you don't see Mimi's pretty shows yourself, and you like them very much, I think.'

Daniel could have wrung his dish-cloth of a neck and squeezed the sweat out.

'Do you suppose I care for that sort of muck?'

'Oh, ah! Mimi says you're not so hurt as you look, and she knows. She's a smart one, Mimi, she's a psychologist.'

'Oh, shut up!' said Daniel. 'You tell her what to do, and I'll confirm it with you tomorrow morning.'

'Yes, yes, yes, yes,' Wouvermans mused, taking little slow skipping steps round and about his islands of junk, 'a psychologist. That's what she is. She could have set up with her own plate and made a fortune in New York.' His eyes twinkled. 'I knew you liked Leda. I said to Mimi, "Depend on it, it's Leda he'll go for".'

Daniel slammed out, his stomach churning. The injustice of things sickened him. He led a sober life, he did harm to no man, he had a sole secret. And surely anyone might be allowed one shameful secret only, one tiny spot of pus at the root of one little fingernail in an otherwise perfect body, without pigs like Wouvermans crying it out to all the world? It was not fair. If he could have cried, and he had never cried since his seventh year, he would have cried now at the unfairness of it all.

He hardened his heart. This was no time for thoughts of anything but the immediate problem: how to command an audience. He would have to get hold of the secretaried brutes by tonight, somehow. He knew a stab of panic: suppose he had made haste a little too slowly and lost them forever?

But fortune was with him. When he got home he found that another invitation had been delivered, and that the hotel page was waiting for a reply. They had invited him to dine, on the following night, at the restaurant on the Quai du Rosaire – the most expensive in the city – at eight o'clock sharp.

In a hilarity of spirit he sat down to write another note, an addendum to the letter he had written earlier that day. The note had to be written: the idea had taken him with such force that it might have been blown into his mind by the swing of a bell in a steeple. Everything he did now was right, it must be right. He went a second time to the post.

Six

The gale had not quite blown itself out. Even now, though the sky was sapphire and a star or two, like a fallen earring, sparkled in the water, a hard breeze whipped at the flowers banked along the terrace built out over the quay, and scampered over the floors. Daniel had often stood in the little square opposite, looking across at the diners in this bright rich place, and hating them. It made his flesh crawl to think that other poor brutes might at this moment be looking across at him, and thinking he was one of the smart. Anyone, he thought, might well have done so, for he was wearing his white tie and his only good shirt, and on his right forefinger was his father's chalcedony seal ring.

He had looked forward to the food, to the cheese *fondue*, the rare steak, the rum baba; but it was making him feel sick. His stomach had shrunk, he could no longer digest these things.

Duncan Moss, his ball slung in a colourful string bag from the back of his chair, was digesting everything, 'tucking in', Daniel thought disgustedly, like some steel-stomached schoolboy. Cosmo was eating little, Matthew was pretending to eat sparingly but putting a surprising amount away, and Dorothy Merlin, hieratic in red velvet, was eating like a horse, stuffing food into her small frame with the miraculous effect, but in reverse, of a conjurer drawing an infinity of rabbits and national flags out of one small top hat. All around them were Americans, women with hard silk hair, mauve or blue or silver-gilt, men with faraway blue eyes, grey cheeks, and solid munching jaws.

Towards only one of his party did Daniel feel in the least cordial, and that one was Matthew, who had somehow obtained a copy of *The Damask and the Blood* in Brussels the day before, and was halfway through it.

'It is really quite remarkable,' Matthew had said in his gentle, surprised way, turning his head slowly as he spoke, as if to distribute his words like Maundy Money among his friends, 'I don't think I have ever come across anything quite like it.'

A fool, Daniel thought, a fool: of course there is nothing either quite like it, or like it at all. Still, a man who had actually taken the trouble to get his novel could not be wholly bad.

Dorothy was talking now. She had eaten her last crumb of cheese, had scraped up the last little bit of butter from her plate, put it on the last crumb of biscuit and made away with that too. She was now replete and could give her attention to higher things.

'You see, Mr Skipton' – she fixed him with exophthalmic eyes – 'my plays have to be read on two levels.'

Daniel knew all about levels and expected his work to be read upon six or seven.

'There is the simulacrum of the individual condition, and the reality of the universal.'

'The fellow in the *Times Lit Supp* seemed to me to miss that point, you know,' said Matthew. 'Betty Hedingham said what a dunce he was.'

She pushed her hand in his direction, silencing him. 'You see, the womb in my verse is not just *my* womb. It is the womb of everyone.'

'Well, of half the human race,' Duncan said gaily, 'I haven't got one. – No, no, no! I'm sorry, Dotty! Do forgive! – Just being silly.'

Daniel shrank back into himself. He loathed women even more than he loathed men, loathed their cosy, glutinous, boa-constrictor sexuality. Dorothy shocked him.

Her eyes, however, were upon Duncan. 'Why do you pretend to drink when you *know* you can't? It makes you quite idiotic.'

Leaning across the table he seized her hand and gave it a courtly, splashy kiss.

'There, there, you're a sweety, you know how I venerate you. I make jokes because I actually venerate you too much to talk seriously. I get tied up inside.'

She said coldly that she hoped this was the case; but she did not snatch her hand away for a moment or so, and when she restored her attention to Daniel she was visibly appeased.

'What I mean is, that it is a symbol not only of my womb, or humanity's womb, but of the womb of all creation. That is why I so often introduce a cluster of kitchen images, to make people feel at home with the ineffable. You will notice –'

Cheek, Daniel thought.

'– how the Flemish masters introduce, behind the figure of the Madonna, perhaps through a small window, little scenes of domestic life. My intention is much the same as theirs.'

'Mr Skipton knows a lot about Flemish domestic life,' said Cosmo, who had hardly shifted his steely forget-me-not gaze from his wife's forehead throughout the meal and had scarcely spoken, 'or so he told Duncan. The seamy side, I believe. I suppose even this delightful city has its seamy side.'

Caught him. Daniel knew the inward jet of triumph, delicate, vertical, deliciously playing upon his hopes. He said sharply, 'I have lived here for most of my adult life. What there is to be known, I know. And there is a good deal I would prefer never to have known.'

One of Cosmo's eyes twitched and the lid fell. A tic, a startling one.

Daniel managed to withdraw his fascinated attention from this phenomenon. He had his piece to say.

It was a well-composed piece, spoken many times before, and each time improved in the recitation. He raised his head slowly, so that his Bembo profile should stand out against the white wall, and stared off into the night, at the tumbling of creeper into the waters, the ghostly convocation of swans. As if happened, there was a break in the chatter of the room and the bells swam into it, filling the silence to the brim.

He spoke of the medieval peace he had found here, among Gothic phantoms and faces of five hundred years ago set upon the necks of the butcher, the baker, the postman, the bus driver, the waiter, the lacemaker, the market gardener, the priest. Here, since the sea had silted up and left the city stranded, a useless glory, the past had usurped all time. Here it was not dead but living; its breath was sweet and its flesh sprang violets. It was a fit estate for God, to whom all His vassals paid tribute as a matter of course, being beyond the embarrassment of mystery but living naturally within mystery itself. God spoke quite clearly in the bells, and nobody bothered to remark the fact. One did not remark the fact that a father gave instructions, or scolded, or praised.

'You know,' Matthew said gently, 'that is most illuminating, it really is. And admirably put.'

Daniel could have killed him. He was always, at this point, genuinely moved; he had been speaking with the gift of tongues. But also, Matthew had forced him, by this interruption, to add a further lyrical piece, before getting down to business.

He added it, and it was not so good, being impromptu and therefore unpolished, as what had gone before. Still, it wasn't bad. Then he said: 'And the pity is, that within it all is human ugliness, human perversity, the blackness of human tomfoolery. For we must believe it is tomfoolery. Otherwise, we should be choked by our own disgust.'

'Oh, I say,' said Dorothy, at her silliest, 'you are quite prodigiously gnomic! What are you getting at?'

He was silent.

'Are there fascinating places?' Duncan enquired, resting his cheek upon his cushioned hand. 'Do tell us.'

'It is not fit,' said Daniel, 'certainly not in the company of a woman.'

'I agree,' said Matthew. 'I am out of date, out of step, but I agree.'

There might be trouble with him.

'Oh!' Dorothy cried. 'Are you one of those people who make distinctions between the sexes? Do you think women oughtn't to face evil the same way as men must? How can we think,' she concluded triumphantly, 'unless we *know*?'

She had dealt with Matthew, and Daniel was relieved; but he thought: She is one of those harpies, those rudases, who beat their hands raw trying to batter their way into men's clubs. It was for them, when all else failed, that the shame of the annexe was invented. Daniel had never belonged to a club, but in principle he was on the club's side.

A rudas: a wonderful word. That was what, below the skin, below the physiological-theological poetry, she was. A smile escaped him, which Duncan took for premature encouragement.

'Well, we'll go and wash our hands, and you tell me, and then I'll break it to Dotty.'

'I am sorry!' Daniel exclaimed, and made his eyes flash savagely.

Dorothy rose. Her *hauteur* was such that despite her lack of inches she seemed to be uncoiling scarlet miles; it was like the unfolding of the road in one of those machines on the pier, at which the penny-payer is asked to establish his own skill in the steering of a car.

'Excuse me,' she said.

I have hooked the lot, thought Daniel; and when Cosmo offered him a brandy was too dazed to refuse, though he had no taste for hard liquor.

'Now come along,' Duncan said, 'do tell us, Mr Skipton.

We're all grown up, and I'm panting to know.'

Daniel spoke as if the words were dragged out of him. 'Well, for instance, there is – one would call it— there is a house where people may, if their tastes so incline – ' he sneered and averted his eyes – 'see what would be, what one might call, a spectacle.'

Duncan clapped his hands. 'Oh, I say! I must see that, whatever you think of me. Do you know, I have had such a quiet life? I never set eyes on a dirty postcard until I was rising twenty-eight, and then it was a snapshot of a clerkly lady with no clothes on sitting in the snow in a cemetery.'

'One supposes,' said Matthew, 'that this spectacle is not free.' He smiled thinly, raising his arched eyebrows, then his whole head, and leaned it back against the white panelling. He had such a stuffed air that Daniel thought he looked like nothing so much as a knife-thrower's target. One could imagine him with a neat edging of bowies.

'I am sure one supposes correctly,' said Cosmo. 'How much?'

Daniel detested this sharp approach. He was beginning to dislike this man more than he disliked the others. 'I am told that it varies with the size of the audience. There would be a reduction for numbers.' He spoke contemptuously, as if he were revolted by the whole discussion. 'But it is, I am told, mere childish smut. I have no interest in such things myself.'

'How much, for instance, for three?' Cosmo was pressing the matter.

'Perhaps fifteen hundred francs.'

'Better say two spectators,' Duncan put in. 'I really do doubt whether this is Matthew's cup of tea.'

'I doubt it myself,' said Matthew, 'but if you are going to persuade Mr Skipton, against his better judgement, to lead you to the *bas fonds*, I shall really have to accompany you, if only in order to see that you come to no harm.'

The wind had dropped at last, and the flowers in the window boxes were still. A waiter had opened a window.

Daniel saw, staring across at them from the little square, the Italian. His arms were crossed on the parapet, his white hands outspread like resting moths. The light from a street lamp glimmered on his watch-bracelet.

Cosmo, spotting him too, leaned out and waved.

'You must meet that chap some time. He's a count, and he sings.'

The Italian, starting up with a broad and flashing smile, waved enthusiastically back, as if cheering on a football team.

Cosmo gestured him to come round by the bridge and join them, but he shook his head and, bowing deeply, melted back into the evening.

Cosmo said he had struck up a conversation with him the day before, in the Gruuthuse. 'He's an interesting fellow. He sang at the Scala once, he tells me, but not, of course, under his own name.' He turned back to Daniel. 'Now, can you arrange for us to visit this spectacle of yours?'

'Not of mine. If you insist I will do so, but I should prefer that you did not.'

'We must absolutely insist,' said Duncan merrily, 'so please be nice.'

'I could possibly arrange it for tomorrow night. But you will forgive me, I know, if I take you there and then make my excuses. It is not the sort of thing I find congenial.' Taking out the large white handkerchief he had borrowed from Lotte's room, when Lotte was out, he carefully wiped his hands, backs, palms and between the fingers, as if to remove contamination.

Dorothy came back and glared at them till they rose fully to their feet for her. She was not content with half-risings.

She waited until the last back was straight.

'Well? Did I give you enough time to be disgusting in?'

'Now, my dear,' said Cosmo, 'Mr Skipton is to be kind enough, against his own inclinations, to show us some nightlife that is quite unsuitable for your eyes.'

'When are we going, right away?'

'Tomorrow. And I don't think it is a question of "we". We are going to be most unchivalrous and leave you to a quiet evening by yourself.'

'Well, of all the – !' She looked at him like a head prefect rebuking cheek. 'Oh, I say, Cosmo, you are absolutely the bottom! Of course I shall come. It's my duty to know the worst as well as the best.' She added that nothing human was alien to herself. Daniel thought almost everything was.

'I daresay,' her husband said remotely, 'that there would be an even greater reduction for four.'

'If Miss Merlin insists upon joining you,' Daniel said, 'then I must decline to be a party to it.'

'What do you mean, decline to be a party? Do you just mean you won't come yourself?' Dorothy was furious, as he meant her to be.

'I mean, I must decline altogether to make these unpleasant arrangements. You are a woman; and you are also, if I may speak with the out-of-date tongue of my generation and my particular upbringing, a lady.'

'I am a woman,' said Dorothy, 'and the mother of men.'

A smile so faint that it was scarcely perceptible touched Matthew's mouth at one corner.

No one said anything.

'I'll tell you what.' She banged her fist down on the table, just missing the butter, which Duncan rapidly twitched away from her. 'If I can't go, it's a jolly sure thing you lot won't either.' She was more of a prefect than before. 'Because Cosmo won't. And if you went, Duncan, I should never have anything more to do with you, never!'

'Well, Dorothy,' said Matthew, 'that leaves me.'

'Oh, you! You wouldn't go by yourself. You're only going because Duncan is. You know you'll loathe it, anyway.'

'I am not expecting to like or to loathe it. I am simply mildly interested.'

The waiter cleared the debris away, leaving only the glasses and some clean ashtrays. Dorothy leaned across the table, and cupped her face in her hands. She fixed Daniel with her burning eyes.

'Now, Mr Skipton, like me, you are an artist.'

If you think that flatters me, you silly bitch, thought Daniel, you are on the wrong track.

'You know that the duty of the artist is to see life whole. If he touches pitch and is defiled, then he must endure the defilement. He owes it to his art. The untouched spirit is the luxury of the uncreative.'

'That's rather nice, I think,' Duncan said appreciatively. 'It is nice, isn't it?' He appealed to Matthew.

'Be quiet,' said Dorothy. 'I am talking to Mr Skipton and not to you. The untouched spirit, as I have just remarked, is the luxury of the uncreative. You cannot suppose that I am the type to revel in the obscene. I daresay I shall find it an ordeal. But I am going through with it, Mr Skipton, because I must. You see, I have to.'

He wondered whether he dared to play the game a little longer, decided it was unsafe. She was quite powerful enough to put a stop to the whole project.

He bowed his head. 'Then, Miss Merlin,' he said quietly, 'it shall be at your own risk.' He bit his underlip so that he drew a head of blood. He had found this demonstration so effective before that it was well worth the physical pain. They stared at him in awe as he drew it off into his handkerchief. 'For reasons of my own, I prefer not to call for you at your hotel, or to ask you to meet at my house. I shall wait for you under the belfry at a quarter to ten tomorrow night. In the meantime, I thank you for your entertainment.'

He had to get away quickly. The vision of a rum baba, beaded with gold, pregnant with golden cream, this vision painted with the minutiae of a Snyders, was forming in his mind: which indicated that the baba had done him the most harm, and was to be the finite cause of his being sick.

He pushed his chair back. 'Good night to you!' he barked, and clanked out of the restaurant before they could make their formal farewells. He just got home in time.

Seven

Queasy of stomach but blithe of heart, Daniel rose early next day and finished varnishing a shrine of papier mâché, which he had not had the courage to complete before this. Lotte came in while he was working and admired it, which nearly made him hurl it back into the drawer. It was horrible and he knew it, but Malouel would give him thirty francs for it and sell it to some debased tourist for fifty.

'Aren't you clever?' said Lotte, with a passing grin at the pegged-out socks. 'I don't know where you get it all from, I'm sure. Oh, look at all the little roses! One could almost pick them.'

She set to work making his bed.

'I don't know what you'd do without me to look after you.' Leaning over to tuck the sheet over the far side, she fell on her face, her rump in the air. She was convulsed with merriment, she could not get up again. 'Oh dear, oh dear, oh dear!'

He touched the varnish to see how long it would take to dry.

'Oh, do look at me!'

'I haven't time to look at you.'

'Give me a hand up, go on, be a sport.'

He did not reply. Disappointed, she heaved herself to her feet. 'Fine one you are. I work my fingers to the bone for you, and never a decent word do I get.'

'Your fingers are like bunches of bananas,' said Daniel, 'no sign of bone is apparent.'

This sent her off again. 'Oh you! You're a holy terror, yes, you are. You'll be the death of me some day.'

She was so lovely and healthy, and his spirits were so high, that he indulged her by giving her a smack. Pretending to be much hurt, she clapped a hand to her bottom and shook her fist at him. 'Now you're supposed to be a gentleman, and that's how you carry on! If I told Mamma, she wouldn't let me come up here, she'd do for you herself and a fine thing that would be! You wouldn't have half such fun. We do have fun, don't we?'

Though he shuddered inwardly at her awful playfulness, he had to placate her by agreeing that they did. He was well aware that, but for Lotte's championship, Mme la Botte would have evicted him long ago.

'You ought to take a wife,' said Lotte, 'she'd send you to the rightabouts. Why don't you take a wife, eh?'

'I have never fallen in love,' he replied with a smirk.

'Never too late to begin, I say.'

'Much too late,' said Daniel, carefully putting the shrine into a cardboard box and fixing pieces of cotton across it on drawing-pins, so that it should not touch the sides.

'I don't like young chaps,' said Lotte, 'they get so rough. I say that an older man, he may tire out quicker than one does oneself, but he's far more likely to act the gentleman.'

'Out of the way, I'm in a hurry.'

'I tell you what, there may be some tart left for your dinner.'

'I shan't want any,' said Daniel, feeling he might never desire to eat again.

He went up towards the Steenstraat, and met Cosmo on the step of Joye's.

'Mr Skipton! Good morning to you. Come and have an ice-cream, I have a passion for ice-cream, especially Joye's. Or a water-ice. A lemon water-ice?'

Daniel was tempted. It occurred to him that a lemon water-ice was just about the only thing he would be able to swallow without retching. But he refused, saying he had a business appointment.

'Oh, come on,' said Cosmo, 'you can put it off. I want you to meet the Count, too, he ought to be here any minute— Ah, here he is!'

The Italian came running up, bright-eyed and boyish, full of apologies.

'Ah, Signor 'Ines! I am so sorry I 'ave kept you waiting. I shall never be forgiven, not if I live to a 'undred years.'

41

'Let me present to you,' said Cosmo, 'Mr Daniel Skipton, resident of this city: Mr Skipton, this is *il Conte* Flavio Querini, of Venice.'

'Now I 'ave seen you!' the Count cried out. 'It was at the Cranenburg, I thought I 'eard you speak of the Wigmore 'All'– he rhymed this with *salle* – 'and it was all I could do not to jump up then and there and make myself known to you. For the very name of the Wigmore 'All is sacred to me, and one day there I shall go, I shall sing!'

'Come along,' said Cosmo, 'let us all three eat ice-creams like little gluttonous schoolchildren and have a chat. Mr Skipton's business appointment can wait, I am quite sure of that.'

Daniel was sure of it too. As he followed them into the salon of red velvet, its duskiness sparkled all about with little chandeliers, he wondered whether he would attempt to add the Italian to the night's expedition. He decided not to. It would be rushing matters. Also, with luck, he might be able to take him by himself later on, which would be far more profitable, and would have the additional benefit of offering Daniel a second pleasure.

He thought it all out as he made a start on his ice, and listened to the Count's happy chatter.

He was, it was apparent, rich: he made mention of a palace in Venice, a villa – 'not one of the great ones, no, not like Valinarana, but pretty – oh yes, definitely pretty!' – on the Brenta. He was touring Belgium and Holland for pleasure, and in the hope of recovering from an illness which had left his throat rather weak. 'I am singing not terrible, you understand me, but not as it should be. When I am quite OK again I go to London, there I shall give an audition to the BBC Third Programme and perhaps arrange for a concert. You know, Mr Skipton, I 'ave a dream?'

He leaned across the table, clutching the stem of the frosted cup. His eyes glowed brown and golden, like blossoms of calceolaria. He had beautiful white teeth but most of them were stopped.

'I tell it yesterday to Mr 'Ines, now I tell it to you. I sing at the Wigmore 'All, all the world is there. I sing better than I 'ave ever sung in my life, troubadour songs of the twelfth century, perhaps a little Monteverdi – all very special. When I finish, when I make my bow, all is dead silence, you can 'ear a pin drop. And then all rise to their feet, all throw up their programmes, the ones at the back they climb on chairs, and they cry, "Querin'! Querin'!" '

Daniel, stupefied by this vision, found nothing to say, and indeed would have said nothing had he found it, for he was watching his step.

Exhaling deeply, the Italian tossed himself back into his chair with such gusto that the whole table rocked.

'But you know, Count,' Cosmo said mildly, his tight smile broadening, 'it would not be at all like that at the Wigmore Hall.'

'It would not?'

'No. I hate to disillusion you, but it would be very far from your conception. However great a success you were, they would all applaud politely and go home. You would learn the truth in the morning papers.'

'There might be headlines, perhaps, saying simply "Querin' "?' The Count still looked hopeful, though the first ecstasy had faded.

'I don't think there would be headlines,' said Cosmo, 'it is done differently in England.'

'It is done in a boring sort of way, I think,' the Count observed sadly.

Daniel was trying to work out what Cosmo might be doing with him, or he with Cosmo, and came to the conclusion that it was the fascination of money on the one side, and the hope of an introduction to English musical quarters on the other.

He was aware that he was talking far less than usual, had made no impression. But he did not care. Cosmo would talk about him in his absence, which was well enough for the moment, and he would make good his silence later on, upon a better opportunity.

When he rose to go, Cosmo suggested that the three of them should meet for a drink before lunch tomorrow. Daniel thanked him, and bowed to the Count. '*Arrivederci domani*,' he said, leaving the impact of his linguistic accomplishment to do its work.

Malouel bought the shrine, but would not pay a centime more than twenty-five francs. Daniel cussed him. He danced with rage; if he had been somebody else he would have scared himself stiff. 'Take it or leave it,' Malouel said, 'it's an off-season.'

On his way home he cussed himself that he had not made certain of the Count for Mimi's. It would have meant at least a hundred francs to the good: and if Utterson was going to be his swinish self (he would choke before he wrote to him again in terms civil or otherwise) and Malouel was going to draw in his horns, he would need every penny he could lay his hands on. He dreaded the repetition of the winter's black patch when, for three weeks, he had shivered in his bitter attic, breaking the ice when he needed to shave, had existed on such scraps as Madame la Botte, rentless and merciless, had thrown him, and on one or two occasions had been reduced to rummaging the dustbins for the half of a stale loaf or a few bacon rinds. He believed that hate was a good thing in itself, that a man could not stand up without it: but even he never wished to hate again as he hated in those terrible weeks. It had worked on his body so surely that he had vomited most of the miserable food he had managed to scrape together. Hatred had made his tongue taste dirty, had fouled his teeth.

This benevolent quay, where he walked now beneath the bright green sunshade of the limes, had been the scene of such misery that all his present hopes were forgotten when he looked back upon it. You would think now that butter wouldn't melt in its mouth. Mayflies danced just above the water, as if it were red hot and might burn their infinitesimal feet. Two béguines paused for a moment to throw crumbs to the sparrows who gathered in a velvety sea about their stubby shoes, and flickered from spraying wings the gold dust of the trees. But then the trees had been lichened with frost, and the ice had set in a sheet ten inches thick over the canal. The iron bells had rung death and starvation in their hundred coarse voices. Bring out your dead! they had cried, and the echo had dropped down to clang at the bottom of his soul, like a piece of iron flung down a concrete shaft.

It had been Christmastime. Utterson had sent him a huge flashy card with a picture on it of roistering cardinals toasting one another in bumpers of port.

Daniel closed his eyes tightly to dispel memory. When he opened them again it was spring. The béguines sailed on in the yachting beauty of their coifs. The man with the megaphone shouted to his festive boatload. An American in a pale-grey hat and gold-rimmed glasses was photographing the swans with his Leica.

Eight

They met like conspirators in the arch below the belfry. Behind them the courtyard of the Cloth Hall, in the scattered lamplight, was Shakespearian. An ostler might have entered left, swinging a lantern. Charles's Wain might have pricked out the sky over the new chimney.

Daniel, proud, cold, unforthcoming, was waiting for them. He barely gave them a greeting.

Dorothy, for some reason, was wearing dark glasses and a yellow mackintosh. She trotted at the head of the men, swinging her arms impatiently as if to keep them to heel. Duncan, in his duffle coat, was as gleeful as a boy out for a treat; the ball, in its net, was slung over his wrist. Matthew carried a walking stick with which he kept prodding at the cobbles. He looked older than by day, more tired, more experienced; he was the only one of them who gave no impression of excitement whatsoever, and this made Daniel uneasy. He had known Mimi's effects completely ruined by a stony reception from just a single member of quite a large party. Cosmo, the oldest of them all, was grinning all over his face as he trotted to keep pace.

'Here they are,' he said. 'They have been warned. I have warned my wife. And now, we are yours to command.'

'It is some little distance,' Daniel told them, 'and I shall not, in any case, take you by the most direct route.'

This was to whip up their excitement, to make them think he was deliberately obscuring the whereabouts of the house to which they were going. In fact he led them there by the normal way, which was also the shortest, since he had never relished walking.

Mimi's house lay in one of the streets off the main road to Blankenberghe, about a mile from the Grand' Place. It was a respectable-looking six-room villa, built about 1910, with some fancy wooden carving over the porch and panels of coloured glass in the door. In the asphalted front yard was a motorcycle, with a tarpaulin thrown over it.

'This is simply not my idea of sin,' Matthew observed, as Daniel brought them to a halt. 'I am already disappointed.'

'Oh, I don't know!' Duncan gave a skip. 'Stained glass and all! I am expecting a Black Mass.'

'Don't be tiresome,' said Dorothy, her sharpness heightened by a twinge of nerves, so that she ended on a note both sour and high.

'Will you all be so good as to keep your voices down?' Daniel spat at them. 'I am not taking you to the cinema, and I dislike what I am doing quite enough as it is.'

He marshalled them up the three steps and knocked five times – three short, two long.

The door sprang open. A bonny woman with a perfectly round face and a motherly air welcomed them. 'Well, meneer, if it isn't you! Jan was saying to me, "What do you bet it's him?" and I said, "Not Mr Skipton, he's too grand for us," but here you are, just the same! Come on in and bring your friends, they're all as welcome as roses in June.'

While she was speaking she had somehow whipped them all inside into the narrow hall and had closed the street door. They blinked at her and at each other in the bright light.

'Well,' said Mimi, as if she did not know quite what to do next.

'It's terribly nice of you to let us come,' said Duncan. 'We do hope we're not a lot of trouble.'

'No trouble at all! I hope you're going to have a good time. Wait a minute, I've forgotten to start the incense.'

She disappeared. They waited. In a moment or so the house was pervaded by its strong smell.

Duncan giggled.

'I'm tired of you,' Dorothy whispered to him viciously. 'All this is very, very silly and you are making it worse.'

Matthew studied a picture on the wall, a reproduction of *September Morn*, framed in gilt.

'Art,' he observed to Cosmo, 'knows no frontiers.'

'And now,' said Daniel, 'I hope you will excuse me. I will call back to escort you home.'

They begged him not to go, and after much pressure he yielded.

Mimi reappeared. 'All set,' she said gaily, and switched off the hall light. They heard the music of a very old gramophone; the record was cracked but recognisable: *Le Cygne*.

'First on your left,' said Mimi, out of the darkness.

Daniel knew his way, though he pretended to be unsure of it. The room into which he led them had once been two rooms, but the partition wall had been demolished and division made between the areas by a curtain of dusty-looking gauze. There was darkness behind it: but there was a dim light in the section in which they stood, enough for them to see that it was a sort of drawing-room, with upright piano, pot plants, and mahogany overmantel. The centre of it had been cleared; ranged across it were the seating arrangements for five, a sofa long enough for three persons, an armchair with a loose cover of floral chintz, and a piano stool.

'If you please,' Daniel said bitterly, putting the men on the sofa, Dorothy in the armchair, and seating himself on the stool. *Le Cygne* ground to a stop. Someone lifted the needle and put it on again at the beginning.

'May I smoke?' Duncan asked, with a light and jolly air. 'What fun it all is!'

'No smoking!' The answer, from behind the gauze, made them jump. It was a man's voice, grumbling and deep. 'Anyone who smokes goes out.'

Matthew stretched his long legs, locked his hands behind his head. He wore a smile of detached anticipation.

Dorothy stirred uneasily. 'Why don't they hurry up?'

Cosmo turned his head and looked at her. He smiled and moistened his lips.

'Lights out, please,' the male voice shouted.

Daniel obeyed him, throwing them all into reeking darkness. He returned to the stool and hunched himself upon it, his heart beating.

A light went up beyond the curtain, disclosing a set scene. This room was bare of furnishings. A *portière* curtain hung over a doorway, and that was all. On the floor was a mossy bank, contrived by means of greengrocer's baize spread over pillows, and upon it Leda lay, an imperturbable Walloon with black eyes and a lot of black hair who worked by day in a boot repairer's. (Daniel, who had seen her several times on the stage, as it were, had been astonished to run across her, one day, in a little shop off the Rue aux Laines, where he had been forced to take his shoes for soling and heeling. He had not acknowledged her, nor she him.) She had nothing on and would have been quite pleasing but for her calves, which went straight into her feet without the intervention of ankles.

'So silly,' Dorothy murmured; 'honestly, one despairs.'

Leda began to mime a sort of dissatisfaction with life in general. She sighed, rolled about on her back, passed a hand over her brow and sighed again.

Somebody restarted *Le Cygne*.

The curtain over the door was pulled aside and to her entered the Swan, a coke-washer from the suburb of St Pieter's whom Daniel had known on and off for a good many years. He was a fattish young man with the indigenous pear shaped face of Flanders, the pear inverted, small blue eyes and pink satin mouth. He looked good-natured and not very sure of his part. He wore large wings made of wire and cotton wool, and nothing else except a corn-plaster.

'So sorry,' Duncan murmured, 'I loathe missing it, but I must have a breath of air. It's the smell that does it.' He rose from the sofa, and left the room.

Daniel grinned to himself. It would be hard for the fat Midas to put so worldly a face on things tomorrow morning.

Meanwhile the Swan was circling undecidedly around Leda, half-heartedly flapping his wings, making a few vague ritual movements designed to express his admiration. Leda expressed some alarm.

Dorothy whispered, 'Too stupid, and too sad. But one *ought* to see these things.'

Daniel could just make out their faces in the glimmer shed upon them from the stage. Cosmo was watching, not the performance, but Dorothy. Matthew was still smiling, his legs still extended, the walking-stick gripped between his knees. He looked so detached that Daniel could have struck him.

The Swan fell suddenly to his knees, breaking a wing in the process. Sensibly, he snapped the broken part clean away, pulling little drifts of cotton wool with it, and shied it to the back of the room, out of his way.

The gramophone record began to repeat itself. Somebody helped the needle over the crack.

The Swan moved in.

Daniel held his breath. This was the only joy he knew,

the satisfaction of the spirit that was denied to his flesh: a satisfaction so supreme that it almost played puppet-master to his body, bringing it alive, flushing into his veins those jets of joy that more fortunate men possessed as a birthright. It was not so much the excitement of the classic union as the heart-taking beauty of it, which moved him. He saw the billowy god sinking down upon the helpless breast of the daughter of Thestius, the wife to Tyndarus, making her one with whiteness as a cloud obliterates into itself the peak of a mountain.

'How,' he thought,

> '...can those terrified vague fingers push
> The feathered glory from her loosening thighs?
> And how can body, laid in that white rush,
> But feel the strange heart beating where it lies?'

Tears stung his eyelids. Yeats, immortal Yeats: *rosa mystica*. The mystic bog-rose. It was not the coke-washer whom he saw, buckling to with honest enjoyment and good humour, until Dorothy shot up out of the armchair.

'Oh, too absurd, too piffling, it's too puerile!'

Her voice was shaking.

'Well, we told you to stay at home,' said Cosmo.

She fell back. 'It is *all* knowledge. It is *all* experience. One has to know these things.'

The Swan clambered up, made a flapping and perfunctory circuit of the room, and a rapid exit.

Leda expressed wonderment. She raised herself on one elbow and wiped her hand again over her forehead. Something seemed to be worrying her. Fumbling among the grassy hillocks at her back, she gave a broad slow smile of satisfaction. She was the mother of two large pink plastic eggs.

The music stopped.

At this point the silence was broken by a peal of laughter

so pure, so uninhibited, so boyish and so joyful that Daniel could not believe his ears. He was jolted back from his dream, his head was buzzing, his stomach ached, he was freezing and burning at once. He looked across the auditorium in stupefaction.

Matthew Pryar was laughing his head off.

'Oh, shut up,' Dorothy cried, 'shut up, shut up, shut up!' The stage light had gone off, they were in the pitch-dark again.

'Will you shut up, Matthew? It is nothing to laugh at, it is all quite stupid and infantile. How you, of all people –'

Daniel put the light on again.

Matthew had twisted himself round and was lying over the arm of the sofa, his shoulders heaving.

'Stop it will you? I can't bear to see you making a fool of yourself –'

'I must have an egg,' said Matthew, weeping with happiness, 'for a souvenir, Castor or Pollux, it doesn't matter which. Mr Skipton, I am sure you could induce them to sell me one!'

Daniel had time enough to make a recovery. His pleasure had been ruined, his meagre, makeshift pleasure denied him by the injustice of all earthly things, and he was still quivering under the shock. But he said icily, 'This performance, if one may call it so, is now at an end. I hope you all considered it worth the money.'

He had collected it in advance, had slipped Mimi's share into her hand while they all waited in the hall.

She now made her appearance, like a cook who feels she has provided a dinner out of the ordinary. 'Pretty, eh? We do think it's so pretty. Very nice of you to come, lady and gentlemen. I hope you all enjoyed yourselves.'

She repeated to Daniel, '*Ik hoop dut u zich heet verveeld heeft. Komt u nogeens!*' she added, and let the lashes fall very slightly over one eye.

Dorothy, silent, went past her into the passage.

'Most unusual,' said Cosmo, 'an experience. A classical

51

experience. One could almost consider it an extension of one's formal education.' He bade good night to her nicely and followed Dorothy out.

Matthew could not thank her enough. His natural courtesy at last conquering his mirth, he bowed over Mimi's hand. 'I really am frightfully grateful. It isn't the sort of thing one can see just anywhere. I think it's most kind of you to take the trouble, really most.'

As he passed Daniel, he whispered, 'Skipton. Egg.'

Daniel acquired one for fifty francs, and when he rejoined the others in the street he told Matthew it had cost him sixty.

The walk home was rather silent, except for Dorothy's scolding of Duncan, who had put the net on his head and was bouncing the ball with sad precision along the empty pavements, now starred with rain.

'You have got to face up to life, or you will be *no* good. Why do you pretend you've got guts when you know you haven't? It might all seem pretty silly, but actually it was quite elemental, innocent in a sort of way, it wouldn't have hurt you. Coward!' she exclaimed, unable to contain the venom of her envy that he had succeeded in making his escape.

'I think we should now visit the place where one asks for *gueuse* while holding one's left ear,' said Cosmo. 'Let's get a taxi.'

'I don't want to,' Dorothy snapped at him. 'That awful incense has given me a headache. Matthew! Put that thing in your pocket, if you can get it in, or let me hide it under my mackintosh. I do not know how you can bear to be seen with it.'

Daniel parted from them coldly, warmth in his purse. He would not accept their thanks.

'It was obliging of you, Skipton,' said Cosmo, 'to endure it for our sakes. You must not think too badly of us. We have not your standards.' He clapped him on the shoulder and walked off with the others.

In Daniel, doubt stirred like a centipede, one foot and

Nine

Friday morning brought him a letter from Flabby Anne, *rentier* and hypocrite. Having read the first few lines, he put on his gloves. He did not wish to touch the thing.

'I do what I can for you because Uncle left to me what perhaps you ought to have had, but I can't do any more, really I cannot. You get everything so wrong, I do so wish you wouldn't. I haven't any "broad acres" or "water-meadows", as you put it, there is a paddock where Mr Gravesend puts his old pony and of course one can't charge him anything, not being neighbours, and though the river is at the bottom of the garden it is nothing but an expense, it flooded in February and all the stakes went rotten, I had to have them replaced, and besides that all the potatoes went.

'A hundred a year is *all* I can afford, I only have my pension and what Uncle left. I don't know what you mean by a bleached garden. I am sure your books are wonderful, Daniel, because you were clever as a little boy, but I am over seventy now and my eyesight isn't what it was. Also they have given me bifocals and I can't get along with them. I will try to send you a little extra next Christmas; do make it last.'

He knew her. She was as rich as Croesus. One day he would go back to England, he would take the train to Colchester, he would find her out and confront her. He would bet all he had made on Wednesday night that he had always been right in assuming that there were peacocks on her lawns.

Nevertheless, he felt a smile sliding, not across his face, but across the face of the man who stood within him, strengthening him, giving him courage against his enemies. Flabby Anne might have been proud of herself when she had written these lines; by now she would be proud no longer, for by now she must have received the second note, which he had dashed off in the sarcasm of his spirit and posted within an hour of the previous letter. For it had occurred to him suddenly that, if she were rich enough to keep peacocks, she was unlikely to be particularly strict in matters of financial morality; and the idea had inflamed him. It was abominable that people of her sort should be so loose, while he was required to account for every penny he spent and, which was more, to pay cash. If everybody behaved as she did, the economics of England would soon fall to ruins; and Daniel, patriotism rioting suddenly within him, had been sickened by the thought. He must act at once, he had felt, against this kind of swindling: and so, inspired, had sat down and written her some curt lines, telling her he was considering whether it might not be his duty to bring certain income-tax evasions and concealments to the attention of the proper authorities. Perhaps she could give him some idea of why he should not.

And he had assumed, as he had gone to the box a second time, to post this afterthought, that it would give her something to think about. What would her reaction be? He did not care. It was beneath him to care. But he would have liked to see her face when she read it. He felt better: well enough to take a little walk, as far as the Pelican House and back again.

On the way in, he observed that the outer door of the dentist's ethereal apartment stood wide open, and the inner door also. Daniel knocked loudly: there was no reply. He ventured inside, through the hall, into the drawing-room. On the table was a silver cigarette-case, finely chased, and this he borrowed. He was able to skip upstairs, unseen, a second or so before the dentist came back from the paper shop round the corner. His prize would help him, he believed, to correct any wrongful impression the man Hines might have of him. He looked at the clock. There was time to put in an hour's work before his appointment.

He took his manuscript and coloured pens from the drawer and settled down. He had an excellent idea for a new character, who could be easily and advantageously inserted into the story.

'It was upon the eve of the Feast of Saint Pisca, Blessed Virgin and Martyr, that is to say, the eighteenth day of January in the Year of Our Lord Nineteen Hundred and Fifty, that the hog Butterman, replete from pleasures of the table that he shared with Valentina, his hippophile wife of infinite coarseness and greed, made the acquaintance of Coralie Sterling, woman dramatist, pretentious, pop-eyed, from the purlieus of Purley Downs.'

Taking up the red pen, he obliterated 'Purley Downs'; with the green one substituted 'Putney Heath'. It was the correction of a true artist. He made a further alteration, 'hippophile wife of ineffable crassness and of a cupidity like unto his own', and felt that though this was an improvement, he would still have to give the phrase a greater pointedness. Had a weak spot for him, had she? Condescending cow. 'Oh, how nice to see you again, Mr Skipton, *such* a stranger!' – tossing her mane at him, flaring her hairy nostrils, showing such a terror of yellow teeth that it was as if somebody had flashed a candle across a window pane. Seven years since he had set eyes on her, and he still shuddered at the memory of how she had pressed upon him great gouts of her own risotto. People who could afford cooks and would not, he thought, should have risotto rubbed in their hair.

At half-past eleven, having polished ten lines till he could see his own soul in them, he made himself ready to go out. He had just inked over a shiny spot on his sleeve and slipped the cigarette-case into the inner pocket of his coat when he heard feet on the stairs, a pounding on his door, and a jolly voice crying, 'May we come in?'

He sprang round, trembling, from the glass. 'Who is it?'

'It's only us. We thought we'd call for you.'

Like a trapped animal, Daniel backed away from the door. He was speechless. His attic was the shrine of his poverty and of his art; they were only for his eyes, these sacred make-shifts, the iron bed, the table propped up with a book under its short leg, the washbasin with a crack in it like the course of the Ganges, the wretched carpet like cold ham to naked feet, the little line of washing.

'You can't come in. I'm undressed.'

'Well, buck up. We'll wait.'

'Who is with you?'

'Only Cicely,' Duncan shouted in reply. 'She's an old sweety, you'll like her. Come on, Skip, do open up!'

'Are you drunk,' Daniel demanded, 'at this hour of the morning?' He had partially regained his nerve and was temporising while, soundlessly, he crept to the door and turned the key in it. He burst into a sweat of relief.

He heard a girl's giggle, a tiny scuffling.

'Not drunk,' Duncan answered aggrieved, 'only popular. Popular with all my friends. Why did you lock the door just then? Popular I may be, but I have got manners. I don't barge in without an invitation.'

'Go away,' said Daniel, 'go away at once. I'll meet you at the Vandenberge in ten minutes.'

'You do sound cross. How can I face you in ten minutes unless you prove you're not cross now? Come on, come on, puss, puss, puss!'

'Oh, Duncan!' said the girl reproachfully, 'you are awful!'

'No, I'm not, I'm only playing, he knows I'm playing. Did anyone ever tell you you were like Réjane?' he added, on a cuddlesome note.

'If you and this lady will kindly leave my house,' Daniel said, squeezing his hands against his beating heart, 'I shall be able to continue dressing, and shall have the pleasure of seeing you later. Otherwise, you will confine me here indefinitely.'

'I know!' Duncan's voice took on a wooing tone. 'You're offended with me because I called you Skip.' The direction of the voice changed: it had dropped about three feet. He had fallen to his knees and was trying to talk through a crack in one of the lower panels. Daniel rushed to the door and flung a towel over the handle so that it covered the crack and would frustrate the fat drunk if he decided to put his eye rather than his lips to it. 'I know I was wrong, Mr Skipton, it did sound awfully rude, but it was only high spirits if you know what I mean. Do say you're not offended.'

'Go away!'

'Look, we found the front door open and that jolly maid of yours polishing the floor, and we said we were friends of yours and she said go right up.'

When he saw Lotte next he would punish her for her treachery, he did not know how, but he would do it. He kept his strung silence. For a few seconds he heard nothing but the noise of his own whistling breath. Then the girl said, 'Do come on, Duncan, you are not sober and you are obviously not wanted.'

'Forgive me,' said Duncan loudly. 'Go on, Skipton, forgive me!'

'Go away.'

'I'll be buggered – Oh, Cicely darling, I'm so sorry – Skipton! Skipton, I'll be damned if I go before you forgive me!'

He was on his feet again, the voice six feet up.

'I forgive you!' Daniel screamed. He was on the verge of tears.

'Bless you,' said Duncan warmly, 'I knew you would. All happy again. Now don't be long, there's a dear chap. Cosmo looks all right, but he can be so spiteful if anyone's late except Dorothy.'

To his profound relief, Daniel heard the sounds of withdrawal, the creak, the giggle, the stumble on the stairs, the rush of feet receding as if the two of them were having a race. He lay down on the bed and put his hands across his eyes. He was beset by all the beasts in the jungle of the world. They had torn from him all he had, and now they grudged him even his loneliness. What a poor thing to grudge a man! And how beastly the spirit that would strip away even this. He felt ill and feeble; and old. He was younger than Hines, probably no older than Matthew

57

Pryar; but he was an old man, his youth eaten away not so much by years as by hunger, bitterness, and righteous rage. He lay there so long that he was shocked to hear the bells ringing for noonday.

Late!

Good. Then he would not go.

But he had to go: he had to meet Querini again. Heaving himself from the bed he poured a little more water into the basin and washed his face and hands again, combed his hair. He could not stop his mouth twitching: but it would stop of its own accord, he believed, once he was in the fresh air. Even now, he was afraid to unlock the door, lest Duncan jump upon him with some brutal idiocy such as, 'Peep bo', or 'Guess who'. At last he did so, and peeped out. Nobody. He ran downstairs. Lotte was still on all fours, reddening the tiles. The temptation to kick her, to send her sprawling all among her pails and polishes was so strong that he had to grip his hands behind his back to restrain himself.

She looked up. 'Oh, aren't we smart! Did you see your friends? I bet that was a nice surprise for you!'

He rushed past her out into the hot, soft, mazy shine of a beautiful day.

He found them on the café terrace, Dorothy, Cosmo, Matthew, Duncan, Querini: no girl. They were wrangling, and Dorothy was wrangling louder than the rest.

'No, Duncan, she cannot come, she was not invited! We can't keep pace with your pick-ups, we never could, and we're not going to.' Her eyes were ringed with rage, the coaly pupils sticking out from the whites; the ropes of her neck emerged as she stretched it. Daniel was reminded of the rampant dark demon by Niccolò Alunno, in the Galleria Colonna at Rome; all she wanted was the tail and the fin-like wings.

Duncan, standing, tried to argue with her. She wasn't a sport, she had no generosity. What did it make him look like, turning a jolly nice girl away? She was a nice girl, too, her father was a solicitor in the Isle of Man.

'And you're drunk,' said Dorothy, 'and we saw you yesterday, making yourself ridiculous by prancing round the Minnewater swinging hands with her, just like a butcher boy out with the housemaid. You ought to be grateful to us, saving you from your own mistakes.'

He protested that Cicely was not a mistake, she was a duck, and she had brains.

Nobody paid the slightest attention to Daniel.

'Come, Dorothy,' said Matthew, 'the poor chap is surely free to pick his own young women. You can't say he isn't.'

'Not when he's on holiday with us! It is sheer rudeness to *me*, and if Duncan doesn't know what sheer rudeness is, he must be instructed by those who do. Aren't I right, Cosmo?'

'Naturally,' he said. 'Have I ever denied it?' He looked up. 'Ah, Mr Skipton! We were so afraid you weren't coming.'

Daniel apologised for being late, and shot a savage glance at Duncan.

'Now I am very glad you are 'ere,' said Querini, 'because they say you are a great expert on the Flemish masters, and I 'ave much to learn. Also, if you can tell me any more about the Wigmore 'All, I shall be so 'appy.' He looked sideways, in alarm, at Dorothy, who was continuing to breathe with a rasp.

'Dotty,' said Duncan, 'it is not that I am so mad keen about Cicely as yet, but I do hate to send her away. You must see –'

'Sit down and shut up,' she said.

He did so, a cloud on his gentle, fuddled face.

'Do I know best?' she bullied him.

'Now, now,' Matthew said, 'that is so obvious that none of us needs labour the point.'

'I wasn't talking to you. *Do* I, Duncan?'

'You are quite wonderful, and quite perfect as always,' he said, 'and now let us make Mr Skipton at home and be nice to him, because he is cross with me, too, and one way and another I am having a hell of a morning.'

She subsided, switching her terrible attention, which was none the less terrible for being benevolent, to Querini.

Meanwhile, Daniel took out the silver case and offered the dentist's cigarettes. Cosmo took a quick look at it, and by a scarcely perceptible twitch of the brows indicated that Matthew should observe it also.

'Now what are you drinking, Mr Skipton?' Cosmo said.

'I would like you to drink first with me this morning,' Daniel replied, 'because I have had some pleasant family news in a letter from home. Nothing important, merely concerning a relation of whom I am particularly fond. But I should like to acknowledge it by the recognised symbol of celebration.'

He would not take no for an answer; and a part of his commission from Mimi disappeared in a round of *Stella Artois* for six persons. But it was worth it, he knew it was worth it.

At ease, a host for the first time in he didn't know how many years, he asked Querini where he was staying.

'Ah!' The Italian's eyes sparkled. 'You would never, never guess. It is the most little place, so tiny, so clean, just a little pension as modest as can be. You see, first I do not like big hotels, they are too like the palazzo of my papa in Florence and I am a bad boy, I am afraid I do not love my papa! But also I am very mean, as you would say, a meezer.'

'Miser, we would say,' Dorothy corrected him.

'I am a meezer,' he went on, not easily deterred, 'with myself! I like to buy beautiful things, I do not myself wish luxury, I 'ave a 'earty appetite but I am not for being posh, as I believe it is called.'

Duncan, who had almost sobered off, was set back again by the *Stella*. He burst out, almost in tears, 'Cicely goes back tomorrow and I shan't have another chance of seeing her!'

'Run off to your Cicely then,' said Dorothy, without looking at him, 'but don't think you can come running back to us again afterwards.'

60

His shoulders drooped.

Querini explained that he would pay money willingly for a Lorenzo Lotto, or a Niccolò de Abate, both of whom he adored, but for himself, if he should be hungry he was content as a peasant with polenta or a bowl of *zuppa verde*.

Daniel enquired where his pension was; he knew the city, he said, like the back of his hand.

'Now I shall be naughty and not tell you!' The Italian had long dimples running like sabre-scars down the sides of his mouth; they were both engaging and alarming. 'You see, it is my secret; I go always when I visit 'ere. If I tell, other people find it out: and then they come in 'ordes, and it is spoiled and no good for Querin'. You understand? You are not offended with me?'

'Well, go along, run off if you want to. Why don't you?' said Dorothy to Duncan, who sank even lower in his chair like a discouraged *putto*, Daniel thought, with a flea in his ear from Venus.

'Indeed I am not,' said Daniel, 'I have a peculiar regard for my own privacy, as some people have found to their cost.' He loathed Duncan, at that moment, even more than Miss Merlin did.

'Have you any Flemish pictures in your collection?' Cosmo asked Querini. 'I imagine yours is a fine one.'

'Well, it 'as some fine things. To the great collections, such as the Colonnas', it is nothing, nothing at all: but for a modest gentleman it does very well. I 'ave a little 'ead by Tiziano – the sweetest thing! But my collection is not really posh.'

It said much for Daniel's self-control that the thought of the Wouters, soaring like a firework, did not transform his face. He would have to be careful, very careful, for the man might be more knowledgeable about Flemish paintings than he pretended.

'I believe there is a fine Van Brouwerts in the Mocenigo palace in Venice,' he said idly. 'I wonder if you have seen it? To me, he is supreme among the early still-life painters.'

61

'Ah yes!' Querini exclaimed. 'I know of it, of course, though I 'ave not seen it. I believe it was in Rome for cleaning when I last visited the Contessa. She is so sweet, and not at all posh.'

Daniel bowed his head to conceal what he feared was a flush of exultation. His instinct was right. The Count, for all his knowledge of Italian painting, knew nothing about the Flemings at all.

Daniel had just invented Van Brouwerts.

He made a vague remark, and changed the subject. There was all the more need for going slowly now. When Cosmo invited him to lunch with the rest of the party he accepted with dignified simplicity. He and Querini must make friends.

The meal, however, turned out to be a fiasco from his point of view, since Dorothy, feeling that the Count should be given some idea of her position in the literary society of England, seized upon a reference to the Sistine Madonna to explain her part in reconciling, by means of drama, the motherhood of the individual with the cosmic motherhood of all things: and was more boring than even Daniel, who had met some bores in his time, could have believed possible. He himself, inwardly raging, was reduced to silence; this play-writing vulture was taking it upon herself to silence the greatest writer of the age, who, though recognised by few at the moment, would one day come into his own with such effect that nobody would ever again even conceive the idea of getting a word in edgeways, once he chose to open his marvellous lips.

He had to get Querini alone; and there was a way of doing so. But it was costly, a very costly sprat for so doubtful a mackerel. He would have to invite the Count to luncheon. It need not, he thought, while Dorothy maundered on, be at too smart a place, not, for instance, at the Duc de Bourgogne. Querini had expressed his disregard for the ostentatious, his love of the simple.

As the party was breaking up, Daniel succeeded in

inviting him to a quiet little restaurant, rustic in inspiration, by the edge of the Roya, a little way out of town. The Count accepted with the delightful enthusiasm of a child being offered a trip in a helicopter.

'*A deux?* Oh yes!' He clapped his hands. 'We will not tell the others, it shall be only for us, we will talk of art. I do not want the *Signora* to talk of art any more, not for a little while, if I am not being rude. She gives one such food for thought one doesn't need more food, don't you agree?'

Daniel did. They made an appointment for the following day.

He walked thoughtfully home, taking his time. He was startled when, just as he came to the Stonecutters' Quay, Cosmo stepped over the bridge and accosted him.

'I thought I might catch up with you, Mr Skipton.'

He blinked his veiled eyes and smiled sideways.

'I don't believe anyone thanked you properly for the little entertainment on Thursday night. In fact, no one but myself dare do so. Poor Dorothy was desperately shocked, though she won't admit it, and Matthew is shocked because he wasn't. Duncan, of course – such a big baby, Mr Skipton, you mustn't think Dorothy doesn't adore him really, they make a show of quarrelling but it's all a great big game –Duncan couldn't take it. Poor lad. For myself –' He paused.

Daniel waited.

'Look here,' said Cosmo briskly, 'seeing is all very well, but for my own part, I like my amusements a bit more active.'

He explained that amusement with Dorothy was out of the question. They had seven sons, and that was enough; but she did not think so. She had flatly refused to take or to tolerate the pursuance of any steps that might inhibit an eighth; and he had refused to take Dorothy unless she changed her mind.

'So there is an *impasse*,' said Cosmo. 'Can you direct me to pleasant pastures, Mr Skipton? It is not, I know, in your own line. But I don't think it is beyond your powers.'

Ten

Daniel looked at him.

Cosmo looked back.

Father Vinckeboons passed by with another priest, two cheerful blackbirds who loved life and somehow seemed to get the best of it.

Daniel removed his hat. The bells rang out for three o'clock and the spring day gave a sigh, fluttering down upon cobbles and canal a blessing of blossom, limedust and the delicate down of birds.

He jerked himself to his full height; so that Cosmo and he stood respectively at five foot four and five foot three and a half.

He said, all his pride reeking, 'Mr Hines.'

'Yes?' said Cosmo.

'I must make one thing plain.'

'Do please go ahead.'

'I am a gentleman. That is a thing few men care to say, but I must say it.'

'My dear boy, did I ever suggest that you weren't?'

'You and your company are my compatriots, and you have shown me some kindness. Because of it I was prepared to satisfy, so far as I could, your wants. It would have been impossible for me to live in this place for so many years without having some acquaintances with the sordid.'

'Indeed no,' said Cosmo heartily.

'When it was the sordid you desired, I procured it for you, despite my own conscience. I say "procured" and I say it bitterly, since it strikes me as a word you have compelled me to use.'

'Not at all. I see no reason for you to use words like that. I never do.'

'I am not, Mr Hines' – Daniel swallowed – 'a pimp. I have a competence, and I still draw some sustenance from the translation of my books in various countries.'

Cosmo appeared keenly interested. 'Do you, by Jove? You're luckier than most. Do you know, I should never have thought it?'

Daniel made no comment. He repeated, 'I am not in need of money.'

'My dear chap, no! Am I offering it? I am simply asking, as a somewhat deprived person, for a tip-off.'

'This is not a city for the vicious.'

'Now look.' Cosmo was companionable. 'I appreciate everything you say to the full. But darn it, you're a man of the world. *The Damask and the Blood* was not written by Dean Farrar.'

Daniel asked him icily if he were one of those who read a man's books as if they were his private diaries.

'No. But come on, be a good fellow, where is it?'

'I have shown you what this city has to offer in your line. And that is all it has to offer, thank God.'

'I believe there's a place in Knocke,' Cosmo said. He looked up into the glossy branches, where the sunlight knitted and unraveled its patterns of light.

'I am sorry.' Daniel began to move away. He had calculated a risk of just about five minutes more.

Cosmo started after him. 'Listen, listen, you are behaving as though I were offering you money. I'm not. I'm asking you, as a kindness to a weaker vessel than yourself, to make the arrangements. What do you say?'

When the five minutes were up, and Cosmo's imperturbability was a little scratched, as if the record had been played too many times, Daniel admitted that he had heard of a place at Knocke and, with disgust dripping from him like rain from a November tree, had agreed to do what was necessary, if he could find out the address.

He went back to his room well-satisfied, yet with an undercurrent of anxiety. He could not feel that Cosmo's attitude towards him was entirely as it should be. There was something lacking in it – perhaps not respect but the right kind of respect. Had the cigarette-case failed? And the round of *Stellas?*

Reminded of the case, Daniel entered the house quietly, saw that the coast was clear and prepared to drop it back through the dentist's letter box.

Then a better idea struck him, struck him like a considerate streak of lightning, which, instead of landing with an aggressive bang, had touched its object with the kind of calculated keenness Tobias Matthay might have taken to a single note of Mozart. Shut off from the rest of the house, at the rear of the hall, was a passage containing vacuum cleaners, pails, electric polishers and Lotte's overall. Vengeance is mine, Daniel thought, I will repay. He tiptoed through this door and dropped the case into Lotte's pocket.

Then he raced upstairs to his attic where he dropped, upon his left side, into a perfect full stop of sleep.

He was woken at five o'clock by Lotte, bearing a cup of chocolate.

'I don't know,' she said. 'I really don't! Old Mr Khnopff was carrying on about his cigarette-case, he had Mamma down, he was making such a fuss you'd think it was his head. He'd gone over the road to get the papers, and when he came back, not a sign of it! So Mamma said, "More fool you to leave the door open." But he went on and on, and we said, "Well, it's nothing to do with us," and then he had a patient roaring with pain so no more was said.'

Daniel reared up, feeling the crux of the story was approaching.

Lotte sat down on the end of the bed and made solemn eyes at him.

'So we were saying, Rats to him and his old cigarette-case, and then I went along to put on my overall, because I had the silver to do. And what do you think I found in my pocket?'

Daniel lay down again.

'Why, his silly old case! Can you fancy that?'

She put out a hand and shook him, telling him that she

didn't climb all those stairs with chocolate to see it get cold.

'All right,' said Daniel.

'So what did I do? I tore in to Mr Khnopff, and I said, "Mr Khnopff, you'll never guess where I found your case" – and of course he couldn't. Then I said, "In the pocket of my overall!" and he said, "But how did it get there?" And I said, "I'm sure I don't know," and how we did laugh! I tell you, the patient was sitting in the chair with his mouth all full of those little rolls of cotton wool, *he* couldn't speak, and *we* couldn't speak, we just rocked!'

'How do you suppose it got there?' Daniel asked her, his eyes more than normally shut, so that he could feel the lids creasing like concertinas.

'Oh, who cares?' Lotte demanded joyously. 'Point was, he wanted it, and there it was! I tell you, Mr Skipton, when I think of it now, that poor chap full of cotton wool, me and Mr Khnopff…' She thought of it. Bringing her knees to her chin she tilted backwards over Daniel's feet and laughed until she cried.

'And Lotte,' he said when she had subsided, speaking to her in a voice so gentle that he scarcely recognised it for his own while being grateful that in fact it was, 'please do not let anyone up to my room, no matter who it is. Not anyone. Not even Father Vinckeboons.'

'He wouldn't come,' said Lotte innocently. 'Get along with you! He's far too grand.'

He went discouraged to his polishing, even anger dying low in him, no more than a bead of the flame in a lamp almost dry of oil. Thanks to the incurious dentist, his revenge had been spoiled and Lotte was as loud and as happy as ever. The wicked, he thought, did in fact flourish like the green bay tree, and it was untrue to suggest that in the morning they were not, yea, they could not be found. They were, and they could.

The afternoon brought a note from the hotel, in the third person, in a clotted, spiky hand that he knew, even from the envelope, must be Dorothy's.

'Miss Merlin has been invited to give a lecture this evening, under the auspices of The British Council, at the College of Europe and thinks it might interest Mr Skipton to attend. The subject chosen is "The Responsibility of the Poet-Playwright in the Welfare State", and the time 8.30.'

The effrontery of this communication did more to bring him back to his normal daemonic spirits than almost anything else could have done, even a cheque from Utterson. His first impulse was to write a reply of one word. Then he thought, no, he would go to this lecture to hear what she had to say about him.

It was true that he had little idea of how she would fit appropriate references into the context of her subject: but that was her affair, not his. It was true that he was not, in the formal sense, either a playwright or a poet; on the other hand, poetry was the essence of his entire work, the seed, the bud and the flower. It was true that she had said, like the born fool she was, that she did not read novels; by this time, however, she would have read the copy Pryar had bought. It was, he felt, too much to expect that she would talk sense about him, since he did not write for idiot minds like hers. Still, he might as well hear what she found to say. There was sometimes a seed of interest in the ravings of a lunatic as in the prattling of a child; he had never been one to underrate men such as Christopher Smart.

Her note began to look rather less offensive. It was obvious now that she was anxious for him to hear her analysis of his own achievement; anxiety, not arrogance had caused her to write stiffly. She had not wished to appear over-eager, and so had given the mistaken impression of unmannerliness. Well, that he could to an extent forgive. To what extent he would forgive it must depend entirely upon her treatment of him in her lecture.

He went out and caught the bus to Knocke. He reckoned that he would be able to see Madame Houdin, have a stroll, and get back to Bruges in plenty of time for supper before the lecture began.

By five o'clock the sky had lost its colour, not through a gathering of cloud but of that leaden mist which is the precursor of greater heat. Even by the sea it was uncomfortably warm and sticky. The great ugly hotels and cafés jammed along the wide promenade as far as the eye could reach were locked in the torpor of an off-season. Nothing stirred upon the miles of sand, which unlike the sands further south were not yellow, but the mud-grey of shores in a dream. Far out, a Channel steamer caught upon its funnel, out of nowhere, a tip of light.

Daniel turned up a side-street looking like a crack in the wall between two tattered hotels and rang the bell of a tall house, across the face of which some ingenuous advertiser had once painted the name of an apéritif. The name was almost obliterated now by the crumbling of the plaster, but over one window there remained a starch-coloured B and over another the bottom half of an H. The place, despite these adornments, had an air of England at its worst. There were lace curtains to every room, but not the fine clumping Belgian lace, with its clotting of grapes or roses. This was Nottingham indifferently washed, yellow-white in fits and starts, grey along the edges where it parted to reveal an obscurement of fleshy plants in pots with bands and rings of brass.

Madame Houdin, who in fact was an Englishwoman once married to a Walloon and now widowed, greeted him without surprise; without emotion of any kind. Lean as an alley cat, she hustled him into her lean hall and into a parlour half the size of Mimi's.

He explained the object of his visit, gave a brief verbal portrait of Cosmo and said, 'He's good for a thousand, probably. I shall want twenty percent.'

'I hope you get it,' she said. 'I really do. But I don't envy your chances.'

As what he got was within her power to decide, and as she was the arbiter of chance so far as he was concerned, this was cool.

Daniel said nothing.

'Well,' said Madame Houdin bleakly, 'I suppose he's got to have a choice. He'll take Louise, they all do, but he'll want to feel he's the Sultan, the great Lord Muck, he'll want to walk slowly up and down their serried ranks.'

He disliked her rather less than he disliked most people. For a woman of her humble origin, she had some natural powers of expression.

'Twenty per cent, and three girls will do.'

'When?'

'Tomorrow night.'

She told him he had better make himself comfortable, as she would have to do some telephoning. While he waited he looked through the illustrated magazines arranged, with some attempt at artistry, on the top of the piano, and found there a photograph of Matthew Pryar, at a Leicestershire hunt ball, maintaining his knife-thrower's pose against the panelling with a pie-faced débutante on one side of him and an embittered looking marchioness on the other.

Madame Houdin returned. 'Louise will be here at nine-fifteen, but he'd better pick her quick and not play the fool because she's busy again at ten-thirty. Jeanne and Hendrickje can stick around any old time. Nobody wants them, they've got about two years left to them, and then curtains.'

She would not care, either, Daniel thought, though both sluts had worked for her so long. When the time came she would point out their inadequacies with a kind of ghastly reasonableness, and send them packing. To do her justice, she would not waste tears upon herself when her own time came: hers would be an unemotional deathbed.

'Fifteen per cent,' he said.

She turned upon him her black, lustreless eyes and an expression of comprehending pity. 'Now, Mr Skipton, I hope there's nothing up with you.'

'Up with me?'

'Well, I never knew you haggle before. Take it or leave it,

that's the sort of lord you always were. I wouldn't like to see you any different, Mr Skipton, it would make me feel things was lacking in permanence.'

'I do not haggle because I am particularly in want,' said Daniel, feeling he had turned white, 'but as a matter of principle. There is a point at which anyone –'

'Ten per cent. You've never had more, you'll never get less, so give yourself a pat on the back and try to smile!'

She gave him so appalling a demonstration of the kind of thing she had in mind that he accepted the ten per cent and got out of the place as quickly as he could, only turning back at the door to scream at her – 'And clean up the filth! Wash! Scrub!'

She crashed the door shut on his back.

He walked miserably back along the promenade. As he stopped for a moment to stare out over the mud-coloured sand, the mud-coloured sea, a thought came to him which should have come to him before, not months but years ago: and perhaps it was its very lateness that ran over his skin like an ice cube and made him sick to the stomach. What am I? What have I become?

I am an artist. I am the son of a gentleman.

What have I become?

He had a tiny vision of himself, no larger than a playing card painted on a finger nail, of himself walking across the playing-fields of his public school (not, perhaps, a great one, a snob one, but coming nevertheless within the comfortable embrace of the Headmasters' Conference), a proud, Byronic boy labelled clever by the staff and on two occasions defenestrated by his schoolmates. Not a popular boy, not with oafs: but he had left his mark. The school, one day, would be among the great schools because it had nurtured him, if one could call it nurturing. He saw the football field curving over on the western side towards the willows and the stream, his breath making angels on the frosty air. He saw Puggy Boyle and his mob approaching to remove his trousers, which was for them an entertainment in times when nothing better offered itself: and he ran, clumping in the mud, clutching himself in anticipation, horribly winded with the hate that had not yet turned to despair, he ran and he ran.

He shut off the vision.

When I became a man I put away childish things.

He was still an artist, the son of a gentleman.

He was himself a gentleman, needy, but proud as Lucifer, pride hinged like wings to his heels. Would he demean himself by the action of throwing muck into a sink-basket? No, for this was a means of disposing of muck, and making all cleanly. Did he demean himself by throwing Cosmo Hines to Madame Houdin? The answer was crystal-clear.

A little happier, he turned from the sea and went inland, to catch the bus home.

Eleven

He was expecting a full house, if only for the reason that interest must naturally be aroused in anyone likely to talk about himself. The young Brugeois who attended the University of Liège would obviously turn up in hordes: there would be more Walloons than Flemings, but a good many of the more cultivated Flemings (unless he was seriously mistaken) also, Madame Voerst-Verboeckhoeven would certainly be there, and the Burgomaster; doctors Joos and Van Wierix; the Countess van Haecht, his old friend, too much of a recluse now, it seemed, to receive visitors, and Madame van Bolswaert. It would be far more his triumph than the Merlin's, always assuming anything she did could ever approximate to a triumph: his old friends would crowd round to greet him, he would implore the Countess to rise to her feet, Madame van Bolswaert would call him Master. That would show them all, Hines, Moss, Pryar, even Querini.

The real mistake, he decided, after the initial shock of entry, was the ridiculous choice of hall. It was designed to seat one hundred and fifty persons. It was seating, at the moment, thirty-four, and Cosmo's party, Querini included, wrote off four of them. No sign of doctors Joos and Van Wierix or Madame van Bolswaert or Madame Voerst-Verboeckthoeven, who had doubtless discovered the page missing from her Burckhardt and, in her usual vindictive manner, was sulking: but the Countess van Haecht was there, and when she saw Daniel she started up, despite her weight of years, as if she had sat on a drawing-pin. This gave him an idea, which he stored away for use later on that evening.

He looked round. Such audience as there was had huddled itself instinctively, as if against the cold, in a little clot starting five rows from the front. There were some under-graduates of Liège and Brussels whom he knew by sight, earnest lads who would swallow down any intellectual pigswill in their frenzy for marks, and one or two elderly women. Sitting right at the back were three derelicts from the quais, who picked up some sort of living out of begging from tourists. One had sensibly prepared for the entertainment by falling already into a deep sleep.

Daniel decided to sit by himself, half a dozen rows behind the rest. He desired solitude in which to reflect upon Dorothy's reflections upon himself. But Duncan glanced round and saw him, and deserting his party, came to his side. He looked swollen and sad. His blue eyes were moist, his chestnut spikes of hair were smudged forward towards his cheeks as if he were emulating a Roman.

'I say, Mr Skipton, let me come and sit by you. I like you, whatever you think of me, I really do. Mr Skipton, I think you are a decent man.'

Daniel folded his arms and stared straight ahead.

'They're all being beastly to me,' said Duncan, 'anyway, they all are except Matthew and he never intervenes. It just isn't in him.'

There was an outbreak of routine clapping. Dorothy was crossing the platform in the wake of a bossy-looking Englishman in a bow tie. She wore a sky-blue frock with a cowl collar that was faintly reminiscent of the recognised costume for a Nativity Play. It was too tight for her; her knees had made blisters in the skirt, apparent even when she stood erect. She gave one startled glance at the meagre concourse, then a stare of uncontrolled rage, then forced a smile of modest cordiality. She flopped down into a chair while the Englishman briskly introduced her in Flemish, French and English and announced that she would give her address in the last of these languages.

'When I get home,' Duncan Moss whispered slushily, 'I am going to get that motherly monster –'

'Be quiet, will you?'

'– into my studio if I have to hog-tie her, and photograph her in a dog-collar in a manger –'

Dorothy uncoiled, went to the reading desk and found it too high for her; she could just get her nose above the top of the book-rest. Stepping to the side of it, she surveyed them all. She took her time. She knew how to make an effect. This was marred by one of the derelicts heaving over into a more comfortable position and hawking.

' – for *The Tatler*,' Duncan concluded. He subsided into his own bulk as a pig does when it sits down.

'Mr Chairman, Ladies and Gentlemen, Mesdames et Messieurs, Herren und Damen,' Dorothy began, with considerable thoroughness. She studied their faces again, as if she were making up a list for the tumbrils. Then she gave a curious smirk which Daniel would, had it been on any face but hers, have described as ingratiating. She locked her big bony hands together on the desk and leaned over them, head cocked sideways. 'Since I am a stranger in your midst–'

She started off again in her high and crystalline wail which would have penetrated the deafest ear in the farthest corner of the hall had there been any ear there to listen.

'– you must forgive me if I tell you something of myself

and of my position in English letters, specifically in the field of poetic drama. Most of you,' she continued optimistically, 'will be aware of the various trends in the contemporary drama, the various schools, the conflicts that have often verged upon the internecine.'

She paused.

'Cicely,' said Duncan brokenly, 'Cicely. I don't know what she must be thinking of me.'

Daniel kicked him, a vicious little side blow on the side of the foot, hard enough to shock him into silence but not enough to make him scream.

Duncan turned to him his moist, mild eyes. 'Was that necessary, Skip? Do you think that was necessary?'

Someone shshd. Dorothy waited, grimly, till all was silent. Her smirk disappeared. 'Let me tell you that I belong to none of these schools; I own to none of these trends; I take part in no conflict. It is generally recognised, in England, that in my own, perhaps limited, field, I stand alone.'

Cosmo beat his palms together, with a noise that was like the rattling of laburnum seeds in the dry pod; it was applause in the manner of a husband long trained to respond to certain stimuli.

'But if I tell you,' she continued, 'that I stand alone, that does not necessarily mean that I am *better* than others. That would not be for me to say. There is Eliot. There is Fry. There is Ronald Duncan.'

Cosmo made a noise of disclaimer.

'No, not for me to say. I must leave the relative assessment of such talents as I have to others. All I am saying to you, in no spirit of boastfulness, is that I am unique.'

At this rate, Daniel calculated, she could not get round from the general to the particular for at least ten minutes; and even so, would need another three or four to relate the particular to his own work. He began to think about the old Countess, sitting rockily in her chair, her head trembling.

He did not think she would fall off it, since she had been sitting like this for the past ten years: but he hoped she felt well. He wanted her to do some entertaining for him. He knew with a touch of remorse that he must raise the question of Mimi with her again, since it had upset her so much last time, he would have to do so in order to knock the spirit of hospitality back into her head.

'Motherhood and the infinite,' Dorothy was saying: 'the womb of a bus-conductress and the womb of earth itself.' She gave a light little laugh. 'Does that seem comic to you? Are you amused by the juxtaposition?'

No one seemed to be.

She flung up her hands. 'Laugh, then, laugh! I mean you to. Why should the eternal verities be so solemn? There is humour in holiness.'

She paused. Her face lengthened and became very pure. Her black eyes rolled upward, and to the left.

'The humour of holiness and the holiness of humour.'

Cosmo made a strange rhubarb noise. Querini, told to laugh, politely did so, but Dorothy did not appear to be too pleased and waited till his Latin merriment had died away.

'I wish you now,' she said, 'to recall a poet infinitely greater than I, greatest of my masters, whom some have not recognised as a poet at all.'

Daniel knew the springing of a joyful warmth. Here it comes, he thought. He seemed to perform an act of levitation, rising perhaps an inch out of his chair: nothing ostentatious, but nevertheless infinitely satisfying.

'I refer,' said Dorothy, 'of course, to Adriaen Isenbrandt, painter, 1510–1551, whose *Mater Dolorosa*, in a chapel in the southern side of your noble cathedral, Onze Lieve Vrouwenkerk, as you call it, "Church of Our Beloved Woman", is to my mind the supreme poet of motherhood in the whole history of art.'

Daniel trembled with the violence of hope destroyed. She was a fool and a beast, a piddling ugly silly bird, he would like to gum up her beak with stickjaw.

'You have to hand it to old Dotty,' Duncan murmured wistfully, 'she does *know* a lot.'

But he must be patient. She must inevitably get to him in time. She had already laid the way open, by showing her audience that poetry was found not only in versification, not only in poetic dramas, such as Shakespeare's, Webster's, Tourneur's, but in all things. He steeled himself to endure, perhaps, a music reference before she was ready to introduce the subject of his novel.

A rude young student got up, gathered his books together and went out, tiptoeing for a dozen steps and then clanking the rest of the way.

'I could not pretend,' said Dorothy, 'to have equalled it – no, not to have come within miles of it!' she exclaimed colloquially, smiling to show how ordinary and natural she could be when she chose, 'but in my prologue, now almost popularly, if I may say so' – she gave a little light laugh – 'known as *Should Seven*, which opens my play *Joyful Matrix*, I think I may have caught a pale reflection of the Spirit of Isenbrandt. With your permission I shall say it to you.'

She stepped out from the desk and ambled to the extreme edge of the platform, waving a finger at them. 'Not "recite it", or "speak it" – just *say* it. No craft of presentation should be obtruded between a poem and its hearers. All should be simple, "artless" in the truest sense.'

There was a faint rustle at this. Lecture audiences, as Daniel had discovered long since, having attended all the free lectures available during the lost winter months when it was too cold to sit in his fireless room, loved a change, and any change was better than none. They were instantly refreshed when the lecturer stopped droning on in order to read something somebody else had written: when he wrote things on a blackboard; even when he walked up and down a bit.

Dorothy's face changed, and so did her voice. From being a little face it became a big one; she had filled her

77

cheeks with air. Her voice, from being a high and nagging one became, as she exhaled, plummy and deep. As she declaimed *Should Seven* she appeared increasingly overawed by what she had achieved: towards the end of it she even cast a quick glance over her shoulder, as if the performance had been given by something quite outside herself.

'…and in the pregnant sheaf
My groan,'

She paused.
'Bravo! Bravissimo!' Querini cried prematurely, clapping his hands over his head as if acclaiming himself at the Wigmore Hall.
Dorothy gave him a look so terrible that he flung himself nervously round in his chair, to see what offence he could possible have committed.

'. . . my grief,'

she concluded.
Nothing happened.
She said icily, 'I think I had better repeat the final verse, as the point may have been missed.'

' "…In mirth
the afterbirth,
And in the prayer, and in the pregnant sheaf
My groan,
My grief." '

'It does get you, you know,' Duncan whispered, under cover of the applause that had now broken out at the right time, 'it does something to you inside.' Tears flickered blue along his lower lids, like dew on gentians. 'Say what you like, she is pretty superb. You should have seen her on the screen, she absolutely *loomed*.'

Another student, perhaps feeling he had got what he had come for, briskly departed.

Dorothy was off again now on general theory, and Daniel's heart was hot and hard against her.

To comfort himself, he planned how he should approach the Countess. On the face of it, this would seem difficult; he had been a constant guest at her house in the old days, when he was young to Bruges, and if a coolness had sprung up between them, this was of her own making. Many such friendships, in this city, had long cooled off: all the faults of others, and none of his. They had been fools, they had failed to concede what, as an artist, he should have been able to claim from them without fear of demur. They had even denied him their bread and salt. And so he had drifted away from them all, without regret, hardly with contempt: this pseudo-aristocracy, bone-headed, idle and pigly, was not worth even the contempt of such a man as himself.

But now he had to re-establish relations, for the time being, at least, with Madame van Haecht. He must make it clear from the beginning that he was asking of her nothing but the right to bring to her house, just for a cup of coffee, a gentleman of a family as old and noble as her own. After all, he had his conscience to keep. It did not seem right that the Count, who must by now be rising ninety, should die without hearing his wife's confession, it did not seem right that the Countess should end her days with the lie between them, and the sin on her own conscience. It was true that when Daniel had last broached the matter she had flown into one of the silly tantrums of the aged and had said, 'Publish and be damned!' – but that was because of her impression, which revealed not only her stupidity, but her malice and the lie in her soul, that he was asking of her more than her continued friendship.

Stupid old woman, he thought, as he watched her head quivering lower and lower over the artificial violets at her breast, running up card debts and then taking a cut from

Mimi, of all people, to put herself straight! As if Mimi could be trusted for two minutes. Idiocy, he thought, is worse than crime; idiocy should be punished, so that people learn to keep their brains as clean and sweet as God intended them to be.

Suddenly he pricked up his ears.

'In conclusion,' Dorothy was saying, 'I must speak of the drama-poetry, the poetry-drama, of the Novel. I do not care for novels except when they are instinct with poetry, when they are narrative poems flowing subterranean beneath the rock of Being and Event. But there is one great novel, known to all too few in this age of ignorance, which is as round and pure a poem as *The Windhover*. I wonder how many of you know what I am going to say?'

She put her head on one side. She was a dear little tease, she teased them because she loved them.

Daniel was so excited that, without knowing what he did, he gripped the sleeve of Duncan's duffle coat and held it tightly.

'I know what it is,' said Duncan. 'It's *Kristin Lavrans-datter*. She's never read anything else. That was when she had mumps.'

'By a great Scandinavian,' said Dorothy, 'a woman: a supreme woman–'

Duncan patted Daniel's clutching hand. 'I like you too, Skip. I said I did. I like you most awfully.'

Dorothy lost her thread concerning the novel, and left suddenly with the threads of her entire lecture dangling, went brick red and said she didn't think she could do better than wind up by saying *Should Seven* to them again.

She did so, rather rapidly, backed away and sat down, nearly missing the chair which was shot under her just in the nick of time by the efficient chairman.

Applause broke out as vigorously as she could have wished, taking into account the smallness of the audience. Now they could all go home.

The chairman expressed his thanks, and everyone

clapped again.

Daniel felt like a man made out of shell, nothing inside him but the noisy seas of pure shock. His control snapped.

Jumping to his feet, he revived the flagging applause. *'Bravo! Bravo! Bravissimo! Hommages littéraires! Vervloekte koe! Superbe! Helse idioot van een wif! Hommages, hommages! Ga je verzuinen! Bravo! Lelijke slet! Bravo! Magnifique!'*

The English party, delighted, rose to support him in this ovation.

Some of the remaining students were shouting, some appeared hysterical with laughter: Dorothy, still bowing and beaming, managed to superimpose a glare upon a beam. Two elderly ladies, looking terrified, were making for the door.

'Bravo! Bravo!' Daniel yelled. As she came down the steps from the platform he flung himself upon her, kissing her hands. *'Superbe! Hors concours! Une femme sans égal!* Silly pop-eyed hag and faker!' he added in Flemish.

'Why, Mr Skipton,' said Dorothy, staggered, 'this is terribly kind, but isn't it just a little excessive? It isn't as if it was more than a sort of a little seminar –'

'Vervloekte koe,' he repeated. 'Nothing, for you, is too excessive. My congratulations. And now, if you will forgive me –' He saw that the chairman, who had lived long enough in Belgium to grasp something of what had been said, was gathering courage to attack him. '– but I must leave you. After such an evening, anything would be anticlimax.'

The chairman having thought better of it, was racing round the hall trying to pack the Flemish-speaking section of the audience out as quickly as possible.

'Well, well, Mr Skipton,' said Cosmo, his eyes unspeaking, his lips tight, 'you have done my wife proud. Yes, indeed. You will join us for a drink?'

Daniel smuggled an address into his hand. 'Nine fifteen sharp.' He said aloud, 'Forgive me. I am exhausted. I am not feeling so well.' He bowed to Querini. *'A demain.'*

'Si, si, si, si, si! And then you will tell me what I want to know, to whom one should write at the BBC –'

Daniel escaped; he had seen the Countess retreating, her eyes wild. He was almost at the door when he was intercepted by the chairman.

'Sir, I don't know who you are but –'

'It is an insult to your intelligence that you do not know who I am.'

'I have an idea that a slight has been offered to the lecturer –'

'Then if you have you'll keep your mouth shut, because it will do you no good to talk. Your masters in England may find another job for you. They may pack you off to serve the cause of culture in Punta Arenas, on the Straits of Magellan. And serve you right.'

He gave the man a push and was out again in the starry streets, sweet with the scent of beignets and fried potatoes, gaudy with the noise of the bells. Where had she got to? Yes, there she was, turning the corner by the chemist's shop, making the swivel upon her cane. He ran on soundless feet, whipped round her slow and tottering form, confronted her.

Twelve

Daniel went in good spirits to meet Querini, a Royal Flush up one sleeve and at least two pairs up the other. The first was the invitation, which would establish his social position in the Count's eyes and destroy the effect of any smiling denigration on Cosmo's part. He did not trust Cosmo, not at all. He never trusted suspicious men and he always despised them. He was certain that Cosmo was running him down behind his back, for no reason other than the mere instinct for malice. Not that he had been very effective up to now; Dorothy, after her ovation, had been cordial again; the ridiculous Duncan was offering his maudlin affections; and Pryar, after the evening at Mimi's, had something to thank him for.

The important thing was that he should have Querini on his side. At the least, he would have acquired a friendship of value with a man whose blood ran pure as his own. At the most, he might sell him the Wouters. Wouters, Wouters, he repeated to himself, as if afraid he might forget about it.

The April day was so warm that they were able to lunch in the river garden at a table set beneath the willows, the swans sailing past on water so polished and still that it might have been a blue meadow, dotted with small white clouds like motionless sheep bemused by the sweetness of the day. The restaurant was a square of white clapboard on the tail of a curve of red brick houses, their gardens slipping down like green water to the water's edge. It was more like the Backs at Cambridge than anything else Daniel could think of; and for a moment his serenity was soiled by the memory of the swine who had sent him down after two terms for nothing more than a young man's prank. He had never had the slightest intention of swindling the ridiculous tailor, only of making him suffer, a little space, for his mistrustfulness. His cheques would, eventually, have been honoured.

'Now you look sad,' said Querini, bringing his hands together, opening wide his calceolaria eyes, 'and that is not right! On such a day you should be 'appy as a king. Now we choose something beautiful to eat, fit for a beautiful occasion.' He reached for the *carte*.

Daniel just got it first. He had precisely three hundred and eighteen francs standing between himself and destitution, until Flabby Anne's next remittance turned up. He meant to spend a hundred and fifty on this luncheon, tips inclusive and no more.

'The *fondue au parmesan*,' he said, heading his guest off the *foie gras* and potted shrimps, 'is, as you know, a national dish: and better at this particular place than anywhere else in the whole of Belgium.'

83

'Now you will think it odd, coming from an Italian,' Querini replied sadly, 'but I cannot do with cheese. Cheese upsets me, it gives me dreams. Don't you think that is most surprising? Now fish, a little fish –'

'The *hors d'oeuvre*,' said Daniel, 'is good. In a sense, it is special: there are those who say that it is particularly subtle here, but as I am not a gourmet but a man of letters, I should not know.'

'Ah! You think the artist should 'ave a soul above food? Now I do not. I think the more 'e eat 'is 'ead off, the better 'is art. I do not, it is true, eat much before I sing, but when I 'ave sung! Ah, then! I go to the Taverna la Fenice, and Signor Zoppi, 'e give me turkey with *tartuffi bianchi* – a dream!' He kissed his fingers.

'We will begin with the *hors d'oeuvre*,' Daniel shouted to a passing waiter, setting seal upon the irrevocable.

He steered Querini on to *tête de veau vinaigrette* at which there was no demur; and was profoundly relieved when the Italian himself suggested they should drink beer.

'It is gassy, you understand, yes: and for a singer therefore not good. But wine gives me acid stomach and for a singer that is worse, oh, far worse!'

'For myself,' Daniel said, twinged with sudden disgust at the thought of Duncan Moss, 'I drink very little. The truth is, that all alcohol is filth. But we are compelled to swallow our peck of it, as it were, before we die, in order to conform to the conventions of an idiot society. King Ferdinand of Bulgaria, my father's greatest friend and wisest counsellor, drank nothing but mineral water with a slight coloration of orange juice.'

This might well have been true, since he had no idea what the truth was. In the circumstances, it would have been no more to his credit had he said that King Ferdinand drank only *slivovitz*.

'Fancy that,' said Querini, 'well, fancy!'

The thought seemed to cast a sombreness about him, to darken not only his eyes but the tone of his brown suit.

Daniel waited with a degree of apprehension lest, by the purest chance, his guest should happen to have been acquainted with the intimate habits of the King, and should issue an effective *démenti*. But all he said was, 'As you are an Englishman of culture, a famous writer, you must know everybody in the BBC.'

Daniel regretted that he had been too long out of England to have such contacts, repressing the fact that he had been employed by the Corporation himself. Such persons as he had known there had been narrow and unhelpful.

'I know it is bad form,' said Querini, 'to "swank", but I sing like the angels. That is not boast, it is a matter of fact. I sing really lovely.'

Daniel saw his way through to the Royal Flush. It was an inspiration; he would have been proud of himself had inspiration not been as common to him as a sneeze to a snuff-taker.

Pushing his plate back, he gazed up into the still, soft branches where the little lights flittered about like humming-birds. He spread his hands on the table, looked down at them, tightening his mouth; looked up.

'Count Querini, I shall be frank with you.'

'If you are going to say something nasty about yourself,' the Italian retorted gaily, 'then I shall not listen! I am sure you are a nice man. I am a nice man, too. And Signora 'Ines is perhaps a nice woman when you get to know 'er better, but Signor 'Ines, no.'

What had Cosmo been saying about him? Daniel's heart pounded in alarm, three short knocks and a long one. 'Hines?'

'It does not matter. He tell me people except 'imself and 'is wife are nobodies. But I know 'oo is and 'oo is not.'

Daniel repeated loudly, 'I shall be frank with you.'

'No!' Querini lifted his hand. His eyes sparkled. 'Do not.'

'I was simply about to say that I cannot help you with

85

reference to the BBC. I am, as you say, a writer of some reputation; but by choice I am a solitary. I do not mingle with my kind, or attempt to make contact with them. I live for art –'

'*Vissi d'arte*,' said Querini in a feathery voice, 'it should not have been written for woman, no.'

' – for art, not for its trappings. Not for its mechanics. I am first of all an artist: and next, though I confess to you that I have little wealth, a gentleman. Like yourself, I may lay claim to a title of nobility: absurd, perhaps, but I should insult the very great gentleman who conferred it upon me in my infancy if I were to repudiate it now.'

He related the story of the Order of SS Cyril and Methodius and Querini heard him to the end, making no sound beyond an appreciative interpolation of 'Oh?' and 'Ah?'

'You may well wonder,' said Daniel, 'where all this is leading.'

'Wait! We 'ave to choose. *Intermezzo*, if you please!' The waiter was leaning over them, flapping the *carte*. Querini grabbed it.

Daniel knew a spiritual shrinking. There were wild strawberries, out of season, with kirsch and cream; there was a savoury of chicken livers; there was a huge white pudding, like a crinoline in subsidence, called simply a 'Blanche'. Respectively 45 francs, 40 francs, 45 francs 50.

Querini said, 'No, I am full up. I will 'ave simply coffee.'

Daniel relaxed. There was a great deal, he felt, to be said for Querini, ascetic, inexpensive Querini. Detesting the brutish fancy of democracy that the word 'gentleman' was obsolete, that birth and breeding counted for little against the horny-handed worthiness of H-dropping numskulls, he found himself appreciating the Italian almost to the point of liking. It was not in Daniel to like people; he did not even like, though he admired, himself. He despised those who talked about friendship when all they meant was the sloppy cordiality of the saloon-bar or cocktail party. He felt a tremble of desire for a relationship such as he had not known before; not, perhaps, a friendship, but a closeness between equals.

'And I will have a glass of water,' said Daniel with unaffected majesty.

A skiff went by with a burden of charming girls rowing like blazes, in tight white shirts and tight white shorts.

'Now girls,' said Querini wistfully, 'I can appreciate in the abstract.'

This might have given another lead; but Daniel pursued the first.

'As I was saying, you may wonder where all this is leading. But what I was about to say to you is this: as an artist, I am a solitary. As a man, I am almost a solitary. But I keep up a few old friendships, often with persons older than myself; persons who embody still in this material age, something of the spirit in which I was myself nurtured and reared.'

'Now it is funny,' Querini observed in his thoughtful way, 'Signora 'Ines, she says she give a lecture on the Poet-Playwright in the Welfare State. She says much about the poet-playwright. But I remember damn all about the Welfare State.'

'If you are not otherwise employed this afternoon,' Daniel pressed on, 'I should like to take you to tea with my friend Countess van Haecht, perhaps the oldest, and certainly the most profoundly rooted, member of the ancient aristocracy of Flanders. She would be honoured to receive you. You, on your part – and I take what you are into full consideration – would not be dishonoured in being received by her.'

'She is an old lady?' Querini enquired doubtfully. 'It is funny, you would think it the other way about, but I am not much good with old ladies.'

He had emptied his cup.

'Now,' he said cheerfully, 'I 'ave another, I drink coffee after coffee after coffee!'

Daniel froze. Coffee, at this place, cost an amount quite disproportionate to the meal as a whole.

'It isn't good here,' he said. 'At all other things these people are admirable, but coffee – no. It is like Southend mud.'

'Whatever mud it is like,' said Querini, flinging up his hand in a broad, gay gesture. 'I shall drink it. Cups and cups. *Garçon!*'

He ordered for himself.

'But, Count, we shall be drinking coffee with Madame van Haecht, that is, if you accept her invitation.'

'Of course I do! Though old ladies they are not so bright, and of aristocrats I see too many, they are not bright either. My papa is not. But perhaps she is an artist?'

'It is she,' said Daniel firmly, 'who might give you, at least, valuable contacts with musical circles in Brussels.'

He hoped passionately that the Count was not as unimpressed by his own caste as he appeared to be. If that was so, his Royal Flush was failing to make the customary effect.

'Well,' said Querini, 'Brussels would be better than nothing at all. But I thought you said tea.'

'Tea?'

'That we were invited to tea.'

'A phrase,' said Daniel, 'denoting the hour of invitation. She only drinks coffee.'

'A pity,' said Querini. 'In England I was prisoner of war. I love tea. Indian, very strong, lots of sugar, condensed milk. Never mind. I am an artist and live not for the stomach alone, though as I say, the stomach is important.'

Daniel watched his bill mounting as the coffee poured down. He wanted to cover his eyes. His spirit, however, was sturdy. If one door shut, it was his practice to put a shoulder to the next.

He broached the subject of the responsibility of the artist for seeing all sides of life, for looking unmoved upon good and evil alike. Deviously, he worked round to the point at which he indicated his contacts with the latter, at the same time expressing his nausea that the latter should be so easy to root out of hiding. He had seen things, he said simply, that he had never believed existed.

'Oh well,' said the Count with the air of boulevardier, 'you are a solitary gentleman, life would still have its surprises for you.' The waiter came up in response to his finger. 'I would like more coffee, please, this time with cream.'

Daniel said recklessly, hoping the glutton Querini would sense the rebuke, 'A Kümmel, perhaps?'

'No, no, no. Not for me.'

Thank God for that. 'Reverting to what I was saying: if you had read my books, you would not take me for a person lacking in sophistication.'

'If they were translated into Italian – by *traduttore*, not *traditore*, you understand?' – he smiled lightly at this old joke – 'I would read them all, one by one. But I do not read English very well. And Mondadori, our great publisher, 'as been so bung up with translations since the war that now we get few books from abroad. I bet 'e 'as not taken books from Signor Skipton.'

It seemed to Daniel that the sheep in the river were turning grey, that they were barging along as if the wolf were after them. The colour of the day was fading for him, if for nobody else.

'I do not want to know your *bordelli*,' said Querini earnestly, 'they do not interest me. I only want a friend at the BBC, but you have not got one. Also, I do not for a moment suppose you know of any *bordelli*.'

So much for another outing to Mimi's.

'Certainly I do not,' Daniel said sternly. Now, with the wrench of a taxi-driver turning in a narrow street, he switched the conversation to painting. If he ever came to Venice, which seemed unlikely as he detested travel, he would be much interested in seeing the Count's collection.

Querini's eyes regained their yellow lights. His hands,

surfaced like silk, flew apart in enthusiasm. 'Oh, you must
see it, you must! I have a Basaiti, very big, very 'ideous, I
adore it! You must see it; my papa says it is plain beastly, but
'e knows nothing at all.'

The conversation grew more lively. Daniel threw in the
less common Venetians, Bonifazio, Moretto, Romanino,
Cariani: the Count had something to say about them all.

Then Daniel said casually, 'But you should own a few
Flemish primitives. Though it is not generally known –
indeed one goes to infinite trouble not to let it be known –
there are still some charming things to be picked up here,
for example, in Bruges itself, for a mere song.'

'Nothing which costs a song is any damn good,' said
Querini practically. 'The dealers, they know too much.'

This was received in smiling silence.

'Well, do you know a dealer 'oo is a big baby?'

Daniel called for the bill, stiffening himself to open it. It
was well that he did so for it was terrible: Belgian frcs
248.45. Much, much worse than he had even begun to
imagine. He ran his eye down the items, praying to discover
an error: but the vast figure at the foot denoted precisely the
value of the cups of coffee Querini had consumed.

He laid down two hundred-franc notes and a fifty,
praying that he could whisk his guest away before the waiter
expressed his contempt for the smallness of the tip. He shot
up. 'We must go. Madame van Haecht is intolerant of being
kept waiting, even for two minutes. It is her age, and the age
in which she was bred.'

'The poor old lady must wait a bit,' said Querini, with a
wink, 'for I 'ave to go to the Gents.'

He was in there for nearly five minutes.

Daniel was not surprised.

In the meantime the offended waiter circled him with
the expert, greasy movements of a dancer on skates,
shooting beams from his eye and inaudible pleasantries
from the side of his mouth. One day, Toad, Daniel thought,
I will know enough about you to make you pay for this. But

at the moment there was nothing for him to do but knot his hands behind his back and stare up into the glossy sky.

Querini returned, buttoning himself. He took Daniel's arm. 'Left, right, left, right, we will not keep 'er long now. 'Oo is this silly dealer? Come on, you tell me and I shall not spoil the market by tipping off my papa.'

'I am sorry. I spoke rashly. Furthermore, I was speaking in generalities.'

'Now I 'ave put my foot in it,' Querini said sadly, 'you do not trust me yet. But you will!' he added, brightening. 'I never knew anybody 'oo did not. I am patient as God, you shall see.'

As they turned into the courtyard of the gloomy house in which the Count and Countess van Haecht lived out the last trickle of their lives, Daniel permitted himself to relax. Leaving aside the commission to be collected tomorrow from Madame Houdin in respect of the lecher Hines, he reckoned he had only sixty-six francs left to him in the world. But he had hope. He would have to talk to Wouvermans at the earliest possible moment.

Thirteen

The entire ground floor consisted of a vast, grey-painted hall with a lot of coloured glass in it, something between a conservatory and the waiting-room of a railway station. There was nothing there but a hard wooden bench and two columns of bronze, supporting rubber-plants. In the back wall, flanked by two rows of pilasters, now scratched and crumbling, was a wooden staircase leading to the upper quarters.

After a longish climb, for the first floor was derelict, they were ushered, by an old, deaf maidservant, into the drawing room of the Countess. Both old people were sound asleep, upright in their chairs.

'Keep them waiting two seconds,' Daniel whispered

bitterly, 'and this is what happens. I told you to hurry up, but you would shilly-shally.'

The room had been furnished at the highest point of chic in the 1920s, and since then, it seemed, had barely had so much as a flick with a duster. The skirts of the crinoline doll squatting over the telephone as if it were a privy were faded, dirty and split. The jazz-patterned lampshade had lost half its fringes: the pierrot doll sprawled over the jazzy cushions had lost its nose and several pompoms. One of the tubular chairs had a split seat and the statuette of the dancing girl was filmed over with a greyness like leprosy.

The chairs in which the Count and Countess slept were, however, of the period of Leopold II; and over the chimney-piece was a full-length portrait, noble and very bad, of Albert I. There was a fire in the grate. The room was suffocatingly hot. As Daniel stood there, for once at a loss, one of a sheaf of dry leaves stuck in a majolica vase on the upright piano tumbled out and rattled on to the tiles.

'You must excuse me,' said Madame van Haecht, 'but I am old and sleep is too easy.'

She opened full upon Daniel a glance compounded of recognition and of distaste. She had made the transition between sleeping and waking as easily as a cat who rises from the rug and goes at once to his saucer. 'You must excuse me, too, if I do not rise.' Leaning over, she patted her husband's cheek. 'Frans! Frans! Wake up, Frans, we have guests.'

He woke with a start and sprang to his feet, a tremor running down him from crown to soles like the tremor of a taut clothes-line when a bird alights on it. 'My dear. Yes?'

'Meneer Skipton has brought a friend to call upon us.'

'Yes, yes, I remember, it is very kind of him. I must put a piece of coal on the fire, my dear, it is getting quite chilly.'

Daniel introduced Querini, who greeted them in French. This, unlike his horrible English, was elegant and pure, but the Countess would have none of it.

'In this house,' she said, 'we do not speak that language.

We speak Flemish, or we speak English.'

She had been a fanatical Nationalist all her life, and had got tipsy publicly, on the terrace of the Panier d'Or, in full view of the population, on the day the French street names were taken down and rue de l'Equerre became once more Winckelstrasse.

He apologised to them both. 'But it is sad, I think, because I 'ave an idea my English makes Signor Skipton wince. I sound, as 'e would say, a common sort of chap.'

It was interesting to Daniel to observe how the van Haechts took to Querini. It was true that he himself was ignored by the Countess as much as she dare ignore him: but it did not worry him. Poor, dirty, old, living in their hideous dusty room, they were nevertheless of the old nobility; it was written down every dying inch of them.

The maidservant brought coffee and some stale *Noeuds de Bruges*, confections Daniel had always disliked and which he regarded as a tourist treat on the level of Margate rock; but Querini tucked away at them as if he had had no food for a month.

It was curious, Daniel thought, how a trace of the *louche* was perceptible still in Madame van Haecht's crumpled face. She had been a scandalous girl in her youth, so he had been told, her name a by-word in the Brussels of the 'nineties; but when the Count had come from Bruges to marry her, he had rapidly simmered her down. He was not a Catholic, but a Dutch Protestant; his mother had been Dutch, and it had been with her that he and his young wife had lived stringently for nearly fifteen years.

Typical of the old woman that, when up to her eyes in card debts contracted behind her husband's back, her mind should instantly have turned to the possibilities of a little genteel pimping. If there was anything Daniel hated, it was a pimp; he repressed the natural pity that rose in him at the spectacle of her great age, and remembered that if he were in the slightest sense the instrument of her punishment, then she was damned lucky to get off with an instrument so relatively painless.

'I travelled in your beautiful country in my youth,' the old man told Querini. 'I had a good friend in Verona, the Marchese Guardini. He would be dead now. But he had several sons. One is a wine importer – they had vineyards, you know, or perhaps you would not, they made a tolerable Chianti, not so fine as Antinori but pleasant – pleasant –'

'Don't ramble, Frans,' said his wife.

'No, I must not ramble.' He bowed his head, as if she had told him he must write this out a hundred times. 'I must not ramble. But my dear, what was I saying?'

'The young Guardini is a wine-importer in Brussels,' she said impatiently, 'that's what you wanted to say.'

Querini clapped his hands. 'But I used to know 'im, we were at the University of Padua together, what a snuffy old place! But my papa, that was 'is silly idea. Yes, Guardini, he is very good musician, he plays the piano lovely.'

The last of Daniel's lingering doubts fluffed away like white ash up a chimney.

' 'E must come over 'ere before I go to England! I tell you what, Madame, you 'ave a piano, you could let me give a little recital, yes? Guardini would play for me, I would sing Fauré, Duparc, Wolff, Monteverdi and a 'ole lot of troubadours! It would not put you out?'

The van Haechts looked, in fact, appallingly put out.

'Mr Skipton will tell you that we hardly ever entertain these days.'

'But it would not be entertaining, see? Just a little coffee, a tiny, tiny cup each' – he ringed his thumb and forefinger to indicate how tiny a cup it would be – 'and just the Marchese, and Mr Skipton, and my English friends, one is a great lady writer like Mrs Browning – nothing more! Now you will let me, no? Because they say to each other, "Querini is all big talk, 'e say 'e can sing, but they will never let 'im triumph in the Wigmore 'All".'

On this track Querini was unstoppable. The idea of a piano and a pianist had inflamed him: he disregarded the stony reluctance of his hosts, he pressed them like a touting gondolier.

'Now you see! In all this there is no trouble for you. I ring Guardini over the telephone. We make all the arrangements. I even 'elp make the coffee. All you and Signor van Haecht shall do is to sit and listen, and to such sounds! Do not think I am conceited. It is cold fact.'

'Do me the kindness,' said the Count, 'since you are younger and more nimble than I, to put that big piece of coal on the fire. Give it a poke – there! That's better.'

Freshened flame roared up into the oven of a room.

Daniel thought rapidly. If he put a stop to this nonsense he would get the old woman on to his side, which might come in useful one day. If, on the other hand, he backed Querini up, he would be able to make the acquaintance of another Italian nobleman, more exalted socially, and doubtless just as able to afford the Wouters. He would make Wouvermans demand the equivalent of fifty pounds for it and refuse to budge by a penny.

So he said smoothly to the Countess, 'If you should lend your drawing room to such an occasion, I assure you that it would be an historic one. I do not know if you remember a soprano who gave a private recital in Bruges some twenty years ago. I wish I could remember her name. In one evening, before a small circle of cognoscenti, she consolidated her European reputation. Alas, she died in the war.'

'And what is that to me, Meneer Skipton?' the Countess demanded, her anger overcoming discretion. 'We are not makers of reputations, European or otherwise. We do not keep a *salon*. We know little of the arts and care less. Indeed –'

'Now what was her name?' Daniel mused. 'It is extraordinary how such things elude me. Ah! I know; it was Mimi something. Now, Mimi what? Could it have been Mimi –?'

The Countess did not let him say it.

'All right then!' she screeched, and her head bobbled

violently. 'We give our drawing room to the performance. Did I say we would not?'

Querini in delight, seized her hands. 'But you know what you are? You are old darling, that is what you are, and *il Conte* van Haecht, 'e is old darling too. You 'ave 'earts of gold like my friend Cavaliere Skipton, I cannot love you enough!'

After this, Daniel was glad to take him away as soon as possible.

'It was nice of them,' Querini said, as they passed through the dark hall, 'because they will die soon. It is very sad. They sit there so snug, so sleepy, so old, in a room that smells of death, but they do not know for they 'ave had the smell in their poor old noses now for years and years. They must love you very much, Signor Skipton, if they do so much to please your friend, just as they are about to die. God, let us walk a little by the canal! I am so 'ot I think I shall die myself, and that would not do now we 'ave everything so arranged, ah no, that would not do at all!'

Fourteen

Daniel returned to his attic by no means displeased with his prospects. He found that the afternoon post had brought him a letter from Flabby Anne. Reading it, he felt that he had fallen backwards down a flight of stairs.

'Dear Danny,

'Your second letter has upset me very much. I am an old woman and I don't think you ought to make silly threats. I have done all I could for you out of what I have left for dear Archie's sake which, considering I have never seen you, does seem to me not bad. But I have taken advice, and Mr Pellew, my solicitor, says there is no reason to pay you anything, so with much regret I am going to stop sending. I live in a very modest way since poor James died, the house is too big for me to keep up but I cannot get anything else, the council owns all the cottages. I have only a woman who comes in by the day and the garden is in a dreadful state. So hoping you will remember kindness in the past and not think badly of me, I remain,

'Your affec. cousin

'Anne Wrigley.

'PS. It is a crying shame to say I have ever hidden anything from the Income Tax, Mr Pellew would not let me.'

He looked about him for something to destroy. If he could not find something he would go mad; yet everything in his room was necessary, even precious: here, and on his person, was all he had in this vast meanness of a world, this torture-chamber for the artist and the upright man. His head was throbbing. He looked in the glass and saw his own wild bony face, the dark eyes protruding as if in strangulation, the lips flushing with blood where he had bitten them, like sheep-ticks squeezed between finger and thumb. He must rip, he must tear, he must find symbolic murder for his hands.

Lotte bumped the tray against the door and came in with it sideways. 'Here's your supper! Pigs' feet, and very nice too. You'd have got potatoes, but Mum's had the idea of rent again.'

Daniel turned slowly and regarded her. Setting the tray down she gave a squeal. 'I say, you do look a sight! Something upset your apple-cart?'

He swore at her and pushed her outside, aiming a kick at the door instead of her bottom. He flung the window open, tore the pigs' feet from their glutinous sauce, ripped the flesh off with his fingers and hurled it out of the window into the canal. Sticky, breathless, his hands disgusting, he watched the morsels bobbing below, soiling the water, soiling the city. Then he washed himself, yanking his clothes off from head to foot, going over every inch he could reach with the battered nail brush. He would be clean, he had to be clean, if he were to get through this hour of rage.

The cold water and the hot friction sobered him up. Supperless, and not caring if he were, he sat down to sort things out, to draw up a balance sheet. He wrote the credit in green, the debit items in red. He produced the following statement:

CR.

	B.frs.
In hand, on the feast of St. Mark the Evangelist, April 25, remaining from F.A.'s miserable remittance	140.00
From Malouel, for shrine	25.00
Commission from Mimi, for Spectacle	250.00
	415.00

White tie	6.00
1 Coffee	12.00
Commission to Wouvermans	50.00
Round of drinks for 6 persons	45.00
Tip	2.00
Fare to Knocke	15.50
Luncheon to Conte Querini, Gormandiser	250.00
	380.50

Cr. balance. B.frs. 34.50

Like all personal statements of this kind, the result on paper did not quite tally with the reality. The human element had to be taken into account, the element of forgetfulness. When he turned out his pockets he found that he had not frs. 34.50, but frs. 32.75. In English terms, about five shillings and sixpence.

Flabby Anne, like the fat miser she was, had reneged on her responsibilities.

And Madame la Botte was enjoying the conception of

being a receiver of rents.

He held his aching head in his hands.

Wait! There was yet something to come. One hundred francs, commission from Madame Houdin, plus reimbursement of fare to Knocke, frs. 15.50. He would have to get hold of the lascivious Hines first thing in the morning.

Still, it did not look promising. He might fob Madame la Botte off with fifty francs, but he doubted it. He could, of course, try: he would try.

There was only one thing to do. Crumpling up the balance sheet, he found paper and an envelope. He was so filled with gall that his stomach, never what it should be despite the daily dose of raisin water, went back on him, as mankind had gone back on him, and he retched violently several times, though without result, into his handkerchief.

When it had stopped churning, he wrote a short letter.

'Dear Utterson,
'You demand of me that I should write to you again. I do so. I do not think you can complain that the terms of this communication are uncivil.

'Yours,

'Daniel Skipton

'(Kt of the MN Order of SS Cyril and Methodius).'

He went out with it, this time buying a stamp. As he dropped it in the box his throat constricted.

He ground up his courage like an iron bucket out of a well. He had never been lacking in courage, he had never given way. While there was still a practical course open to him he would follow it.

He went on to see Wouvermans, and banged at the door of his shop till the old man opened up. He was feeling angrier than ever, since he regretted throwing the pigs' feet into the canal; he was desperately hungry.

Wouvermans took him into the back room behind the shop, a grubby den with his meal cooling on the table, fish and boiled potatoes. Daniel spiked a potato and ate it.

'You stop that!' Wouvermans cried. 'I won't have you walking in here and eating my supper, not however high and mighty you are.'

Daniel felt the hot root sliding down his throat to fill just a corner of the vast and windy space below.

'I'm going to be worth more to you than a potato, you old carp. Have you still got the Wouters?'

'You said it wasn't, Meneer. We know how double-clever you are.'

'It's a Wouters from now on. Have you got it?'

'I might have.'

'And I might have a customer. Now listen Wouvermans, if I bring you one, you ask seven thousand francs and you don't budge, not by a centime. And if you get a sale, fifty per cent of that is mine.'

The old man started up. 'Fifty per cent? I tell you what, you're going up the pole, that's what it is. Never did I pay fifty per cent my whole life long!'

Daniel told him this was the time to start. The picture wasn't worth the rotten wood it was painted on, let alone the frs. 3,500 which would be Wouvermans' own share. 'He's an Italian, and rich as Rockefeller. I'll find out whether old Key has got any stuff.'

At the mention of this dealer, who was reputable, Wouvermans stopped chewing his fish and looked up with open mouth, a crumbly mess inside it.

'I will,' said Daniel, 'or may I one day look as filthy as you look at this moment.'

All the same, it was a full hour before he got the agreement he wished.

Next morning he telephoned the Memling Palace and made an appointment with Cosmo to meet him at three o'clock in a café behind the Bourgplaats.

Cosmo turned up twenty minutes late, looking more

bloodshot than usual and tight with ill-temper.

'I hope you found your jaunt to Knocke satisfactory?' said Daniel, accepting the grudging offer of an orangeade.

'All I can say is that I found better places to the rear of Paddington Station.'

'Indeed? That is something I shouldn't know.'

'A flea-ridden hole and a Flanders mare.'

'Louise? I believe,' said Daniel, with an air of casual disgust, 'that there is one called Louise.'

'There was no Louise that I saw. There was a pudding-face called Marie, with a moustache, and an old one, must have been fifty, called Jeanne, and this Hendrickje, who at least looked clean. I told the old woman she'd get five hundred from me, and not another cent.'

This would cut Daniel's commission by half: the street swam before him.

'All I feel is sick,' said Cosmo.

'I am sorry, but you should not have come to me. I know nothing of these places. I had been told of this particular address, and it was the only one I could give you. By the way, I'm afraid I must ask you for my return fare to Knocke.'

Cosmo paid reluctantly.

Daniel, switching his mind to more hopeful things, now told him of Querini's projected recital at the house of the van Haechts: and was stupefied to be rewarded, not by renewed respect, but by a slow, bloodless grin of derision.

'Look here, Skipton,' said Cosmo, 'I've found out something about our noble friend. Dorothy suspected him from the first: you can't swindle Dorothy. She always believes the worst and she's usually right.'

Buffoons around them, still believing the world a good place, were chattering their heads off, gorging ice-creams and cream pastries, and adding to their already grotesque weight of flesh. Daniel could have struck them down, could have called fire upon them from heaven. He was terrified.

'I know where he's staying,' continued the man Hines, 'I

followed him. He's staying in a slummy little pension behind the station, a hundred francs a day all found. I pretended I wanted a room myself, and I heard a lot. His landlady says he sings all day and it's like a sick cow. She's about fed up with him; she doesn't like music.'

Daniel said stiffly, 'There is no question that he is acquainted with the Marchese Guardini.'

'Shone his boots once, I expect, on the Piazzetta. Are you seriously expecting your Marchese to show up? As for Querini – count, my foot.'

'He is a gentleman,' Daniel said, breathing hard, 'more than many people I know. But he is, it is true, singularly mean.'

'Wigmore 'All,' said Cosmo, his grin spreading. 'Wigmore 'All!' He got up. 'You'll see. And now I must bid you farewell I think, Skipton, that you had better refuse to make recommendations in future to persons of my rackety tastes, since you are by no means accomplished in that respect.'

'Mr Hines,' said Daniel, speaking slowly, 'your attitude to me is such that in a more robust age than our own I should have taken pleasure in calling you out.'

'And I should have run like blazes. So where do you think that would have got you?'

'It's only out of respect for your wife and her great gifts that I pursue this acquaintance.'

'I think you were saying rude things to Dorothy at her lecture,' said Cosmo, spitting on a finger and obliterating a spot of beer on his lapel. 'I don't know Flemish, it's true, but I picked up a bit of German in my youth. Well, you will let us know when the recital takes place, won't you? I wouldn't miss it. Indeed, I wouldn't miss it.'

He twirled his hand round in the air and walked off, leaving Daniel to his own thoughts.

Daniel smelled danger: though he was too shaken by Cosmo's assurance concerning Querini to think of much else, he knew that he must watch his own step. If Hines, the hyena, the coward (Daniel ought to have replied, to his announcement that he would run away, 'In that event, sir, I should have been compelled to cane you'), was getting a wrong impression about him this would have to be readjusted. For it had occurred to him that Dorothy, if her good will held, might be useful to him, and it would be a disaster if her ridiculous husband poisoned her mind.

In deep perturbation he made his way along the quays, round the back of Notre Dame, down Sinte Katelijnestraat and through the Wijngaardstraat to the Minnewater and the Béguinhof. He came through the Archway into the lovely Square of grass and poplars, surrounded by houses that were caskets of quietude, and of stern, gentle lives. The daffodils were almost over, but there were galaxies of daisies streaming over the greenness. The custodian of the gate knew him too well to try to lug him into her cavern and sell him lace or postcards. He began his slow perambulation of the paths, his shadow before him, in the sharpness of the sun, like the shadow of a trousered bird. Here he could think in peace. No eyes peeped at him from behind the closed shutters, for the béguines did not peep. A breeze sprang up. The gold and silver of the flowers was sifted through the mesh of grass, the poplars heaved a sigh of contentment as they showed the white side of their leaves. The white coif of an old woman at the door of her little house flared up as if it were a sail that might carry her away, so big it seemed, so frail she was.

Fifteen

He was just passing by the chapel when something fat came out of it, and collided with him.

'My dear old Skip!' cried Duncan Moss, embracing him, 'How nice! What fun! What on earth are you doing here?'

This being a rhetorical question, Daniel did not reply, but bowed as well as he could, taking into consideration the fact that Duncan had both arms around his waist.

'This is marvellous, you can meet her straight away. She's inside with Matthew, but they won't be long. Do you know, she's been here three days. Simply *nobody* knew!'

'Who has?' Daniel asked, disengaging himself by the undignified device of slipping under Duncan's arms rather than through them.

'My dear fellow! Mrs Jones!'

'Mrs Jones?'

'But you must know! *The* Mrs Jones! She's so smart it's not true. Matthew's in the seventh heaven. I'm afraid he's a snob, but I do think that's the least of the vices, don't you? – Like card-sharping or being a fence. I simply cannot get up the slightest moral indignation about either of them. She goes everywhere out of season, she makes a point of it. That's why seasons are inevitably a flop, because if they're the out-of-seasons they're wrong anyway, and if they're the in-seasons, Mrs Jones has buzzed off to Gozo, or somewhere extraordinary.'

Daniel was just about to ask for more concrete information when a woman emerged from the chapel, Matthew just behind her.

'Darling Mrs Jones,' Duncan cried, 'I want you to meet a terrific friend, that is, I want him to meet you. I never get introductions right but you're too big to hold it against me.'

Coming to a halt, she looked Daniel up and down.

She was a minute woman, very thin, with a prodigious nose arched like a waterfall; it would have made four of Dorothy's. She was probably in her late fifties, but it was hard to tell, for though she wore age in her face it had not lined her. Her clothes were rather shabby, a navy-blue suit, a damaged-looking straw hat of the same colour. She had long, narrow blue shoes and beautiful kid gloves wrinkling up past her elbows.

Matthew shot round her, somehow succeeding in obliterating Duncan. 'Mildred, darling, may I present Mr Daniel Skipton, Knight of the Order of SS. Cyril and Methodius, who has the great good luck to live in this delightful city? Mr Skipton, allow me to present you to Mrs Jones.'

She shot out her hand silently, gripping Daniel's with a kind of electronic force; it was difficult to believe she had no machine concealed in her palm.

'How 'j do. SS. Cyril and Methodius, that's a Bulgarian Order. Know the King? No, you're too young. How 'j get it?'

As Daniel explained, she kept her foot tapping, her hatpin gaze steady upon his face.

'Skipton? Was he in Sofia with Puddefoot? M' father respected Puddefoot, always said he was far from a fool.'

Daniel, glowing, though he did not know why her attention should give him such a feeling of acceptance, acknowledged Puddefoot.

'Mr Skipton is a most distinguished writer,' Duncan said eagerly, 'but an awfully special sort of one. For the few.'

'Don't 'j want to be read?' Mrs Jones demanded. 'Can't think why you plug away at it if y' don't. Matthew, I want m' tea. Mr Skipton can join us and tell us all about those books he doesn't want people to read.'

They all passed out of the Béguinhof together, the men clustered like leaves about some spiky and uncompromising flower.

Mrs Jones did most of the talking on the way, this consisting of enquiries about the friends she and Matthew had in common. 'Ever see Norfolk?' – or, ''J know poor Alf Dorset's marrying that gel who sings on the wireless?'

They came into the Grand' Place, noisy with holiday, the excursion coaches pouring in, the carillon pouring down. The red, black and yellow flags rippled in the breeze, the cassocks flapped, the skirts of the girls ballooned. Stepping back in line with Duncan, Daniel asked, 'Who is Mrs Jones?' but got no reply, for at that moment Dorothy bore down upon them in pink, a cartwheel hat stuck right on the back of her head. She looked like a mushroom. She addressed Duncan and Matthew.

'Oh I say, you two! Where have you got to? What's the use of saying we're all going to have a holiday together when you know you don't mean it? Cosmo and I are starving, we want our tea.'

Matthew, looking as excited as a man could who had so unmomentous a face, seized her arm.

'Oh, Dotty, this is splendid! Mrs Jones, will you permit me to present Miss Dorothy Merlin, Mrs Cosmo Hines?'

'How 'j do,' said Mrs Jones. She looked round. 'I don't see Mrs Hines.'

'Dorothy *is* Mrs Hines. Dotty, darling, this is Mrs Jones.'

She just about acknowledged the introduction.

'Duncan, if you've been picking up any more ghastly little girls, we don't want to meet them. Didn't you say –'

'Miss Merlin is a most distinguished verse-dramatist,' Matthew said, 'as of course you know.'

'I'm afraid I don't; never see plays, never read 'em. 'M sorry.'

'I write for the few,' said Dorothy.

'Do you? Now that's queer. Mr Skipton here says he does, but if I wrote books, I'd want people to read 'em,' said Mrs Jones. 'I expect it's m' generation.'

'Listen,' said Dorothy, 'I want my tea. Cosmo wants his tea. If you are *all* coming, then do for heaven's sake come. We're at the Vandenberge.'

'Oh, but we are all coming,' said Matthew, 'that is –' He looked at Daniel, who said, 'You must excuse me.'

'I expect you want yours, Mr Skipton,' Mrs Jones said, 'I

don't think y' eat enough. Come along.'

Taking command of the party, she swept it forward. 'Vandenberge? Where's that? Ah, yes, I see. Mr Skipton, that is a remarkable tie, very interesting. What is it? Oh, a white tie painted. I never saw anything like that before. I must take one home to Wulfric, that's m' nephew. He's just at that stage.'

Cosmo, when presented to Mrs Jones, looked puzzled and put out, though he was relieved when it became obvious that she was in the role of hostess. Belgium was an expensive place to live in, and it was the oddments like teas, beers and coffees which mounted up. Both he and Dorothy seemed bewildered by the deference paid by Matthew and Duncan to this new acquaintance. Daniel heard him whisper to his wife, 'But who is *Jones*, if I may ask?'

Mrs Jones commanded the waiter to set two tables together so that they should not be crowded. Daniel wondered about her. Despite her shabbiness, her near-rudeness, she had a certain style. He wondered if she were the principal of a women's college, but dismissed the idea. If she had been, she would have heard of Dorothy.

'All this cowardice about a pack of bombs,' Mrs Jones was saying, 'perfectly absurd. Stops people getting on with their work. Nasty way to die, I grant you, but no sense in puling about it. All the same whether you pule or don't pule, so where's the sense?'

Dorothy pulled out a grave, sweet smile unbecoming to her avian bone structure and clasped her hands before her on the table. 'As the mother of men,' she said, 'perhaps I feel differently.'

'Oh? How many men?'

'Seven,' said Dorothy, 'between two and eighteen.'

'Eight,' said Mrs Jones concisely.

'Mildred,' Matthew exclaimed, 'do tell me what's happening to Freddy!'

'Freddy? Well, he's not marrying the Greek. Emrys put a stop to that, said money wasn't everything. Not so sure m'self.'

He called the roll of her other sons, expressing delight and interest at the news of each. Dorothy was furious. Feeling obscurely that she had better not take things out on Mrs Jones, she decided to take them out on Daniel.

'Mr Skipton!' she called in her most penetrating tones, 'are you writing anything at the moment?'

Daniel non-comittally showed his teeth.

'Because you haven't published anything since 1946. Don't you think there's value in actual fertility?'

'I shall publish nothing till I am content that it is perfect.'

'Yes, but how will you know it is? I mean, *you* can't possibly judge.'

He looked away.

'He can, Dotty,' said Duncan eagerly, 'he has the most remarkable assurance of anyone I have *ever* met.'

'Now don't be silly, he's got a tongue, he can answer for himself.'

'I do not choose to answer for myself,' said Daniel.

She burst out, 'There you go!'

'What do you mean, Dotty, "There he goes"?'

'He's like the rest of you, forever taking umbrage about something. It's a fair cow.' She had forgotten herself, or perhaps had remembered. 'You are making it a perfectly beastly holiday for me, I'm fed up with the lot of you.'

Cosmo begged her not to upset herself. He explained hurriedly to the others that she had been working on her first act all the morning, and was strung up. Daniel fancied that at this point he kicked his wife under the table.

But she was not to be deterred. It seemed to her that a tantrum was the best means of attracting attention away from her hostess, and she let it rip. She cried out, addressing herself to Mrs Jones, that nobody could imagine just how miserable it was, to work like a dog all year, struggling to write and to keep a home together, giving absolutely all her emotive residue to her sons, with just one glimmer of light ahead – the thought of a holiday with friends: and then to have those friends being as selfish and disagreeable as possible, never taking into account that she was an artist and that her nerves were on the stretch, never wanting to go where she wanted to go, always wandering off like a crowd of demented trippers, picking up strangers and dragging them in, keeping her waiting for her meals...

'Don't, my dear,' said Cosmo in a priestly manner, 'it is not worth it. Nothing is worth it. Your creative work is all that counts.'

'Now let me get this quite straight,' said Mrs Jones. She finished her slice of *cramique* before she continued. 'Is Mr Skipton of your party?'

'Mr Skipton is just somebody we met here –' Dorothy began.

'Then why, Mrs Hines, are you so annoyed with him? I can't for m' life see what the poor man has to do with it.'

Dorothy's neck swelled up. 'I am awfully sorry, Mrs Jones, but this is a difference of opinion *en famille* and I couldn't possibly explain it to you. It is purely domestic. And I don't use my husband's name as I prefer to be a person in my own right.'

'Well, he's quite a person in his,' the hostess said unexpectedly, 'best bookshop in W1, Wulfric says, like a good club; he reads, *I* don't, he ought to know. You must know Wulfric, Mr Hines. Doesn't call himself that, of course, hates the family forenames, anyway, he doesn't have to use it. You know him, you must. Breckenridge,' she said encouragingly.

Cosmo knew him. He went so bright red that the pale hair on his cheeks took on a sparkle. This time he certainly kicked Dorothy, for she gave a suppressed yelp of pain.

'Lord Breckenridge,' he said distinctly, for her benefit, 'is one of my most amusing and knowledgeable clients. Yes, of course, we've known each other for years. Years and years and years,' he mused idyllically.

At this point Duncan smuggled into Daniel's hand a strip torn from a cigarette carton on which he had written,

'Duke of –'s granddaughter, by 2nd son, m. Jones but madly grand.'

Daniel was torn by three emotions. The first was fury, that snobbery like this should exist, that the duke's descendant should be prized above the great artist. He thought of Shakespeare's bootlicking to Southampton, and was ashamed both for Shakespeare and himself. The second was consolation, that he should find himself in the company of a woman of his own kind, who had his own standards. The third was hope, that she might come in useful, in some way or other.

Dorothy, unstoppable, was demanding to know whether Breckenridge bought poetry or just the latest smart rubbish by one lot of Etonians and praised by another lot.

'Don't follow you,' said Mrs Jones, 'five of m' boys went to Eton and none of 'em writes.'

'Now I am going to exert the authority of a husband,' said Cosmo, 'and insist that my wife goes back to rest. She has worn herself out today and when that happens I have to be stern with her.'

'Put your feet higher than your head,' Mrs Jones called after Dorothy good-naturedly as she angrily withdrew; she did not appear to bear malice. 'Best thing to do is lie on the carpet and put your feet on the bed. Nothing like it.'

They watched Cosmo and his wife retreating, and for a few moments nobody said anything.

Then Duncan murmured that Dorothy was a sweety really, though this was not one of her good days.

'Silly gel,' said Mrs Jones, 'crosspatch, m' father would have called her.' She finished another slice of *cramique* and paid the bill.

'Are you in Bruges for long?' Daniel asked her remotely, as if it were a mere politeness and of no real moment to him.

'Two days, three. I don't know.'

Somehow she must attend Querini's recital, if (qualms assailed him) it were ever given.

He asked her casually if she knew the Count.

'Don't think so,' she replied. 'May do; Emrys don't like Italian food, so I haven't been there since I was a gel.'

Matthew offered eagerly to escort her back to her hotel in the Noordzandstraat, but she shook her head.

'I'm going to ask Mr Skipton to walk a little way with me,' she said, 'if he's nothing else to do.'

Something moved in Daniel which was as like love as anything he had ever known in his life, love not for Mrs Jones, who was too spiky to inspire any gentle emotion, but love for that beautiful instinct, born of generations of breeding, which had known him instantly for what he was.

'I shall be honoured,' he said. 'I am at your service.'

As they walked away he turned the conversation to Flemish painting, and to his own contacts in the world of dealers: but this did not touch her at all. She did not like pictures, she had got far too many. She and Emrys had long forgotten what the wall looked like, since her father was forever presenting them with huge canvases of which he had himself grown tired.

'He's mean, y' see,' she informed Daniel, 'and it saves him birthdays and Christmas.'

She then asked about his writing. She did so not as one who has any interest in or knowledge of the subject, but as one who likes to give pleasure: and Daniel was not in the mood to split hairs. No Frenchman would have described Mrs Jones as especially *sympathique*: yet Daniel found himself pouring out to her the splendours and miseries of his whole career, summoning up for her his works of the past and his works to come. He told her of the envy and malice that had stood like Apollyon in his path: of the greed of publishers, of the bitterness of lesser men in the presence of the artist. For once he was putting into words thoughts that stood alone, with no calculating thoughts standing like policemen at the back of them. His spirit expanded. He felt, as he felt so seldom, like a free man.

'Don't make much out of it, do y'?' she said at last.

They were nearing her hotel: the time was short.

'Got y' troubles?'

He admitted that he was in some financial straits; but, he added, he would overcome them. His life had been one long process of overcoming. It was an art in which he was profoundly experienced.

'Debts?'

He did not answer.

They were at the hotel door.

'Now I could lend you some money,' said Mrs Jones thoughtfully.

He stood silent, his heart racing.

'But I'm not going to. It would be degrading to you and degrading to me. I've a certain respect for you, Mr Skipton, and I'm not going to make y' an offer y' could only refuse.'

Holding out the hand in its lovely glove, she took his own in her terrible grip.

'Mrs Jones,' cried Daniel, drowning, 'there is this question of Count Querini's recital –'

'I'll come if I'm here,' she said cheerfully, 'though I don't know one note from another. Come round here y'self and let me know the details,' she added. 'Matthew's a nice boy, but too much of a snob. Father in trade and never got over it.'

With a pecking motion of her head, she disappeared. Dorothy was a small bird, she was a smaller one. Daniel could have wrung both their necks and afterwards slept like a sated lover in the sunshine.

Sixteen

For the moment, one thing only was left. Creeping indoors, for he was afraid of meeting Madame la Botte, he set his table for work. He was going to interpolate two paragraphs, one a miracle of place, the other a miracle of characterisation.

Where was he?

112

With Billy Butterman among the islands.

He took out the green pen and looked at the tip of it, reverencing the spring from which the words would tumble in their joy and crystalline freedom, till they reached the discipline of the river. For him, words were not simply sounds, single or in combination: they had forms as visually distinctive as oriental ideographs. Even when he was at his hungriest, as he was now, since he had eaten only bread and butter that day, a word standing in its heavenly shape like a girl with a jar upon her shoulder could make him forget the cruelties of man and of nature. Sometimes he would fall in love with one word only, and scheme to use it: today he wrote 'fritillary', retracing his pen in delight down the wing-curve at each end, the antennae in the middle. It filled his room with its mothy light, it flickered the paper all over with peacock eyes of gold.

He wrote:

'The rim of the approaching isle was a crust of verdigris on the metal of the sea. The smell of it was wafted across the water to greet the voyagers, a scent like a singing, an invisible siren-sailing of welcome. As the motor launch drew nearer, other colours glossed into their vision, the clovy-mauve of clover, the far, faint purple of fritillary. White clouds came floating towards them like welcoming hands.'

He stopped. He didn't think much of that last sentence, it spoiled the colour. The verdigris, the mauve, the purple, the implicit slate-blue of the sea: white was too sudden, white was bad. And the clouds were not like hands, but like sleeves, sleeves drifting back from soft, possessive arms. He struggled to get it right, but without success.

'Clouds came floating towards them like sleeves flying back'... 'drifting back'... 'from soft, possessive arms'... 'from amorous arms'...

No good.

He got up and rinsed his forehead. He felt very hot, as if he had a fever, and there was a humming in his head.

113

Fortunately Daniel knew what to do with such a humming, how to make it work for him. He would let it spend itself on character. With his long falchion he would make these fellows skip.

Refreshed, he sat down again to his manuscript.

'As the cur Butterman set his padded feet upon the shore of the island, he became aware of the blasphemous presence of Coralie Sterling, mammalian playwright, with her hyena spouse at her side. Even Butterman, essentially coarse of fibre, his sensibilities blunted as his little snout, from which the hairs stuck out like whins from a heath, felt the pollution of their presence.

' "Oh, I say," Coralie moaned, in her Antipodean whine, "why did you say you weren't coming when you knew you were?" The hyena, who had snuffled up so much of the dead flesh of other men's labours, who had battened on their creative agony, who had taken his percentage of their souls, patted her bony arms. "Perhaps, my dear," he said, "Mr Butterman hoped to escape us?" '

Daniel stopped. It wasn't bad: but it presented new problems. What had Butterman to do with these new characters, and why did he hope to escape them? Butterman was a dirty Barabbas of a publisher, the hyena was a bookseller. What dirty tricks might they conceivably be doing each other and where did Coralie come in?

At the thought of her, his pen raced again.

This bit could be put in later on.

'She read to them, in the glutinous accents of self-love, imbecile verses engendered in the tripes and filtered through the clogged sieve of her mind, dropping finally on to the paper with such an irrelevant accretion of stale orts and rotting scraps that the tripes moved at the sight of them, thus bringing, in this meanest work of art as in the noblest, the end into holy fusion with the beginning.'

Not entirely satisfactory, Daniel thought, though he knew by the diminution of his head noises that it was nearly so; however, it must do for the moment. One can't have her reading verses, and see them on paper at the same time.

'She slid across the table, with a glutinous smile of self-love, a sheaf of imbecile verses…'

It was time for the sunset. He would not work any more.

Leaning out of the window, he saw the step-gables waver in the wind-stirred water, saw the river slowly fill with light red as the ancient brickwork, the great tresses of ivy tremble in the flow. He thought, struck with terror. How much longer shall I be able to look at all this? What will become of me?

With the reimbursement of his fare to Knocke, he now had frs. 48.90; and would have to go to Knocke again to collect his now miserable commission from Madame Houdin. He could not wait for her to send it, for soon he would have to pay some more rent. Well, he would at least insist that she pay his fare this time, which would mean a total of frs. 65.50. Add that to what he would have on arrival: and there would be frs. 98.25 in his pocket. He might fob Madame la Botte off with frs. 50, if he happened to be in the mood. That would leave him with frs. 48.25 to carry on with until he heard from Utterson or sold the Wouters.

When he did get his money from Utterson he could put his other plan into effect: which was, to change his publisher for Dorothy's. From a new publisher he could doubtless get another advance, and Dorothy's was a rich amateur who splashed advances all over the place like flowers and fruit from a cornucopia of the purest gold. So he must not quarrel with her. He must do something to please her. If he had to fawn upon her he would bring himself to do it, in the knowledge that she would laugh on the other side of her face when his book came out.

Seventeen

He worked all the next morning upon his book in a kind of hopeful frenzy. He had always known that, as a work of art, it was beyond criticism. How could one criticise a thing that was perfect? Yet today it seemed to him that he was writing a masterpiece of such universal appeal that riches were within his grasp, the joy of lordliness, the majesty of the peaceful mind in the well-fed body. He had only to finish the novel, and all would be well. There was no time to lose: he must not spare himself.

And so, in not sparing himself, he forgot all about time; morning slid imperceptibly into the bronze-blue of the afternoon, and it was four o'clock, and he had struck the rush-hour.

The journey to Knocke was disagreeable; he had to stand all the way in the hurtling bus, crushed against sweaty women with shopping baskets, men spreading out the evening papers on one another's backs. His head ached, his stomach was empty. It was a relief when they had left the cobbled streets behind and were on the road out of the city, rattling past suburban shops and houses, past fields blueing now into the twilight, where pigs like sunset clouds rooted under the orchard trees.

Indeed, he felt so tired when he arrived that he did not go at once to Madame Houdin's but sat down on the promenade looking out, with no thought but to breathe easily once more, over the violet spread of the sea. The disappointments of the day ranged themselves up before him like insolent servants proud of their own bad manners. He could so nearly see them that he closed his eyes.

When at last he got up, he was aware that his left foot was hurting him with a sharp, sore twinge at every step. Sitting down on the edge of the *digue*, he took his shoes off. One of the little knitted toes had a great hole in it, through which his own toe, protruding, had rubbed itself raw. It seemed to him, at the moment, like the final insult. So he was to walk three hundred yards there and back to her house, another hundred and fifty to the bus stop: and when he got back to Bruges, a quarter of a mile back to the Quai de l'Aube. After that, up three steep flights of stairs.

He had to take action. He fumbled in his pockets for something he could pad his toe with, but there was only an empty book of stamps with some stamp-paper still adhering. It had been sent him by Flabby Anne, the abominable hypocrite, as a Christmas card. Things might be worse. Stripping off the stamp paper, he wrapped it stickily around the rubbed toe, so that it took off some of the friction from his shoe. When it was done he rose and limped away, promising himself one thing. He would have Madame Houdin's commission: and out of it he would pay for a taxi to take him back from the Grand' Place to his home. It was years since he had sat in a taxi; the thought of doing so now, and damn the expense, was like a small sprig of greenness bursting out of the wilderness of his heart.

He was almost in spirits again when he knocked at her door.

Nobody answered.

He went on knocking, mildly at first, and then with mounting anxiety, till he was beating a devil's tattoo upon the flaking wood.

'It's no good you doing that,' said a woman, looking out from the house next door.

Daniel spun round. 'Why in hell not?'

'She's not there.'

'Where the bloody hell is she?'

'She's had an accident.'

'For God's sake what accident?'

'She had a fall, poor soul,' said his informant reprovingly, 'and don't you use language to me because I don't like it.'

'Was she badly hurt? Where is she now?'

'Oh, she was ever so badly hurt, it was those back steps, see? I always said, "If you don't get a light put there you'll go right on your back some day." And so she did. Just as I told her.'

'*Where is she?*'

'By God's mercy she's with the blessed angels in heaven,' said the woman, crossing herself and dodging indoors.

It was her door at which Daniel battered now.

She opened again, thoroughly indignant.

'Haven't you more respect?'

'She can't be dead,' said Daniel. 'People don't die like that. She dodged off, she's trying to swindle her creditors!'

'You ask Father Van Reymerswaele if she's not dead,' the woman retorted furiously. 'Six o'clock she must have done it and not discovered till ten when the man came to read the meters! If he hadn't, she might have stayed there for days.'

Daniel repeated that it was not true, it could not be true.

'And if that's what you think,' she shouted at him, 'my sister went the same way, only it was in the cellar.'

By now half the street was aroused, windows shed their orange and lemon lights upon the thickening dust, heads stuck out of windows, voices hastened to confirm what their neighbour was saying.

'Whom do I go to?' Daniel pleaded. 'She owes me two hundred francs.' It might as well, by now, be this sum as another.

'You're a nice one, trying to grab money off a corpse!'

'I don't believe she's a corpse. People don't fall down and die. It's a trick!'

'They do if they're her age,' said a disembodied voice, female, from a high window. 'She was seventy if she was a day, so you bugger off!'

'That's right,' said his informant, and slammed her door with a finality which made a clang in his soul like the violent closing of a life.

He limped back down the street; he was distraught. He did not, he would not, believe it. It was a trick of a coven of whores, they had brewed it up in their filthy cooking-pot, they were trying to rob him. He would get even with them somehow, he would creep up when they least expected it and catch the old bawd gossiping on her own doorstep. And then it would not be fifty francs she had to pay him, not a hundred, but two hundred, not five hundred, but a thousand!

He felt the eyes, like fireflies, watching him; not four pairs, or a dozen, or a score, but hundreds of eyes, blazing with joy at their successful cruelty.

His taxi. He would not be able to take a taxi. It was years since he had been in one, ten years, fifteen, twenty years.

At the junction of the street and the promenade appeared a cluster of lights bewildering to him, a golden pagoda blossoming against the dark, each lamp a lotus.

As he approached he saw it was the pavilion where they sold croquettes of shrimp and parmesan cheese, open for the first time that year.

Tugging around him every ounce of his cunning, he came softly to the window and found to his relief that the woman inside was unfamiliar. When she asked him what he fancied, he cut her short. He was looking, he said, for the house of a Madame Houdin, whose name had been given him by an English friend; he knew the street but not the number. Could she, he wondered, oblige him? He mimicked, as best he could, the Eleusinian smile of the sex-prowler who has been given a good tip.

The woman stared at him; then was lighted up like her own pavilion with mirth. Feeling this was, perhaps, unseemly, she straightened her face as if she were pulling down blinds.

'You're out of luck, mate. Died this morning. Now isn't that a shame?'

The delicious smell of frying, with its intimacy and its hot tickle, was too much for Daniel. He bought a *fondue au parmesan* for six francs and wolfed it down. He now had frs. 11.60 between himself and eviction.

'But I tell you,' said the woman compassionately, 'if you call at number 36 and mention my name, Wiertz, they'll see you get what you came for. Don't thank me, mate. Happiness is what I care about. What else is there? I liked a bit of happiness myself once.'

Daniel came home, slowly, on his fiery foot, grinding his teeth as each rod of pain probed upwards from his toe into his forehead. He hauled himself up the three flights, clinging to the banisters as he went. For the first time in his conscious life he went to bed unwashed, his teeth uncleaned.

Eighteen

It was a day of soft, invisible, interminable rain. Unobservant persons going to mass without their coats, having failed to notice the silvery sparkle of the roadways, were drenched within five minutes' walk from their front doors. Everyone was busy, for it was only a week now until the Procession of the Holy Blood, which fell that year upon the ninth of May. Mothers of little girls who were to be *Pucelles de Bruges* were sewing blue capes for them. Adam and Eve were repairing the skins handed down to them from generations of their forebears. The girl who was to be Mary was praying to be delivered from vanity and the little boy who was to confute the doctors studied his important speaking part.

Daniel lay in bed. For twenty-four hours he had not dared to rise lest Madame la Botte, ceasing to consider him a sick man, should also cease to send up his food. He felt trapped. He wanted to go out to see what was happening. For all he knew Dorothy and her party might have left the city, and Querini with them. But how could he go to see for himself? He would be trapped on the stairs, and rent would be demanded of him.

He had got up once or twice, to wash himself, to make a note or so in his manuscript, to see what the weather was like; but the moment he heard feet on the stairs had hopped back again into the sheets and rolled on his side, his eyes closed, pretending to be asleep.

But it could not go on like this. He was in a fever of anxiety. What was Querini up to? Had he made contact with the Marchese? Was Wouvermans keeping his word to hang on to the picture? For he was a wretched old bag of lies, was Wouvermans, he would sell his daughter or a candlestick to the first customer who made him an offer, without any stronger feelings about parting with one than with the other.

The bells had changed their tune and were pacing his griefs step by step. The rain, making everything cold, was rusting the iron tongues so that they clanged and stuck, jangled sour notes, cracked upon the giant semibreves till the steeples shuddered in distress.

In this hideous world there were still beasts insensitive enough to sing. A boatload of rainsodden trippers, Cockneys, bawled their way along the canal; *Roll out the Barrel* came clearly to Daniel's ears and the dirty vowel sounds blocked his Eustachian tubes, so that he could hear nothing else.

'If I were you, lying there all day like a lord,' said Lotte, who was giving the socks a quick darn, 'I'd think myself lucky. And I wouldn't sham sleeping; I'd have a cheerful word for anyone who traipsed up and down half a dozen times a day to see how I was getting on.'

He glanced at her under his lashes. She was a cabbage rose blooming in this grey room, her fat cheeks gathering to themselves what light there was, her broad beam, broadened further by the full skirt of pink cotton, taking up the half of his bed.

'I saw you,' said Lotte, 'you were peeping.'

'Who is that?' Daniel asked feebly. 'Did someone speak?' But he did not do it well enough, for she pushed at his face with her sock-covered hand and said, 'Oh get on, don't think I don't know you. I know who's playing the old soldier.'

121

Daniel gave her a shove with his feet that sent her flying off the bed.

'You devil!' she cried, as she scrambled for the chair. 'After all I've done!'

He sat up, too furious to worry about appearing to her in his night clothes, which consisted of a vest and a pair of pants too ragged for day-time.

'Who asked you to squat in my room, you tart? Haven't you any modesty? Don't you know what the priest would have to say to you? Get out now, because I'm going to get dressed, I won't stay cooped up here for ten minutes longer even if your damned mother is lying in wait for me.'

'Hoo, hoo, hoo,' said Lotte, 'we must be feeling better.'

She made no attempt to budge, however, until he made a move as if to fling back the bedclothes; and then she ran. Daniel looked after her with his first smile of the day. It hurt him like a split finger. Despite all appearances, she was a modest girl. She was also, certainly, he had no doubt of it, a virgin.

When she had gone he crawled out into the dank room and put his coat and trousers on over his nightwear. Painfully he cleaned his teeth, then remembered that he had not drunk his raisin water. This meant that he had to clean his teeth a second time.

He did not smoke and he scarcely drank: but occasionally, when things went well for him, he bought a few sweets. One was left in the pocket of his overcoat, a clove-ball. He sucked it slowly, making it last.

He was just thinking that he might make some attempt to go out when a noise broke out of so crashing, stumbling and slithering a character that it sounded as if a drunken cavalry officer were trying to ride his horse up the Duke of York's Steps.

'Oh no, you can't, no, you can't,' Lotte shouted in Flemish, the only tongue she knew. 'You let go of me!'

'*Je veux voir mon ami! Je crois que mon ami Skipton est malade, peut-être mort!* You get that broom out of my way, or *j'appellerai les gendarmes!*'

A girl's voice chimed in, mirthful and scared. 'Duncan! Leave her broom alone! Stop it!'

'*Si vous voulez le tug-de-war,*' Duncan shouted, '*vous l'obtiendrez.*'

Lotte screamed: something must have given way, for there was a violent thump, a rush of feet and the door flew open, revealing Duncan in duffle coat and a kind of pixie hood made of mackintosh, out of which his eyes darted their blue fire.

'Skip! I guessed you were ill! May I bring Pauline in? She's done a bit of nursing.'

Daniel cowered against the wall under his clothes line. The dirty soup plate was still on the table, his bed was rumpled, the night vest with all its darns showed in the gap of his jacket.

'Get out!'

'Now, Skip,' said Duncan, advancing, 'when a friend's in trouble one doesn't let oneself be prevented from helping him, even by that friend.'

'Keep your woman out of here!'

'But she's a sweety! She did six months at the South London Hospital for Women –'

'Keep her out!' Daniel screamed, in a voice he hardly recognised as his own.

Duncan shouted, 'Sorry, Pauline, you'd better wait downstairs, I won't be long.' He banged the door shut. 'What's the matter, old boy? Not 'flu, I hope? Do stop glaring, it's so awfully silly. You may not like me but I have immensely taken to you. Have you been ill? I say, you do want to know all the news, don't you?'

Daniel did, and the thought of it quietened him down. With as much dignity as he could muster, he switched the plate out of sight, kicked the chamberpot into darkness and turned up his coat collar.

'What funny socks!' Duncan said simply. 'Are they socks? How very odd. Is that what you wear?' He sat down on the chair and composed his round face, which had been struggling with an impulse to smile.

'Will you say what you have come to say, and then leave me?' Daniel demanded. 'I have had a chill. I have spent twenty-four hours in bed. I have had every care.'

It was repulsive to him to see this stout, happy stranger sitting in his room, observing the material wretchedness in which a proud spirit was forced to dwell. Nobody ever came here but Lotte and her mother. Here, at least, in this contaminated place, he had kept himself from the world's contamination.

'Are you getting anything to eat?' Duncan asked. 'I say, they ought to keep you a bit tidier than this. It's a shame, Skip, taking advantage of a chap like you. Don't they know you're – you're – '. He made a big hopeless gesture of admiration.

'I have asked you, Moss,' said Daniel, regarding the peach-fed hog with loathing, 'to deliver your message and go.'

Duncan protested. He didn't carry messages, not for anyone, not even for Dorothy, who, duck as she was, did like to queen it a bit. He had come on his own account, and had brought Pauline, whom he had met at yesterday's band concert, in the belief that her professional assistance might be welcome. Pauline was wonderful, she was learning the flute and piano at the Royal College of Music. She was awfully pretty; Dotty was hopping wild.

'I do not wish to hear about this lady,' said Daniel. He huddled himself on the bed. Out of some wall-building instinct he had wrapped the blankets round him from his waist to his feet.

'You look a bit like a merman,' Duncan observed, 'yes, that's what it is! "Where great whales come sailing by, Round the world with unshut eye –" Now don't look so cross, there's a good fellow. Won't you ever get it into your head that I actually *like* you?'

'What,' said Daniel, feeling the rasp of tartar on his teeth as he clenched them, 'is happening?'

A good deal was. They had decided to stay on for the Holy Blood, though they would have to pay a bit extra for their rooms. Querini had asked them to hear him sing at the house of some people on Wednesday, that was, next day: someone was coming from Brussels to play his accompaniment. 'You're invited, too,' said Duncan cordially.

Daniel acknowledged this with a nod, and with a look that would have stricken anybody else to the soul.

'There's a bit of trouble in the family, though: as it were. Dorothy's being so silly, you can't imagine. Just because darling Mrs Jones has one more son than she has, she wants to catch up – you know, "We want eight and we won't wait" stuff – and Cosmo is quite adamant. He says no. It would have been all right if he had only said no, but he also implied that poor Dotty was past it, so you can guess how frightful it all was! Matthew just crept away because he cannot bear obstetrical chat-chat except in her plays, when of course it gets transformed and sort of noble, so there was only me for her to shout at except Cosmo: and it was all outside on the terrace, and who should come up but Pauline, so I had to introduce her, and though I hate to say it, Dotty actually verged on the discourteous.'

Duncan, running out of breath, was content to sit and glow, while he pumped up some more.

'I must see Querini,' said Daniel. 'The recital will be at the home of *my* friends, who are of the most ancient Belgian aristocracy, and they will not tolerate arrangements being made by anyone but myself.'

'Well, that's all right. We're all foregathering with Old Q at the Cranenburg in an hour, so you just come along, that is, if you're fit enough.'

Duncan rose, towering up in his pixie hood so that the point of it just touched the bulb of the electric light.

'Don't be cross, Skip, I know you hate visitors, but I'm not a visitor, I'm a friend. Do say you don't think of me as a visitor!'

Daniel rose also, the blankets falling away from him as the bandages from Lazarus whom, indeed, he fancied he must resemble, so clayey-white he was above the untrimmed border of his beard.

'Mr Moss,' he said, 'there is something I must say to you.'

'Do,' said Duncan cooperatively. 'You go right ahead.'

'Since you have intruded upon me thus and have, by so doing, discovered the straitness of my circumstances, you can at least give me your word as a gentleman, if you are a gentleman, to remain silent as to what you have seen. You have subjected me to humiliation. As an artist –'

'Look, old boy,' Duncan said warmly, 'you can't feel humiliated in front of a chum, as it were. Now can you?'

'– as an artist, poverty, even hunger, matters to me little, But as a gentleman –'

'Skip, you've got gentlemen on the brain. Nobody cares, you know, not in this day and age.'

' – I am bitterly ashamed that I cannot receive you in the same fashion as my father used to receive his guests. I stand before you at this moment, and I feel shame. Are you satisfied? Is your curiosity appeased?'

Whether it was the way he spoke or the way he looked which at last went home to the uninvited guest, he did not know: but Duncan looked at first uncertain and then downright troubled. His blue eyes filled. 'Oh damn,' he said.

He sat down again.

'It is abominable, Skip, it really is. I'm so sorry. You ought to live in a palace like old Querini, chandeliers, that's what you ought to have, I can see you coming down one of those cracking great staircases… Oh, damn it! And here am I, I've got quite a bit of money which I don't deserve, I'd look an ass in a palace even if I had one.'

The ichor of hope fermented so suddenly in Daniel's veins that he felt giddy. Clutching the edge of the wash-hand stand, he waited.

'And the awful thing is,' Duncan continued, 'that I could have helped you out. But the truth is, I've run through

126

almost all my travel allowance, what with Cicely and now Pauline, and I'm having to borrow from Dorothy as it is. Oh, what a shame!'

'If you will go,' Daniel said, forcing up the words somehow, 'I will be at the Cranenburg shortly.'

'If I hadn't been a simply bloody fool, I could have got an allowance from the Treasury, to take photographs, you know. But I didn't happen to think of it.'

A voice cried out, spiralling itself up the stairway, 'I am not going to wait for you all night! What on earth are you doing?'

'Pauline,' said Duncan apologetically. 'Must run.'

Daniel, alone, said his prayers to a Creator who had been as poor as he, but, up to a point, seemed to have had more friends. The rain was heavier now, falling with its boring hush into the swollen waters of the quay.

Nineteen

They were sitting inside the café, still and silent in the yellow-plum light; they might have been there always, they might sit there forever. They were all there, all, that is, but Duncan, who had probably found it impossible, as yet, to part from Pauline. The place was crowded by a new influx of visitors getting out of the downpour, for the rain was spurting off the cobbles as it fell, the gutters were running like millstreams, and the thick flat grey of the sky had changed to ochre.

As Daniel joined the party, Cosmo smiled sideways, Querini bowed, Matthew raised a tired-looking hand. Dorothy simply glared, and shut her lips tighter.

'I understood,' he said, 'that you were expecting me. If that is not so, I will go elsewhere.'

'Mr Skipton!' She had spoken at last. 'When you say you're going to arrange something, we expect you to do it, not to disappear off the face of the earth just when you're wanted.'

The Count explained, exaggeratedly cordial in the hope of neutralising her unpleasantness, that all was well: his friend Guardini would arrive that night; all was to be quite splendid and at last they would be able to hear him sing as lovely as he could manage it. 'You will like my friend, too, 'e is artist *manqué* but so nice! I 'ave not seen 'im for, it must be twenty-five years, fancy that!'

Then Querini, Daniel thought, must be getting on for fifty: and the moment he had taken and absorbed the shock, he saw that his, like Matthew's, was one of the strange young faces sometimes achieved by middle age, tight-fleshed and polished, but dry: vivacious, but never relaxed.

'Well, we're waiting,' Dorothy said. 'What steps are you going to take?'

She was not really angry with him: but there was a deep brooding anger within her that needed release.

'Now, my dear,' said Cosmo, 'don't bully the chap. He may like it no more than we do.'

She looked at him as if he were a rotten apple on which she had trodden unexpectedly. 'Than *we* do? Who is "we"? Does Matthew have any cause for complaint? Or Signor Querini?'

They disclaimed this. Daniel did not. 'I am not going to this trouble for my own benefit, Miss Merlin. I have come here from a sick bed, and am in no mood to be brow-beaten by a woman.'

Her mouth stretched into an O of pained surprise. As she spoke, her voice soared, and made its switchback descent. 'Oh, I say! Are you an anti-feminist? But an artist can't be, it's a contradiction in terms.'

'There is no question –' he began.

'I loathe anti-feminists. I think they're contemptible. Where would all you men be if we didn't bear you?'

He resisted the obvious retort. 'If you will let me speak –'

'You're all the same,' said Dorothy, falling alarmingly on to the verge of tears. 'Why do you say you think of women as your equals when you know you don't? Duncan and

128

Matthew lurking in their beastly clubs which are *nothing* more than places where they conspire to do women out of the best jobs, Cosmo even refusing me the natural functions of my sex because he despises motherhood –'

Daniel pushed his chair back. 'I shall go to Countess van Haecht now and make the necessary arrangements. If Querini will accompany me, he can come back and tell you what has been decided.'

'And now it's you,' said Dorothy, 'without the moral courage to stay and listen to what you *know* is true because you might have to face the truth of it in your heart! Oh, it's so mean, so pusillanimous!'

Cosmo observed that since she now had the full attention of the entire café, she might consider a change of subject.

Starting up, she pointed to a figure, much distorted by the rain-streaked window, which was lumbering across the square.

'And there's that miserable, lecherous brute who calls himself a friend –'

'You can't accuse Duncan of not respecting women,' Matthew said idly, with his fleeting, mothlike smile, 'he has respected at least four since we came here.'

Duncan Moss dashed in, splashing off water like a wet dog, pushing back his hood with such vigour that a jet of rain went all over a woman in mauve who was eating cream cakes. She jumped up, protesting, her husband protesting in concert.

'Sorry, so dreadfully sorry, do forgive me, you cannot possibly think I meant it!' He hung the mackintosh on a peg on top of someone's relatively dry overcoat and brought a fresh protest upon himself.

When he had soothed those whom he had offended he came across to Dorothy and kissed her hand. 'Bless you, darling, you look so cosy and nice in here. May I have a big pot of tea and some pastries?'

There was a moment's silence.

Then – 'Do not kiss my hand!' she exploded. 'It is a

129

bogus trick, you know you don't mean it, you are hours late, and you don't show the smallest respect for me though you haven't the least objection to taking my money!'

He opened his eyes so wide that the copper lashes rayed out against the rosiness of his upper lids. 'Dotty! In a tizzy! Come on, come on, you tell me why you're so sad and then we shall all be happy again. Honestly, Cosmo, one can't trust you to look after this marvellous wife of yours for even five minutes. The moment I'm out of the way she gets all sorrowful. Don't be sorrowful, Dotty, when life's so splendid!'

The café was jammed with people now. A stout smartly-dressed man with white hair and pebble glasses was circling around them as if in search of a chair.

'There is no room here!' Dorothy told him savagely, but he was not looking at her. Instead he pounced suddenly upon Daniel, seizing him by both hands.

'My dear Querin'!' he cried in Italian. 'I should never have known you, never, never! My dear good chap!'

Daniel was stunned. He allowed himself to be pressed and pumphandled. He could make no sound.

'No, I should never have known you. But I daresay you would not have known me, eh?'

Daniel found his voice. 'I would never have known you because I do not know you. This is Conte Querini.'

The man dropped him at once, swung round and stared at the Count who by now was on his feet, trying to lean out in welcome over Dorothy's chest.

'Is it?' said the man doubtfully. '*You* are?'

'Guardin'! Guardin'!' Querini cried. 'How good to see you! Now you I would 'ave spotted at once. But I must not be rude, I must make you known to my friends.'

He introduced them to the Marchese who, still in a puzzled fashion, greeted them in excellent colloquial English and dropped into the chair Dorothy had forced Duncan to vacate. 'Well, well, I expect because I have grown old and fat myself I think all my friends must have grown the same.'

'You are a bit fatter, per'aps,' Querini said, 'but you are still my old Guardin' 'oo plays the piano so well and get into so much trouble with the Rector. When did you get 'ere? We did not expect you till tonight.'

The Marchese explained that he had decided to be driven over earlier in the day as he had business *en route* in Ghent. 'So I thought if I looked around a bit I'd be sure to find you. My dear lad, you have kept your figure quite remarkably well!'

'I do not believe he knows him from Adam.' Cosmo spoke quietly but clearly into Daniel's ear, and he smiled.

'Now you will come and play for me tomorrow night, and I will sing more beautiful than ever. Do you remember when you play for me Puccini and you put it up so 'igh I scream like a mouse? 'E was so unkind,' the Count explained, ''e know I cannot protest, I 'ave to go on – Oh, 'ow they laugh!'

The Marchese, too, dissolved into laughter. 'It was a filthy trick, really quite filthy. But hilarious, honestly, it was hilarious.'

'Yes he does,' Daniel whispered to Cosmo, who widened his smile and drew a face in the ashes upon his plate.

By now Dorothy had recovered her poise, had forgotten the slights to which she was daily exposed by those who called themselves her friends. The atmosphere lightened. Duncan was allowed to share the edge of a seat with Matthew provided he held his tongue, and Querini was boyish with pleasure. Daniel, who had been offered nothing to eat and had ceased to expect it, took his leave. He would, he said, go alone to the van Haechts' and report details of the recital later.

'But I shall not be free again till seven-thirty,' he said hopefully, 'as I have some business to transact.'

'Will you give my personal regards to the Count and Countess?' Guardini asked. 'They are such charming old people, but of course too old. People shouldn't be as old as they are. It is no kindness on the part of nature.'

'Join us for coffee after dinner, then,' Dorothy said to Daniel. 'We'll be at the Duc de Bourgogne. You'll dine with us, Marchese, I hope?' She added, 'Nine-thirty will be all right, Mr Skipton. We'll have eaten by then.'

Duncan broke in, 'Perhaps Skip would dine with us as well. He –'

'We have imposed on Mr Skipton quite enough!' Clytemnestra could not have looked more blackly upon Agamemnon than she upon Duncan. If I were he, Daniel thought, I would ram her head down into that disgusting cake and hold it there till she choked in cream. 'We are not going to take up any more of his time than is strictly necessary,' she added, with an assumption of gracious firmness, as if working together with him for his own good. '*Au revoir*, and thank you so much. So kind of you.'

Daniel went off into the downpour. His clothes were sodden, water squelched in his shoes. The painted stars on his tie had bleared and run into each other. In this condition, his heart swollen with rage, he went to call upon the van Haechts.

Twenty

There was no question that the gathering, so hardly achieved, so resented by the hostess, had at least the merit of making the social position plain. The company had somehow fallen, though without physical division, into two groups. Daniel knew what the van Haechts thought about him personally – at least, he knew what the old woman thought: the Count was rather too old to think, and was doing no more than totter about between his guests saying 'Ah ha?' or 'Is that so?' in a cordial, desperately anxious fashion as if he knew what his role ought to be but could not remember how to play it. But whatever the Countess thought, he knew that she had grouped him instinctively with Querini, the Marchese and Pryar; Cosmo and Dorothy were shown up for what they were: white trash, on the other side of the line, irretrievably *petit bourgeois*. As for the fat and ridiculous Moss, becking and beaming, prancing round with coffee-cups, he appeared to inhabit a half-world, not quite in the drawing room, not quite in the servants' hall, one of life's tutors, perhaps, a paid hobnobber within recognised limits.

Daniel, in a clean shirt, the white tie cunningly transformed by a patter of green polka dots painted over the smeared stars, was warmed by a feeling now very rare to him: the feeling of acceptance. He would be even more accepted, he hoped, when Mrs Jones turned up.

When he called on her she had been out; he had left a message. In return he had received a note saying that she would be pleased to come but might be on the late side.

So now they were waiting for her.

The rain, when it stopped at last, had left greyness behind it; but it was a humid greyness, steaming gently from the canals as from swamps of crocodile and hippopotamus. Even the Countess, suffocating in the heat of her own fire, had had to open a window.

The house was far enough from the centre of the town for the bells to make no more than a distant commentary upon the hour, the office, or the saint for which they rang. From the window one could just see, over the jumble of the roof-tops, the nineteenth-century tower of Saint-Sauveur, the turrets of eight pinnacles catching a faint snow-light from the rising moon. The wind was blowing from the north-west, bringing with it a drift of scent from the sea.

'It is quite extraordinary, Flavio,' the Marchese was saying to Querini, 'how you have changed, or haven't you? Perhaps the trouble is that you haven't. One expects it, one has a different image in mind. Look at me! My hair is white.'

'My 'air,' Querini said simply, 'would be a bit whiter if I did not use the excellent colour rinse. As a singer one 'as to look young, or the audience do not feel so like cheering, it is a very sexy thing, singing.'

Cosmo touched Daniel's sleeve. He seemed to be quivering inwardly with a kind of derisive joy.

'I do think people ought to be punctual,' Dorothy whined. 'I do loathe bad manners, especially in people who claim to be so *grand*.' She might have picked out the word with forceps and dropped it into a jar for sterilisation.

'I do not know what you mean by the word "claim", Mrs Hines,' said the Countess, sparkling into sullen life. 'I take it Mrs Jones is not an impostor?'

'Oh, I say, you know what I mean!'

'She did say she might be late,' Matthew murmured, looking put out.

'Well, then, it would have been better if she'd simply said she couldn't come.'

The Marchese bowed to his hostess and asked her permission to remove from the top of the piano a vase full of paper flowers and a photograph of the late Queen Astrid, so that he could open it.

She had, however, fallen back into her resentful dream. She muttered something like, 'What does it matter to me? I didn't want them,' and shut her eyes.

'She do not mind,' Querini whispered, 'she is old darling, we open the piano. OK.'

As they lifted the vase on to a table, dust like carpet-pile dropped from the flowers, making Dorothy sneeze.

'Oh, do be careful what you're doing! This place is filthy!'

'Oh, ah?' said the old Count, smiling uncomprehendingly, giving her a friendly little nod, and tossing his head back so that his yellow teeth were bared in something between agony and appreciation. 'You think so? A great treat in store.'

'I think we will not wait longer,' Querini announced, 'you must want to 'ear me sing so much, I want to sing to you. I love to sing ever so much. My voice is not strong again but it will still be lovely, you shall see.'

'We shall indeed see,' Cosmo murmured into Daniel's

ear. 'He is a bloody wonderful faker and his friend does not know him from Adam. I am going to enjoy this.'

He settled himself in one of the tubular chairs and crossed his hands benignly over his stomach, like Father Christmas in a big shop waiting for the children to be let in. Daniel could have burrowed both hands into the silky white hair and torn it out by the roots till his head was bald as his beastly soul.

'Do let's get on with it,' Dorothy moaned. 'No, Duncan, I don't want any more coffee. It always keeps me awake as I've told you a dozen times, but you never listen.'

The Marchese sat down on the rickety stool, got up, folded a cigarette carton and put it under one of the legs. He ran up the scale and winced.

'Oh, 'ell!' said Querini. He made a comical face. 'To say it is not in tune, that would be putting it mild. It would not do for the Wigmore 'All. But,' he added, brightening, 'they all make allowance. You do? No?'

'Of course we do!' Duncan exclaimed. He had plumped himself down on to a dirty mauve pouffe at the feet of the Countess, to whom he had taken one of his curious and unreciprocated fancies. 'Anyway, I wouldn't know all that much.'

Guardini shrugged and smiled. Broad-shouldered in his dark business suit, flexing his square hands, he looked unlike a pianist.

'Now you are all ready?' Querini cried. 'All comfy?'

They were posed, Daniel thought, like waxworks in a seaside show, and they looked as grubby and as nasty. The Countess was sleeping in one tall chair, Dorothy was glaring from the other, her feet not quite touching the floor. Cosmo lay relaxed. Matthew sat on the extreme edge of the chair with the split in the seat. The old man had retired to the sofa, and had courteously pushed the pierrot doll out of the way so that Daniel might sit there too: but Daniel preferred to stand.

'Then I explain. I start easy, because some of you may not know the 'ighbrow music. We 'ave the troubadour songs last, when you 'ave got into the swim: OK?'

'I hardly think,' Dorothy said with a small, quincelike smile, 'that we need quite such an elementary approach.'

The carillon tumbled its faint noise over the rooftops and in at the window, soft, sorrowful, expressing regret for time past and to come.

'Ah, ha!' Querini held up his finger. 'But you do! You let me do it my way, you will be satisfied. It will be lovely and all as easy as pie. I will begin with Duparc, 'e is easy as pie and so beautiful, you all cry like children. You see.'

For Daniel, this was a moment of such suspense that for a moment he went stone deaf. When his ears unstopped themselves, the Marchese was playing the introduction, and Querini, his face miraculously cleared of foxiness, open and eager as a boy's, his yellow eyes shining, was parting his lips.

'*Mon enfant, ma soeur.*'

Though Daniel had little interest in singing, he knew that this voice was, at least, not a bad one. It was a little weak as might have been expected after illness, but it wasn't unpleasant. At least he knew that. He sneaked a look around, but the listening faces told him nothing at all. Dorothy had assumed an intense peering look. Cosmo was still benign. Duncan was looking merry and peaceful. Matthew was looking blank as usual. The Countess slept. The old Count stared anxiously at the far wall, as if trying to recall some courtesy he had somehow failed to extend. Nothing. No clue at all.

But if Daniel did not know about singing, he knew about poetry; and this poem he had first read as a young man, at Cambridge, heated by dreams and inexpressible hopes, believing there were no heavens or hells which he would not be able to prise open for himself and enjoy as master.

So, at these words recalled to him after so many years, he felt a dreadful writhe of desire, destructive of his resolve, of all the strength he had lived by. It was not the *beauté*, the *calme*, the *luxe*, the *volupté*: it was L'ORDRE. That was the word, terrible in its capacity to ruin the soul with hopeless longing. To be offered the rest – that was nothing: a man could resist them. But to be offered them plus *l'ordre*: that was the thing, that was the torment, that was the deepest point of the heart's sick longing. For we live in a mess, Daniel thought, in a sickening, formless mess; we have beauty in a mess, we are luxurious in a mess, we are calm in a mess, voluptuous in a mess. And so we are vulgar: men or beasts: never gods. But *l'ordre* – that was the difference between man and God! Man is for ever miserable because he is set in competition with God, and God wins; God, in His order, inevitably, callously, in His cold calculation, wins.

Silence had fallen, only the idea of the bells, rather than the sound of them, dropping down and down through the silence of the sky, the silence of the room, into the bottomless seas of the night.

Someone clapped. The clapping was taken up, racing, rattling, sore-handed, all of them clapping but Cosmo, who was patting his palms together, pat, pat, pat, I'm sure that's very nice. Then Daniel looked at Dorothy and was stupefied by what he saw. The tears were pouring down her face, magnifying her protuberant eyes, trickling down the sides of her birdlike nose on to her lips. She looked ridiculous, hideous and entirely human. She got up from her chair. Advancing on Querini, who was still bobbing up and down in a satisfied acknowledgement, she grasped both his hands.

'But you are a glorious singer!' she cried, with a great snuffle to clear her voice. 'You are absolutely glorious, you really are! Why didn't you *tell* us you were glorious? And why don't you take better care of yourself?'

'But I tell you, I sing lovely! And I tell you, I 'ave trouble with my larynx. But I get well, and you tip off people at the Wigmore 'All, no?'

'You've come on since Padua,' Guardini said, 'a tremendous improvement. But you're having to strain a bit.'

Daniel had moved over to stand behind Matthew. He whispered passionately, 'Does she really *know*?'

'Know?'

'Does she know what she's talking about?'

'Oh yes,' Matthew murmured, 'she's frightfully good on music, Dotty is. She would certainly know. And so do I. The chap is good.'

Daniel knew so profound a wash of relief that he could have spread his hands and ridden the wave like a swimmer. He returned to his place behind Cosmo who muttered, 'He can obviously sing. He is equally obviously a third-rate tenor from the back row at the Scala. And he is a fake.'

Dorothy had stumbled back to her seat. The concert continued. Daniel ceased to listen, because he had learned enough for the moment. But the anxiety drummed on behind his ears, and he still felt sick.

Twenty-one

Querini, elated to the verge of apotheosis, was just opening his mouth to begin his fifth and last troubadour song, when the cut-glass voice of Mrs Jones was heard outside the door.

'No need to disturb 'em if they're still singing! I'll make myself comfortable out here and take a glass of –'

There was some confused mumbling. Guardini dropped his hands into his lap with more artistic irritation than was shown by the singer, who simply shut his mouth again.

'No *schnapps*?' Mrs Jones's voice rose in sheer incredulity.

Querini sprang to the door and pulled it wide.

'My dear Signora Jones, for you must be 'er, better late than never! I am Querin'.'

Matthew leaped forward to introduce her, but she pushed him aside. She was still staring at the singer.

'But my dear man, I know who you are! Why didn't Mr Skipton tell me?'

Daniel, released from his stupor, jumped up to tell her that he had.

'No, no, no, you said Crespini. Never knew any Crespinis in my life. Querini – how astonishing! Don't you remember, in 1932, at...? Remind you later. Must meet m' hostess.'

Daniel led her to the Countess who, whether asleep or awake, did not respond.

'Madame van Haecht!'

'Well, what? Isn't it over yet? Do get them all out of here.'

The old man was upon her. 'My dear! A guest! Wake up, wake up, you've had your little nap, you're quite refreshed.'

Daniel introduced her to van Haecht, while the old woman laboriously surfaced from whatever submarine world she had inhabited during the past three-quarters of an hour.

'Mrs Jones,' she said at last. 'I met your father once, when we were at the Embassy in London.' She inclined her old head which, for a second, hung and swayed like a white chrysanthemum broken off at the top of the stem. 'Frans and I were not there long, Frans had lumbago so badly. Your father, too... Emilio!' She beckoned Guardini. 'Mrs Jones, may I present the Marchese Guardini, also his father... not lumbago, Frans and I knew his father. I am afraid we have no *schnapps*, we drink only beer. I don't know whether we have any beer...'

Daniel would have grinned to see Mrs Jones very slightly discomfited, if he had not been so strung up. He was in an agony of impatience, an impatience Cosmo's ventriloquist's dummy grin did nothing to dispel. Mrs Jones had recognised Querini: Querini had not recognised Mrs Jones. He was longing beyond all things for the Count's complete rehabilitation, to see him fling off the rags of suspicion as St George, in an idiotic and vulgar children's play he had been forced to endure at the age of six, had flung off his rags to reveal a mighty golden sunburst of breastplate, cuisses and greaves.

'Please go on singing,' said Mrs Jones. 'I'm tone-deaf but I don't mind it.'

She bowed to the others, patted Matthew's arm, raised her hand in Duncan's direction. Van Haecht offered her the seat next to him upon the sofa, which she accepted, first

139

admiring the doll. 'Amusing, that. Long time since I saw one of those, Betty Hedingham had one, didn't she, Matthew?'

'I 'ave really stopped singing,' Querini said, looking at her with a frown between his eyes. 'I sang lovely, but my throat is tired now. Miss Merlin is going to give me an introduction to a friend of 'ers on the BBC, so my cup is pretty full up.'

'Y' ever see George Wickman these days?' she asked him. 'Y' seemed to be thick when I met you at Longleat.'

'George...' He blinked. Then his face cleared and he gave a little skip. 'Ah, that would be Carlo you met! Now I understand!'

'Carlo? Aren't you Carlo Querini?'

'No, I am Flavio! Carlo is my brother, the little one, 'e can't sing for toffee, though 'e is the dead spit of me only not so gay.'

'Weren't you at Longleat in '32?'

'I 'ave never been to England. I am the throwout of my family, you understand, the bohemian one. They get jobs all over Europe, you understand, I sit tight and sing. But now I shall sing everywhere, and you shall 'ear me at the Wig –'

'Flavio!' Mrs Jones exclaimed.

'No, Carlo does not see George Wickman because my papa made 'eavy weather. My papa is not broadminded, and besides, 'e said poor George 'ad bandy legs.'

'So he did.'

'Me, I don't care what people's legs are like if they have good 'earts. But poor George was a bounder, I think.'

'They wouldn't have him in Budapest,' said Mrs Jones. 'I don't blame 'em. What is Carlo doing now?'

He told her. And as Daniel listened to their gossip, he felt that relief which is a total exhaustion of body and spirit, leaving behind it hunger and thirst and the desire for good sleep.

'There is no more coffee!' the Countess said very loudly. 'It is all gone, all gone, all gone.'

Only Daniel, it seemed at first, heard her. Dorothy, Cosmo and Matthew had all risen to cluster around the sofa, to pay court to Mrs Jones and Querini alike. Butter would not have melted in Cosmo's chapped-looking mouth. Guardini, head cocked on one side, was very quietly and surreptitiously attempting to tune the piano. Ping, ping. And then, after a pause, Ping, ping ping.

But Duncan had swivelled round on the pouffe, and was looking up into the old woman's face. 'You're awfully tired, aren't you? And we're such a mob. None of us wants more coffee, honestly we don't.'

She swayed her head feebly from side to side as if badgered by house-flies.

'I think you're so nice. I don't wonder you feel sleepy. May I come again?'

Her head dropped to her breast. She folded her hands in her lap.

Duncan got up. 'I say, Monsieur van Haecht, I think we all ought to be going now.'

'Oh, be quiet,' said Dorothy, 'mind your own business.'

'Skip, I think we all ought to be going. Be a good chap and drag them away. We can all go and drink *gueuse* with the left ear. She's dreadfully tired Skip, do be nice to her.'

Daniel stole a glance at the Countess. Her eyes were not quite closed. Under each lid was a millimetre of dark, venomous light, raying straight in his direction. He thought she might be silly enough, senile enough, to forget how much she had owed to his silence and his self-restraint, for though, apart from the dark twin rays, she might have been asleep or even dead, there was something dangerous in the set of her shoulders. It was as though an ancient moribund lion, long written off as a menace by his trainer, was summoning up the last of his resources for one last awful spring.

So he joined forces with Duncan in inducing the party to leave, though he was told repeatedly by Dorothy that it was for Signor Querini to decide the hour of their departure.

They came out into the full cascade of the moon, which was pouring into gutter and puddle, sparkling in the little moat of water that surrounded each cobble so that a whole quay was criss-crossed with silver. The swans riding up from the Quai du Rosaire were argent upon argent, scarcely visible until they swept under the shadow of a bridge. The wet leaves were silver, and still as stone.

Mrs Jones and Dorothy walked in front, the one as if by right, the other by conviction. Both backs were stiff, but Dorothy's was stiffer.

'So sorry I missed all the singing, but I had a call from New York.'

Daniel shuddered at the thought of so much money expended upon minutes' talk, crass talk, hollow talk, the talk of persons so filled to the crop with money that it dribbled out of the sides of their mouths.

'M' husband,' she explained. 'He gets bored, then wants all the news. He's never been much good at amusing himself,' she added, not at all pejoratively, but rather as if pointing out some peculiarity unique to Jones.

Duncan repeated his suggestion that they should go and have a drink. They all agreed with the exception of Mrs Jones, who said she was moving on to Brussels next morning so must get up early, and Daniel, who could not accept for fear that he might be called upon to buy a round, not merely of beer, but of whisky.

He said to Mrs Jones, 'I should like once more to offer you my arm, back to your hotel, if I may,' while he sweated with fear lest she refuse. He had something he must say to her; he had screwed himself to do it.

'Very nice of you, Mr Skipton,' she said, 'but I'm going to borrow Flavio Querini from his friends for half an hour – It's all right, Mrs Hines, I'll send him back when we've had a chat.'

It might have meant that she did not wish for Daniel's company as well; he dared not, however, entertain this thought. Placing himself firmly at her side, he said goodbye to the others. Mrs Jones also said goodbye to them, intimating that she might possibly see Matthew or the Marchese again in the course of life, but not extending the hope to anybody else.

As she moved away with Querini and Daniel she observed, 'Odd sort of gel, Mrs Hines. Can't pretend to like her. But I daresay she must grow on her friends. Mr Skipton, I don't want to take you out of your way.'

'As it happens, I have an appointment in Koning Albertlaan,' Daniel replied quickly, 'so your hotel is on my route. But if it were not, it would still have been a pleasure for me to accompany you.'

The great lady's glare with which she greeted this was not unfamiliar to him, since in his younger days he had not lacked opportunity to see great ladies at work. It chilled him, of course, for she knew her business: but he put it resolutely out of his mind and tried to concentrate upon the job in hand.

Querini, still excited by the success of his recital, got along with her splendidly. It was surprising how many acquaintances they had in common. She marked her acceptance of him as a person within her own social ambience by indulging in genial abuse of people they both knew, an exercise at which he also, gentle as he seemed, was by no means inept. Daniel repressed a hot twinge of anger at the great truth this suggested to him: which was that his own acceptance had not been complete. The Mrs Joneses of this world, he thought, were polite only to their inferiors, and impolite about persons on their own level only to other persons on their own level.

But this was not the time for anger. He walked silently, squinting at his moon-thrown shadow, while the other two chatted away.

'Now we shall say goodbye, Signora Jones,' Querini cried, 'but we shall meet again. You must not 'ate Venice or you will never see my sweet little Tiziano, my beautiful Niccolò de Abate! Promise you will not be so insular a lady, but look me up, as they say. Now promise!'

'I don't make promises,' she said briskly, 'but I expect I shall run across you some time. Give m' regards to Carlo, tell him George Wickman came to no good end. People don't see him now, y'know. Goodbye, Mr Skipton,' she said, less cordially.

'Now I shall call 'im Skip like 'is great friend Duncan,' said Querini, 'and we shall go off and join our friends for a drink, yes? And be 'appy.'

'No!' Daniel almost shouted it. 'If you'll excuse me, I must have a word with Mrs Jones.'

Querini was taken aback. 'You will not come? Not to celebrate?'

Daniel promised, in a frenzy, that he would join him later. He would not be long. He would celebrate, it was what he wanted most.

'Well, run along, Querini,' said Mrs Jones, 'can't y'see the man wants to talk? Heaven knows what he wants to talk about. This is all very odd.'

When they were alone together she looked straight at Daniel.

He said, 'I stand before you and I feel shame.'

Well, he began. When he had said these words to Duncan they had made him wince with pain; this time they came almost with ease.

'Y' mustn't do that,' Mrs Jones said heartily, having no understanding of the situation.

He saw his shadow sideways. One of the points of his collar had come loose and was sticking up; it gave the shadow a crow-like look, the look of a pecked crow cast out by filthy gormandising birds of the upper class of birds.

'I am about to ask you,' he continued, moistening his lips so the words would slide out and not stick upon them, 'to degrade both yourself and me. To be brief, I am asking you to lend me a small sum of money.'

'How much?' asked Mrs Jones, showing interest of an abstract variety.

'A thousand francs. Even five hundred would do. I am destitute.'

She was standing in the peachy circle of light radiating out on to the pavement from her hotel. He stood a little beyond it, still in the company of the shadow.

'D'y' mean it?' she enquired. 'Because if so, Mr Skipton, I advise y' to think again. If y' borrow money *once*, you're on the slippery slope for good and all. Emrys always says so. First time hard, second time easy.'

'Oh God,' said Daniel, and the sound he made had the hollowness of the place where God lived, and turned His face away.

'Struck a bad patch?' asked Mrs Jones.

He bit his lip and the bead of blood, no larger than the head of a hatpin, appeared on it; but she did not seem to notice. If she did notice, he thought, she probably would not care. Blood, to people like Mrs Jones, was stuff not to make a fuss about, necessary, displeasing, of no account. He supposed she had been smeared with it when they caught the first fox of her life, and had not objected to the filthy initiation.

'I am destitute.'

'Now, look,' she said, and gripped his arm companionably, drawing his rags into the light. 'Things may seem difficult to y' now. But you're a spirited chap: you'll come through. If I lend y' money, that will be the easy way out. Come, Mr Skipton, y're not made of sugar and spice. The easy way is not for you.'

'It *is* for me, Mrs Jones!' he almost shouted, the lump in his throat as hard and as fragile as an egg in its shell. He was afraid it might burst, choking him with its beastly yolk of emotion. 'Mrs Jones, I cannot pay my rent.'

'Y' actually can't,' she said thoughtfully.

He did not reply.

'Well, do think what y're doing.'

'I could not have spoken to you as I have done, had I not thought about it. I am a gentleman.'

145

'Cuts no ice,' said Mrs Jones wisely. 'Known some doubtful gentlemen in m' time. Antecedents beyond question, but shady, shady. All borrowers. Get on the slippery slope –'

'I am on it. And I am sliding down it at a rate too great for me to bear.'

She looked beyond him into the brilliant street, where the festival spirit was already casting its mysterious beauty.

'Well, Mr Skipton, y're out of luck. Can't change a travellers cheque tonight, and I leave early tomorrow.'

'I could call –' Daniel began with difficulty.

'Never see anybody before ten, I've made it a fixed rule. So I can't see you, because I leave here at eight. Sure you won't change y' mind?'

The smart shops glittered, massing their delights, the lace, the diamonds, the limitless, desirable truth for people with full stomachs.

'Don't you see,' he burst out furiously, 'that I can't? Do you think I like to stand here like a mendicant? I am an artist, a great one, born before my time. I –'

Mrs Jones was feeling in her bag. She said mildly, 'Now y' mustn't put that point of view, we had such trouble when Wulfric thought he could write. Here y'are, and good luck. Don't do it again.'

It was astonishing how such a woman could disappear utterly, as if the light itself had first made her transparent, then sucked her outlines away. There was a rush of wind from the swing door, and that was all.

Daniel stood alone, holding a hundred-franc note.

Fifty for Madame la Botte. The symbol of rent. And fifty to spare.

He jerked the loose point of his collar into place and his shadow stood erect. He looked, not a crow, but a man. A man degraded, perhaps: but he had survived such degradation before, and for less.

Refreshed, his spirits soaring, he nipped back through the streets into the peace of the quays. The moon rose clear

146

above the chimneys, a fed, euphoric moon. There was plenty to live for, the Wouters to deploy.

The heel of his sock had slipped under his sole. He bent down to adjust it, and as he did so a curious thing happened. It was as if his soul had turned into a man inside him: a small, strong man in his image, fitting into the greater shell as the lesser shell in a Russian toy. And that soul made a very slow, deliberate somersault, involving itself with Daniel's entire physical organism, with his heart, his lungs, his liver, his bowels.

When he recovered from this peculiar experience he let go of the parapet, which he had been holding, and drew a deep breath. Yes. All was well. His head was on his shoulders, his body balanced itself nicely enough on his legs. He took a step, he could walk.

But I shall have to go carefully for a while, he thought. I have been worrying too much. I shall have to watch my step.

Twenty-two

When he awoke next day it was upon a spasm of energy that sent him hopping straight out of bed. The sun was shining, the sky was a pale, silver blue and judging by the way the flowers in the window-boxes across the water wagged and flipped with the breeze, the wind must be keen and in the east.

He drank down his raisin water, scrubbed and dressed in haste and ran downstairs, tracking Madame la Botte down in the pail-cupboard and giving her enough money to keep her romantic imagination quiet. In consequence, the breakfast that followed him upstairs was more lavish than usual, three rolls instead of two and a dollop of jam on the side of the plate.

He worked for an hour on his novel, bringing Billy Butterman into a farcical and degrading situation *vis à vis* the repulsive bookseller, then went briskly out in search of

Querini, whom he expected to find taking coffee in the Grand' Place. No time to lose. Not a second.

He found him breakfasting with Guardini, who had a valise at his side and, it appeared, was waiting for a car to pick him up. They greeted Daniel with enthusiasm and ordered him a second breakfast.

'I shall never forget 'ow you were to fix up my recital, no, I shall never forget. And to give me a chance of meeting my old friend. What could be nicer?'

'The Marchese didn't seem to know you at first,' said Daniel, frightened that this was too blunt, but unable to resist the touching of his tongue to the hole in the tooth.

'Well, I know him now,' said Guardini, in his cultivated, infinitely English tone, 'and he knows too much about me, ha, ha! I tell him, he's an ass to dye his hair —'

'I do not dye, Emilio, it is a colour rinse.'

'– and starve to keep his figure. For myself, I am content to be an old codger. More comfortable. If my friend Flavio had any sense he would relax and let himself go to seed; because really there is nothing so young as seed.' They had reverted to Italian.

Querini retorted that this was the last moment at which he meant to let himself go, not with the BBC and the Wigmore Hall in sight. He outlined to the Marchese his dream of triumphing at the latter, only to be met with the same disappointing response as Cosmo's.

'I assure you, old boy,' said Guardini, 'they will not jump on chairs. Nor shout "Querin', Querin' ". Bordone's wife sang there once – Nina – you remember?'

'Too fat,' said Querini, 'that's why they did not shout.'

'She's gone to skin and bone now, poor girl. Stomach ulcers. – As I was saying, when she sang there all she got was six lines in the *Manchester Guardian*.'

'Because she was too fat,' Querini repeated stubbornly.

'May I revive a matter of which I spoke to you before?' Daniel asked him in Italian, and was complimented upon his linguistic gifts.

On receiving permission to do so, he said he had word of an interesting painting, now in the hands of a dealer who did not know his arse from his elbow. It was a small wooden panel, in indifferent condition, certainly of the early sixteenth century, and in his opinion – 'but I am not, you understand, a Friedlander or Berenson' – almost certainly a Johannes Wouters. If they were interested, he could almost certainly get it for them for no more than seven thousand francs. If it were not a Wouters, it would be worth the money: if it were – he need not tell them how much it would be worth then.

'Well, Mr Skipton,' said Guardini, rising at the sight of a Cadillac, chauffeur-driven, which had drawn up before the café, 'it's no use talking to me. I don't collect paintings: coins are my hobby. If you are ever in Brussels I'll show you my stuff. And now I must rush off, or I shall be late for my board.'

He and Querini embraced, with mutual expressions of gratitude and affection.

'No, no, no, it was I who had the pleasure of playing for you. Keep it up, Flavio, and let me know how you get on.'

The Marchese was ushered into his car and his knees covered with Mackenzie tartan.

'*Arrivederla! Arrivederla!*' the Count shouted after him, quite tearful at the loss. He turned to Daniel.

' 'E is a good chap. 'Is playing is quite mechanical and 'is soul is in trade, but 'e is definitely good. And rich as anything,' he added. 'My papa, 'oo is so mean, 'e says the Guardinis could buy up the Papadopolis tomorrow without so much as cashing a cheque. But my Tiziano, it would mean nothing to 'im. Not a damn' thing.'

Daniel brought him back to the Wouters. He did not wish to press the point, he said, but the dealer would certainly get rid of it within the next twenty-four hours, God only knew to whom: and a treasure would be lost. 'At least, I think it is a treasure. As I told you, it is simply my opinion; I have a certain amount of knowledge and experience, but I am not –'

'Oh, I know, I know,' Querini mused, his mind still on his departed friend, 'but I think you are modest. I 'ave always thought you were the most modest man.'

'But at all events, you would be interested to see it?'

'Oh yes, I see it! Very nice. A look would not 'urt me, don't you think?'

Striking the iron while it was hot, Daniel said they might as well stroll along to look at it now. He would first telephone the dealer to say that they were coming.

Leaving the Count to settle the bill, he went to the booth inside the café and gave Woutermans a few brief instructions.

'All right,' said the old man, 'but forty per cent is all you get, meneer, and if there's going to be any arguing you'll find the bird has flown when you get here.'

Daniel could not control himself. '*U zyt een vervloeckte dief!*'

'I am not a bloody thief,' Wouvermans retorted calmly, 'I am a business man. And if meneer goes on abusing me, I shall have to dock another five per cent to console myself for the insult.'

'Fifty,' said Daniel between his teeth, and hung up.

He returned, with furrowed brow, to the Count. 'Have you paid?' he said shortly. 'Because there's no time to lose. He had a dealer in from Brussels last night who seemed interested in the picture, and of course his nose has started to twitch.'

'Say I buy this painting,' Querini said carefully, 'and it is not a Wouters. Could I sell it again for what I pay?'

Daniel permitted himself to smile. 'Easy.'

'And if it should be?'

He named a figure, one on the cautious side had the painting been genuine. 'You could certainly get that in any sale-room in Europe.'

'OK!' Querini sprang down from the terrace to the cobbles, like one of the young men in English light comedies of the 1920s who invariably made an entrance through french windows, waving a tennis racket. 'I go and see. I must not seem too pressing, no? I must look cold and stern? Very 'ard for me, since I am not like that at all, I am always joyful.'

'I think you had better stay in the background,' Daniel said, 'and allow me to act as your agent.'

'Oh, but be careful! You would not, 'owever, make an offer without getting my OK?'

'Certainly not. Let us arrange a code. If, at some stage, you definitely wish to buy, or at least, to enter into negotiations, you might make some sort of unobtrusive signal –'

'I know!' Querini routed in his pocket and produced a mauled packet of chewing-gum. 'I think I 'ave one bit left – 'ere 'e is! If I want to buy, I put 'im in my mouth and I chew, chew, chew. It will be quite distinguished, I think, since I do not chew as a rule except in private, not even with my best pals. It makes one look a bounder, yes? – though it is good for the teeth.'

They walked along in the bright, battering light to Wouvermans' shop.

The old man, cleaner than usual, and looking benign, was waiting for them at the door.

'*Conte* Querini,' Daniel said, 'of Venice. Have you still got that panel you showed me last Friday? I want to see it again.'

Wouvermans bowed deeply and held the door for them to enter. He had tidied the place up a bit; it would, indeed, have looked respectable but for a ginger cat who had dragged the last of its breakfast fish on to a Persian prayer-rug and was messily finishing the meal. Wouvermans kicked it. 'Ah, dirty brute! Look what you've done, filthy pussy!'

'It's not to be wondered at that you don't prosper,' Daniel said disdainfully, fingering a lapel as if it were the ribbon of an eyeglass, 'if you let your stuff get in such a state.'

'Oh, but 'e is a nice, nice pussy,' Querini cried

reproachfully, making an attempt to chase after the cat but losing him among the junk-heaps, 'and 'e is only wanting to eat nice, on proper tablecloth, like the rest of us. *Gatto, gatto, gattino!*' he wheedled, holding out his hand so that the gold bracelet threw off a spasm of light.

'*Er staat u iets aangenang te wachten*,' Wouvermans muttered to Daniel, expressing his belief that he was on to a good thing with the Count. He said aloud, 'You sit down, *mijne heren*, I find you what you want. But I must warn you, I am not sure I wish to sell.'

'Come on, come on,' said Daniel, 'this gentleman hasn't the whole morning to waste.'

They had a distasteful fascination, the manoeuvrings of Wouvermans, who now made a pretence, first, that he was not one to be moved by clamour, and second, that he had mislaid the panel altogether. Tortoise-like, his rosy wattles trembling as he moved to and fro, he peered into cupboards, climbed up to high shelves which had obviously been untouched for years, carefully lifted every rag in the place to see what lay beneath, and at one point, as if he had forgotten the purpose of Querini's visit, insisted upon showing him with cries of enthusiasm, a filthy Kakemono of the poorest workmanship which, he said, he could let him have for two hundred francs. At last, pouncing upon some shadowy pile of muck beneath a table, he produced the panel, which he had carefully wrapped in a piece of sacking in order to give it a faint air of preciousness.

Daniel ripped the sacking off and snorted.

'I have had an offer on this,' said Wouvermans. 'I must be honest. I had a visit from one of the big men from Brussels. He has offered me eight thousand francs for this little piece of wood.'

'Get away, Wouvermans. Why should he?'

'He says it is early sixteenth century, perhaps late fifteenth.'

'Not on your life. Late sixteenth, at best, and worthless in its own right.' He handed it to Querini. 'Take a look at it yourself.'

Querini looked at it, blankly. 'It is not so pretty, no? And it is all dirt.'

'A simple cleaning job,' said Wouvermans, 'nothing to it.'

'I can't see a bloody thing in this murk. Why the devil don't you get yourself a better light? You might get more trade.'

'Well, meneer, it's sunny enough in the street. Take it outside, look at it there, I don't mind.'

Daniel sauntered out with it, turning his back upon the shop. He made his inspection a very long one indeed. Now: he braced himself. This was the moment of failure or success. He formed upon his face a look of repressed ecstasy, constricting his throat muscles till he could hardly speak. He let his eyes flame. He went quickly back into the shop, seized Querini by the sleeve, drew him aside, and spoke to him rapidly in Italian.

'*E vero?*'

'*Certamente.*'

'Here, here, here,' cried Wouvermans. 'What is it? I know you, Meneer Skipton, you're no fool. Have you discovered something? It's not a Memling?'

Daniel collapsed into a chair, holding on to the picture casually with one hand, with the other mopping his forehead. He was the embodiment of a man who has come to the end of his patience with simple-minded idiots.

'Oh, for God's sake! It's a nobody at all. Memling! Why don't you ask me if it's a van Eyck? A van der Goes? Eh?'

He glanced at Querini and his heart sank. The jaws of the Italian were motionless. He had to carry on, to temporise.

'If your chap from Brussels wants to buy this under the impression that it's late fifteenth, then let him have it and serve him right.'

'But, meneer, you saw something. You would not try to deceive an old man who has known you for years, a poor old man who always tried to help you when he could.'

'All I found out,' Daniel said coldly, 'was that it was middle sixteenth. A bit better than I thought, but more

153

damaged. There's a tricky repair job here.'

He heard a cough. Hardly daring to turn his head, he stole another look at Querini who was now chewing steadily, bearing the whole structure of his jaw from side to side and accompanying each movement with a click of the teeth.

'I'll tell you what,' Daniel said, tossing the picture back on to its sacking. 'If *Conte* Querini here is interested – which he wouldn't be, if he hadn't some Flemish stuff already and is short of middle-sixteen-hundreds – I shall advise him to offer you six thousand.'

Wouvermans gave an old man's scream.

'Six thousand? You're mad. I tell you, I've been offered eight.'

'By some ass with more cash than sense who will never come back again.'

'You know I would rather sell it to you, you being a friend, than to a stranger, but not for six thousand.'

'Take it or leave it.'

Rising with a gracefulness he could feel in the back of his own legs, Daniel took Querini's arm. 'Listen,' he said, 'it won't hurt if you let this go. You'll get something better in time. No, thanks, Wouvermans, there's nothing doing.'

With a cunning repellent to Daniel even though it suited his own purpose, since he despised that low and puny cunning with which modern man had replaced the princely strategy of the Renaissance, Wouvermans let them get out of the shop and almost as far as the corner of Sinte Katelijnestraat. Querini, not used to these manoeuvres, stopped chewing and threw Daniel a glance of baffled disappointment.

Then the old man chased after them, padding on his greasy carpet slippers over the cobbles. 'Seven thousand five!'

The haggling, the end of which they both knew, had begun. For Querini's benefit they kept it up for a long time: and when seven thousand had been agreed, went into the parlour at the back of the shop and drank to the modest deal in *schnapps*.

'It is not a big picture?' Wouvermans pleaded rheumily. 'You have not cheated me?'

'God,' said Daniel, 'another suggestion like that and the deal's off.'

Querini, who had said nothing up to now but was beaming like sunshine, explained that he could not put down so much at once in cash. He had not got it with him. But he would pay frs. 3,500 tomorrow, and the remainder the following day, when he could get in touch with his bankers in Venice.

'I will not keep it after tomorrow,' said Wouvermans, 'not even for my old friend Meneer Skipton. I dare not. I am a poor man, I have to take care.'

'Tomorrow midday,' Querini assured him gaily.

Daniel secretly admired him because he did not give the picture another glance, but let it lie on the sacking. It was true that Wouvermans knew quite well it was worthless; but if he had had his doubts, how convincing this lordly gesture would have been!

He did not speak to Querini again until they were back in the paddock of Notre Dame. Then he said seriously, 'May I congratulate you? You have made a fine acquisition, and I shall not be the last to envy you deeply. If I were a man of substance, I am afraid I should not have brought it to your attention.'

'You are my good angel, Skip,' Querini said, throwing an arm about his shoulder. 'I shall never forget you, you are as nice as Signor Moss says you are and that is something. Now I must go and 'ave a word with the bank 'ere, or we shall both be in trouble tomorrow morning!'

He went swinging off over the bridge, so boyish, so gay, so aristocratic in the cut of his head, the shape of his shoulders, that Daniel would not have been surprised to hear him burst into *La Donna è mobile*.

Daniel, too, had he been able to sing, would have felt like singing. So blue the water! So white the swans! So green the trees! So like topaz and cornelian, the bricks of ancient houses doubled in the quivering water, so giddy the tower of Notre Dame! Joy made him feel a little faint. He closed his eyes and the wind swept cheerfully over his lids.

Twenty-three

For once, he had a midday meal. Madame la Botte had never provided this, and he had long trained himself to do without it whenever the need arose: which was often. Today he went to a workmen's café near the site of the old station, and here he ate stewed beef with prunes, and a slice of apple tart. He felt at ease with workmen, he was a workman himself; he could never understand why they were not at ease with him, unless his caste betrayed him. He tried not to let it when he ate in such places, addressing himself in fellowship to everyone about him, and using dirty language as freely as they did; yet somehow these men never opened to him the mysterious porches of their comradeship.

Had there been any room for bitterness in his heart this morning, he would have felt it bitterly that parasites such as the van Haechts, the Marchese Guardini, the Count Querini, accepted him without question, whereas these humble men whose sweat he shared, whose labours he understood so profoundly since he himself had laboured as they had, though in a different fashion, should turn their upholstered backs upon him and chew their pigs' feet only with their social peers. But there was no room for bitterness. In the square outside the military bands were practising for the Procession, and the lion of Flanders was streaming and flapping with the wind. Fast wind! Daniel loved it. It was cold, it was sharp, it was pure, it was a killer. He understood the east wind, it was of his kind.

On his way home, he dropped into Count Thierry's underground chapel and said a word of appreciation to Our Lady of Succour. When he came out again the light blinded him, the clang of bells, the seething of the trees, made him deaf. He felt as if he were part of a festival, not a spectator but a participant; and he knew a strong, jealous adoration of his beautiful participating city, where every man, woman and child was involved in the common mystery, and jolly hogs like Duncan, tailors' dummies like Pryar, posturing bitches like Dorothy, white snakes like Cosmo Hines, were forever outsiders, trippers, foreign yahoos.

He found a letter awaiting him from Utterson. Folded inside it was a cheque for twenty-five pounds, drawn on the Banque de Flandres. This so intoxicated him with pleasure that he was not even so much as irritated by the letter itself, when he could bring himself to read it, though it would have driven insane a man small enough, unsure enough, to resent the mere nip of a louse.

> 'Dear Dan,
> 'Cheque herewith, in advance of royalties on that novel which I expect to receive from you within a week. Let me warn you, though, that if it should contain any caricature of myself as absurd and vindictive (not to say childish) as that of my partner, in your last unpublishable manuscript, you must find another sponsor for it, always provided one exists who is prepared to pay the thumping costs of a thumping libel action. (If you are not already insured against libel, I advise you to remedy the matter without delay. You are quite the most vulnerable writer I know, in that respect.)'

Daniel smiled at this. When Utterson saw the book he would plead on his knees for the privilege of publishing it, whatever portrait, cruelly accurate, it might contain.

> 'I could hardly say your last communication was uncivil; and I suppose I have to settle for that negative virtue and keep my word to you. You had better make the enclosed last, as there is nothing more to come unless you can earn it. And no one hopes more cordially than myself that this is what you will be able to do.'

This sinking patronage left no mark on Daniel, who was merely amused by the cur's vision of himself as a patron.

Publishers were tradesmen, and should be reminded constantly of the fact. If he had his way, they would all be compelled by law to wear some simple symbol of trade, such as a green baize apron.

'Why on earth,' Utterson rambled on, 'don't you come back to England? You would at least get free medical services and free teeth to bite your friends with. Though you scarcely make yourself lovable, none of us would like to see you in real want.'

Daniel imagined Utterson's secretary yawning covertly at this point, recrossing her silken knees, glancing at the clock.

'Incidentally, when I was week-ending in Suffolk recently with a friend of mine, who is a literary agent, he introduced to me a Miss Wrigley who appears to be your first cousin once removed. She is a nice old thing living in a gone-to-seed manner in a house far too big for her, and if she's not on her uppers she's not far off them. She says that so far as she knows you are her only living relation. So what you ought to do is to write something like *The Damask and the Blood*, which has a tolerable chance of selling, and try to give the old lady a helping hand. I mention this because it might give you something to live for, other than yourself.'

Daniel greeted this at first with a stare of incredulity, and had to read the paragraph twice to see whether his eyes had not deceived him. Then, so good-natured was his mood, he started to laugh aloud; it was quite hard to stop. What a wonderful old hypocrite she was, and what a superb actress she must be! He almost admired her for the way in which she had succeeded in making a fool of Utterson, winding him round her cunning finger. He could see her trotting home to the house that was 'far too big', her shoulders shaking, could see her gloating in the gleeful fashion of the senile over her last bank statement, her last rent statement. Wonderful, wonderful! And if the Commissioners of Inland Revenue ever caught up with her, she would undoubtedly bring tears to their eyes, reducing them from monoliths to simple, sentimental men with mothers of their own. He would like to see her do it. What a show! It would be better than Barnum and Bailey's.

Wiping his own eyes, he went on.

> 'I think you ought to make an effort to pull yourself together, Dan, as I have always thought there was good stuff in you. Have you run across a woman playwright who is holidaying in Bruges, called Dorothy Merlin? I believe she's going to lecture. You might make yourself agreeable to her husband, who is a bookseller, and could sell a pregnant rabbit to an Australian farmer if he put his mind to it. (DM is Australian herself, by the way, but doesn't like it rubbed in.)
>
> 'Buck up with the book, now. It might be saleable, if it's not chock-a-block with your usual silly abuse.
>
> 'All good wishes,
>
> > 'Yours,
> >
> > > 'W H Utterson.'

Daniel hesitated between two bales of desire: one, to go straight down to the bank and cash the cheque; two, to add a few flawless lines to his book. He felt the warmth of self-congratulation at the ease with which the artistic impulse triumphed.

He wrote: 'The effrontery of Butterman was beginning to break all bounds. Even the most patient of his friends felt a longing to kick the great, flabby backside which he swung from left to right as he walked as if under the impression that it had the baroque magnificence of a peacock's tail. It was sickening to see him bear down with unctuous refulgence upon a great artist, whom he was in process of sucking dry, to smear him with the honey of patronage while picking his pocket.'

Much polishing would be needed here: but the conception was right, the essence of Butterman was there.

He went happily to the Grand' Place and collected his

money.

As he came out of the bank he ran into Cosmo.

'Ah, Mr Skipton! Just the man I wanted to see. We're leaving tomorrow, not staying for the Holy Blood; that is, I shall go on to The Hague for a day or so, but Dorothy and the others will go home. We had, I regret to say, miscalculated how far the travel allowance would stretch.' He went on to invite Daniel to a farewell dinner at the Vandenberge that night. 'After all, you've put us in the way of some amusement. When I think of that swan –'

Cosmo went through the pantomime of a man convulsed with reminiscent mirth. In fact, that sort of laughter was foreign to him. Like all snakes, Daniel thought, he could only laugh quietly within the confines of his coils.

He replied that he would be pleased to dine with them, but only if he might first offer them an aperitif. He had, he explained, received an advance on his new novel. 'I shall not pretend,' he said, 'that my circumstances have always been easy. But they are readjusted now, I am happy to say.'

He could not resist the small triumph. Had they thought him poor? Had they imagined he had taken them to Mimi's with any sort of profit in mind? He would show them the kind of man he was, a proud man, in need of no one's charity. He was relieved nevertheless when Cosmo, after congratulating him, said, 'No, you don't. Dorothy would never permit it. You are our guest.' He added regretfully, 'I shall be sorry to miss this feast of gore. I believe it's all about blood, from beginning to end. So appropriate for this country, with its peculiarly blood-sodden history.'

Daniel flinched. It was as well the hyena was going. He would be incapable of understanding the sacredness of the great spectacle, he would pollute it by his jeering presence. What would he do when the Blood was displayed to the crowd, in the shrine borne by two bishops? There would be a great sighing as the people fell to their knees upon the stones, a darkening of the air as bright faces drooped upon breasts burning with worship. What would Hines be doing?

Standing erect, his blood-mapped, madman's eyes stony above his grinning mouth. In the old days, before God had settled upon a policy of temperateness and detachment, lightning would have wriggled from His hand to strike the blasphemer down.

'On this spot,' said Cosmo, still with the same derisive grin, 'they blew up heretics with water.'

Daniel changed the subject by mentioning his part in the sale of the Wouters to Querini.

Cosmo stared. 'He's paying fifty quid for a picture?'

'I must ask you to keep this confidential.'

'Why?'

'If the news got round, he would have half the dealers in Belgium round his neck.'

'So he's on to a good thing?'

'If you put it like that,' Daniel said distastefully. 'It is an exquisite painting. He has not bought it for the sake of investment.'

'The point is, has he paid?'

'There is no point,' Daniel said with careful irony, 'at which we should cut our losses. You did not, I believe, credit his *bona fides*. Yet he can certainly sing, or so your wife assured us –'

'Admitted.'

'And he is a man of birth, as Mrs Jones testified beyond a shadow of doubt.'

'Also admitted.'

'Well?'

'Well, what?' Cosmo asked blandly.

'Nothing,' Daniel said in disgust. 'Nothing at all. I shall see you, and Querini presumably, tonight.'

'You won't see him. He is going to a little performance at Mimi's.'

'Who the devil – ?' Daniel shouted.

'I thought he might care for it, so I fixed it up myself. You don't mind? I knew you only did so for us with the greatest reluctance. I hadn't the heart to ask you again.'

Daniel sucked his breath and held it. If he were not still borne up by elation, he would have struck the hyena across his grinning jaws. They would do Leda again, and he would not be there. Who would get the commission? No one. That filthy dog in the manger would not have accepted any – that was certain: and had taken care to see that no one else profited. Slowly he exhaled.

'I appreciate your consideration,' he said.

'I thought you would. One can't try one's friends too far,' said Cosmo with a feigned sententiousness that was peculiarly displeasing, 'or we find we have none left.'

Twenty-four

It was good to be among them for the last time, and not to need them. He was strong again, secure, pride burning high in his head like the wick of a lamp newly filled. The days of humiliation were over; and it sickened him to look back upon them. There were times, disgusting times, when he had been compelled to unleash submerged and horrible delights by thinking of humility; to frame images of himself standing cap in hand, trailing the mantle of his genius in the muck so that swine might safely cross to the other side of the way without soiling their trotters. He had seen himself lying in the gutters of the night, being kicked in the face, the buttocks, the groin, by those who at this moment were smiling upon him, assiduously refilling his glass. He had seen himself upon his knees polishing Pryar's toe-caps with his tongue, tying Duncan's laces with his teeth, while they patted him, and called him Good Dog, and put a lump of sugar on his nose. Beastly delights; and it was not long since he had been reduced to them as the only ones within a pauper's reach.

But that was all over now. He was Nebuchadnezzar, the mud washed away, his hair clean and barbered again, the last shreds of grass scrubbed away from his teeth; back on the golden throne among the kings of the earth.

He sat at Dorothy Merlin's right hand and she was gracious to him.

'I did have a look at your book, Mr Skipton, that is, I skipped through it. I thought it had something, though my own taste runs to the austere.'

Daniel bowed, and accepted another *fondue aux crevettes*. Turning to Duncan, he asked whether he meant to take his yellow ball home as a souvenir.

'Pauline pinched it,' Duncan replied sadly, 'she took a fancy to it.'

'Now, don't mention that ghastly girl again,' Dorothy wailed at him. 'You're lucky to have got off so lightly. I don't know what would happen to you if we weren't here to keep an eye on you.'

'She wasn't ghastly,' he said bravely, but beneath his breath.

'Why are you mumbling at me? Why do you pretend you don't want me to hear things when you know you do? She was ghastly, and would have been no good to you at all. And I am sure she was barren.'

Duncan was heard, but only by Daniel, to say that in the circumstances he hoped so.

Matthew said to Daniel gently, 'I'll tell Betty Hedingham I've seen you. She will be so pleased.' He tilted his head back, poised for the knives.

'I don't know how you stick that Hedingham woman,' said Dorothy, whose graciousness seemed to have been dispelled by Duncan's unfortunate reference to his girl. 'Honestly, Matthew, you must see she's essentially vulgar, whatever her –'

'Quarterings,' Cosmo suggested, smiling upon his wife with his usual air of decisive proprietorship.

'My dear,' said Matthew, 'it's just possible that Betty is a little coarse-fibred, but I don't see how she can be vulgar. She is Alf Dorset's sister, after all, and the whole family is pretty stuffed.'

'I wish you wouldn't fall into that trick of calling people

things to us that you wouldn't to their faces.'

'But I do call him Alf,' Matthew said, looking puzzled.

'It's the *pretentiousness* of the name,' she retorted, changing her ground. 'I mean, calling yourself "Alf" just to show how democratic you are, pretending to be a costermonger when you know you're a duke. Don't you agree, Mr Skipton?'

Daniel imitated her quince-like smile and cast it back upon her. It was not a matter, he said, on which he had any strong feelings. Any interest he might have in dukes was purely intellectual, and he was not particularly concerned, one way or the other, with what this one chose to call himself. He was an artist, pure and simple: and in this matter no artistry seemed to be involved.

'Oh, I say!' Dorothy appeared to start at C in alt and make a spectacular *glissando* down a couple of octaves. 'Are you suggesting it has any more than an intellectual interest for me?'

'Pauline is a nice girl, Dotty!' Duncan exclaimed suddenly. He had been brooding to himself for the past few minutes. 'She's an awfully nice girl, and I simply won't have you saying she's not.'

'Oh, be quiet! Was I talking to you? – Mr Skipton, you are an expatriate and I dare say you've lost the feel of English life. But Cosmo will tell you that my own name is infinitely more respected than the name of any of Matthew's smart friends. After all, half of them haven't got names, they're only places.'

She was, Daniel thought, an expatriate herself: probably an educated Aborigine. That was it; that would explain her. Though he did not really believe a word of this, he permitted himself to fancy her in the bush, in a loincloth, a boomerang or digging stick in her little hand.

'Skip,' said Duncan steadily, 'you tell Dotty Pauline was nice.'

She rounded upon him. If he was going to be tedious, he could go home. She wasn't interested in this girl, she didn't want to hear about her.

Matthew, who disliked contention, slipped quietly away to the lavatory.

'I had not the pleasure of meeting her,' said Daniel, 'so I can't make an assertion of any kind.'

'But you did hear her voice; didn't you think it was a nice voice?'

'Oh, be quiet,' said Dorothy. 'Where's Matthew gone?'

'To the gents', I daresay,' Cosmo replied, equably. 'Do simmer, my dear. We're trying to have a convivial evening.'

Dorothy denounced Matthew. He might talk about manners, but he had simply none. He might have been brought up by nannies, because his mother was too lazy and unnatural to *be* a mother, but in that case the nannies should have taught him to go *before* he came to the table. 'And he is such a ghastly snob,' she said. 'Why do you stick him, Duncan? I should have thought you had more pride.'

Daniel noted that she had now attracted the attention of nearly all the other diners. It was easy to see which of them understood English well, from the grins upon their faces.

The room was very full and noisy, not only with voices, but with the noise of the carillon and the military band penetrating from the Grand' Place. The wooden stands for the procession were now in place, they had finished hammering that day. Nevertheless, she dominated the row with the ease of Flagstad.

'Now I will tell you,' she said, leaning across the table, her eyes bulging, 'why he is such a snob. It is a sort of sublimation. Because he has never married, because he has not had the fulfilment of parenthood. And why has he never married? Because he was so madly in love with that absurd mother of his, who clung to him like an octopus. Oh my God, I don't believe any of you realise just how appalling it really is, the curse of Oedipus! Talk about the curse of Cain,' she went on, though nobody had, 'the curse of Oedipus is ninety thousand times worse.' She had fallen into a conversational tone, fluent, instructive. 'The whole struggle of the child is to fall *out* of love with the mother. The greatest act of heroism any mother can be called upon to perform is to destroy that love. It is an agony to do it, but one must. I know how, with my own sons –'

Matthew re-seated himself. 'I'm so sorry. What are you all talking about now?'

'I know,' Dorothy repeated, 'with my sons, how passionately careful I have to be.' She broke off for a second to rebuke Matthew with a glare, and went on, 'It's true, Cosmo, isn't it? They adore me – that is a matter of fact, not of opinion – and I know my duty is to *smash* that adoration' – her fist came down into the butter this time, as Daniel had been hoping it would – 'if I am to make them whole men!'

'Here's my handkerchief,' Cosmo murmured, 'it's quite clean.'

'What do I want with a han –'

'Butter.'

'Oh! Damn!' She wiped her hand and tossed the handkerchief negligently back at Cosmo: it struck his lapel and transferred some of the butter to it.

'Waiter!' He stood up. 'Waiter! Have you got any petrol? I want to get some grease out.'

'Do be quiet,' said Dorothy, 'I'm talking. Who cares about grease?'

'I do.'

'Well, he'll bring something.' She sighed, as if it were a tremendous effort to her to suffer fools as gladly as she did. 'You are not married, Mr Skipton?'

He did not reply. He was thinking she was the beastliest woman he had ever met, and that he would be unable much longer to keep this opinion to himself.

'May I ask you, and I do so out of purely intellectual interest, why?'

'Because I do not like women,' said Daniel.

She coloured faintly, and seemed put off her stride. 'Oh, I see.'

'And I do not like men, either.'

166

'Oh.'

'So you did not see.'

'If you think I meant – '

'I am aware of what you meant. I am not a homosexual and nor, I think, is anyone round this table, Mr Pryar included.'

'Really,' Matthew protested, with his mothy twitch of the lip, 'I should, of course, be included, but I do not know why I am specially included. It seems a backhanded compliment.'

'Dotty,' Duncan said, 'you really are an old sweety at heart, I shall say so till I die, but you are quite preposterous sometimes, you know.'

'I see no reason, when I ask Mr Skipton, who is my guest, a perfectly ordinary question, why he should give me a rude reply.'

Her voice was rising again, and the interest of the room was reawakening.

Daniel felt glorious. This was his hour: a free man, he would act out his most profound desire, which was to put Dorothy Merlin, half-witted lyre-bird, pretentious rudas, in her place. He had not forgotten how she had ignored him in her lecture. He would not forget that she had just thrown her hospitality in his teeth.

'I gave you a rude reply because the question you asked me was impertinent. Furthermore, it is my habit, call it my luxury, the luxury of the artist, to speak rudely in response to plain idiocy.'

'Mr Skipton!' Dorothy said. She meant to shout, but her throat had shut down.

'I have sat here listening long enough to your chorus-singing. Have you ever done anything but sing in chorus?'

'Now look here, Skipton,' Cosmo began, with a show of anger; but he was filling up with amusement as the quays filled up with rain.

Dorothy got a grip on herself. She managed a sick smile of disdain.

167

'Now, Cosmo, don't stop the man. He has a perfect right to talk, don't you think? Nothing human is – '

'I am alien to you,' said Daniel, 'utterly so. I do not sing in chorus. I do not rattle out, in a half-baked fashion, the Freudian claptrap which has been so successful because any dirty-minded dunce can understand it. Not that I am accusing you, Miss Merlin, of being dirty-minded. Where no mind exists, it is impossible for there to be either dirt or cleanliness.'

She said with dreadful charity, 'I don't think you can be well. Do let us help you. I'm not in the least offended with you, I – '

'You are going to be. Oedipus-complex, my foot! It is the greatest error of human understanding that has been made in two centuries. Your sons do not love you, they hate you. All children hate their parents, all of them. That is why they prattle and cling and coo and fawn on their mothers, to cover their loathing. And do you know why they loathe them?'

'I think, Skipton,' Matthew began, 'that even I can hardly sit by and – '

'Oh, do hold your tongue!' said Dorothy. 'When I need your help, I'll ask for it. Can't you see I am terribly, terribly interested?' Resting her elbows on the table, she cupped her hands and put her chin into them. She looked, Daniel thought, like a crystal-gazer on the pier.

'Children loathe their parents,' said Daniel, who had for a moment been afraid of the internal somersault of the midget standing inside him and wanted to be done with them all as quickly as he could, 'because they can never forgive them the sickening physical humiliation of birth, the bloody entry into the world, the repulsive captivity of the navel cord.'

A waiter, his face impassive, murmured in Flemish into Daniel's ear that if he did not lower his voice he would be thrown out. At the back of the room, an over-excited Walloon had actually climbed onto a chair.

'He has asked me,' Daniel said to Dorothy, clearly and distinctly, 'to lower my voice unless I want to be thrown out.'

She rallied at once to his defence. 'But how *petit-bourgeois*!' she cried sharply to the waiter. 'This is a *private* conversation.'

'Oh, Dotty,' Duncan murmured, 'you're so wrong!'

'So as I do not wish to be thrown out,' said Daniel, 'I shall lower my voice.'

'But this is fascinating.' She was fighting back: no coward, Dorothy. He had to admit that to himself, though he liked her none the more for it. The only women for whom he had ever had the least flicker of liking had been cowardly ones.

'Your myth of the beauty of maternity,' he continued, 'makes me vomit. Were you ever actually present at the birth of a single one of your children, or were you full fathom five under ether?'

'Do excuse me,' said Matthew with a sick, polite smile, and he slipped away. Daniel never saw him again.

'I studied relaxation,' Dorothy retorted proudly, though she was scarlet up to the hair-line. 'I had *no* artificial aids. I was a natural mother – '

'You have insulted me,' said Daniel, 'your friends have patronised me. I am prepared to believe that Moss means well, but he has invaded my privacy and his pressed upon me a friendship for which I have little taste. I have eaten your food, and you have insulted me because I did so. May I say therefore, before bidding you farewell,' – he was on his feet now, exultant, but still holding his voice down – 'two things. I am a great writer. To me, nothing is of the smallest importance beside that fact.' He paused.

'Do let us hear the second thing, Mr Skipton,' said Dorothy, who was dewed with sweat all along her beak, 'we are listening.'

'The second is that a public capable of being swindled by such unctuous, owlish, stomach-turning drivel as *Should*

Seven and *Joyful Matrix* will always get the literature it
deserves. I bid you good-night.'

He looked his last upon her, briefly.

She had half-risen, was smiling tenderly, but on the
wrong side of her face. 'I bear you no ill-will,' said Dorothy
Merlin. 'But why do you pretend to hate my work when you
know you – '

He was rippling down the stairs as lightly as a young
man, he was throwing a franc to the waiter who gave him his
hat, he was out in the fresh, cold, starry night with the
lovely bells dancing all about him and *Maritana* crashing
away from the bandstand like the triumphant chorus of all
the heavenly hosts at the final banishing of evil from the
earth.

It was Duncan who ran after him, his face round, earnest
and tearful above the bulge of his duffle coat. He looked like
a deep-sea diver just hauled out on to deck.

'I say, Skip! Skip! Do look at me! You really are a dreadful
chap, and so nasty to poor Dorothy, but I do like you, you're
genuine to the core. Look, she lent me twenty francs this
morning, it isn't much, but I – '

Daniel picked up the big round coin from the fat palm
and turned it about between his fingers. He looked at
Duncan and smiled.

'Well, damn it, Skip, you can't starve. Even after what
you said about *Should Seven*, I can't bear to let you –'

Daniel had seen, passing nearby, one of the derelicts who
had attended Dorothy's lecture, an old, hairless man
without a collar, who carried a malodorous bundle of
something or other wrapped up in newspaper. He stopped
him and spoke to him rapidly, made the presentation and
clapped him on the shoulder. 'Go on! Off with you. Go and
stuff your guts. Go and get drunk!'

'It was for you,' Duncan said, his lower lip drooping.
'Oh, honestly, Skip–'

Daniel clapped him also on the shoulder and went
jaunting off across the square, his eyes on the floodlit

banners that streamed across the sky in bat-black, blood and amber. He did not look back.

Twenty-five

Too stimulated to sleep, he set out his manuscript and pens, and a ration of three clove-balls from the packet he had bought this morning. It was late. No lamp but his own would be shedding its light over the Quai de l'Aube, that steady ray from the lighthouse of the creative mind.

He wrote:

'When he had thus triumphed over his enemies, he knew a sensation of peacefulness so delicious and so strange that it was like the discovery of a joy entirely new, tasted for the first time by himself out of the whole of mankind. He strolled down the stone steps on to the hard flat sands, stretching mile upon mile, unbroken, unspotted, into the breathing darkness of God, whose breath was in the hush of the sea, whose mighty breast rose and fell in angel-guarded sleep below and above the heave of the turning world. The full moon, low hanging, had an aureole of gold; so that the midnight sands were golden, and the rim of the surf was golden as the beer in God's crystal tankard, which was made out of the glassy crowns of seraphim and cherubim who had cast them down before Him in Millennial tribute.

'This peacefulness first spoke to him and then invaded him. It was purely good; and as it rose throughout his being, he also was aware of that pure goodness which had always been a part of himself, and was now himself in totality. His scissored shadow lengthened over the sands as upon cloth-of-gold. The rocks of low tide were stranded on the beach; in minuscule caverns, anemone, starfish, leaf-green, leaf-frail crab, limpets indigo and gold, were lifted above the delicate wash to praise their Creator.'

Daniel counted the number of lines and the words in each line. Two hundred and forty words, roughly. A day's work. Now he slept without dreaming.

Next day he waited till noon; giving Querini ample time to make his first payment on the picture. Then, removing a clove-ball from his mouth and putting it carefully aside in paper, since he was too fastidious to be seen eating in the street, he went off to see Wouvermans.

'What's happened to his lordship?' shouted the old man, who was teetering around on the threshold, waiting for him.

Daniel stopped dead. 'What do you mean? Hasn't he been in?'

'Neither hide nor hair of him. I never thought there would be, meneer, come to that, duke, baron, or whatever he's supposed to be.'

'Then he's ill.'

'Ill? Ha! If ever I saw a gentleman in the pink –'

'I'll fetch him. Something's held him up.'

'I won't let my dinner spoil waiting,' said Wouvermans, 'nor will I give up my nap. You fetch him, meneer, if you can lay your hands on him.'

Daniel started off at a run. He was half-way across the bridge by Notre Dame when he realised he had not the slightest idea where to look. What had hyena Hines said? Querini lived in a pension where? Yes: behind the station. But in the snarl of streets there, where was he likely to be found? Heart pounding in his ears, both from anxiety and from unaccustomed physical exertion, he sat down on the stone seat below the parapet. What should he do and where should he go? Better try the Grand' Place. He tore through the garden of the Groenings Museum, invaded now by a hideous mob of sightseeing schoolchildren, on to the Dyver. He must find him, somehow he had to find him. Who did keep boarding-houses by the station? Mrs Rogier, Mrs Joest, Mrs Geertgen. If the worst came to the worst he could try them; if none of them housed the Italian, they might at least know who did. He would have been a conspicuous enough figure in those parts.

Daniel was running again. His stranded hair had come

loose from the meticulous combing and was hanging down his cheeks. His toe had begun to hurt again and pierced him with a red-hot needle at every step. He knew from an unwanted sense of freedom in his right arm that he had ripped open the armhole of his shirt.

He was seized and held in remorseful arms. Calceolaria eyes shone in his.

'My dear Skip, why do you run like that? It is so naughty, it does you no good.'

Daniel had not enough breath for reply.

Querini released him. He was wearing a suit of beautiful silky brown-bronze, a green-bronze tie, pointed shoes shone to green-bronze also, amber socks.

'Now you see, Skip, you should not do these things. You are not an old man, yes? But you are not a boy. I am not a boy. I cannot run. So it is all very silly.'

'I like to run,' Daniel said feebly. He wanted to drop. Querini steered him on to a bench under the limes and tenderly, with no air of presumption, put the hanging hair back into place.

'It is not so, Skip,' he said sorrowfully, 'you 'ate to run. You were looking for me, OK? You know I 'ave not yet paid the old man and you get in a 'orrible state. Well, now I tell you.'

Daniel looked at him, and his heart began to slow down like a steam train approaching its terminus.

'It is all silly,' said Querini. 'I go find you, the fat girl say you are out. So off I tear, right, and back you tear, left. It is a waste of energy, I think.'

The bells rang out, Geertgen tot Sint Jans, Tot Sint Jans. The schoolchildren passed in a crocodile along the quay, their faces as pure, as blank, as ravishing, as musician angels by van Eyck. They should have carried harp and psaltery.

'First I must explain,' Querini told him and he was smiling now as if at the sum of human tomfoolery, 'that my papa 'e is not only mean as a meezer, 'e is 'uman octopus. 'E live in Florence, Carlo live in Rome, I live in Venezia. But

173

we 'ave to go up and down, back and forth, paying 'im visits, and if we miss one 'e is like a raving lion. 'E hates us out of 'is sight. So when I come 'ere 'e says, "You be back in a fortnight, or I make things nasty." And I am not back. So when I cable 'im for francs to buy my Wouters, 'e cable back that 'e will send me nothing, first I 'ave to come 'ome.'

'But look here –' Daniel began.

'When I get 'ome 'e will give me usual enormous allowance. But not till then. So you see, if I pay the old man three thousand five 'undred francs now I 'ave not enough left for my fare to England, to fix things with the Wig –'

'You said you were getting funds from Venice.'

'Because I am an ass!' said Querini passionately. 'I forget I 'ave run low with the bank there, since my allowance is due and I do not mind running low. I could cable them to sell some securities but it would take time, and I am off to England tomorrow. If the old man would wait –'

'Can't you raise three thousand five?' Daniel demanded.

'Now look,' said Querini, 'I am off to try: Signor 'Ines is still 'ere, 'e will 'elp me, I am sure. So I will see 'im now, and at two o'clock I will call at your 'ouse and we will go to get the picture together. That will do? You make the old man wait, I see Signor 'Ines. And do not worry, my dear Skip, because I will 'ave that picture by 'ook or by crook. I know where I will 'ang it,' he said excitedly, 'in my own study, which is quite little – so nice, Skip, it looks right across the Canal Grande – there is a panel right over the chimney piece, with beautiful carvings of flowers and *putti* all round, it is early sixteenth century, just right. And there I will put my Wouters, and all my friends will come to see it and cry "Bravo, Querin', bravo!" So you see I must go now, I must lose no time.'

He was off, with his elegant fleeting stride, his tie fluttering over his shoulder in the keen wind like a Carpaccio pennant.

Daniel put his head in his hands and tried, just for a moment, not to think at all.

Then he returned to Wouvermans, who received him with a mouthful of sausage. 'Well?'

'He's coming about two-thirty. You be up and about.'

'I'll believe him when I see him,' Wouvermans said, closing the door with a bang an inch from Daniel's nose.

So there was nothing to do but to wait. Wait for an hour and twenty minutes. He returned to the Quai de l'Aube, pushed aside the plate of mussels Lotte had brought him and sat on the edge of the bed, trying to see faces in the dank marble linoleum.

By five minutes to two he was so tormented by impatience that he went downstairs and prowled about the hall. The door to the dentist's apartment stood wide open, and Lotte was inside vacuuming the sitting-room carpet.

'I'm cleaning him up while he's away,' she called to Daniel cheerfully. 'Know where he's gone? Off again to see that ex-wife of his in Ostberg. Mark my words, they'll make a match of it again some day. Not that I know how he could, you'd think it was like going back to yesterday's dinner.'

Feeling too weak to stand, he walked in and sat down in one of the dentist's pink plush chairs.

'You all right?' said Lotte. 'You look rather peaky.'

'I'm waiting for a visitor.'

'Well, here he is,' she said, turning her head at a step on the flags, 'I expect.'

He sprang up.

It was not Querini. It was Cosmo Hines.

Daniel gritted his teeth. He threw a terrible glance at Lotte, silencing her. 'You can do all that later, there's no hurry now.' He said to Hines, 'Please come in.'

'Pleasant place you have,' said the hyena, entering with an insolent saunter.

'Tolerable,' said Daniel, 'it's an agreeable situation.' Upon the bubble-glass of the door at the far end of the room was the shadow, not unlike a bird with a nose of enormous length, of something initiated persons would have taken instantly for a drill. He hoped Cosmo would not

175

glance in that direction or, if he did so, that he might be one of those untroubled by dental caries, who would not recognise a drill if he saw one.

He waved his visitor into another armchair, pushing across at him the dentist's silver cigarette box.

'Now listen, Skipton,' Cosmo said, ignoring this symbol of hospitality, 'you were so damned rude to my wife last night that most men in my situation would not have called upon you at all.'

'I am expecting someone,' said Daniel, 'so I shall be grateful if you will come to the point.'

'You're expecting Querini. Well' – Cosmo looked at his watch – 'he won't be here for fifteen minutes yet. Reverting to Dorothy.'

The last thing Daniel wanted to do was to revert to Dorothy, and he said as much.

'Reverting to Dorothy.' Cosmo crossed his legs, which were rather short, and made a St Andrew's Cross of his navy-blue arms behind his silken hair. 'I am fond of her. I have fathered her seven sons, who all, some think fortunately for them, others think the reverse, resemble me. We have learned to live together, which is just as well. But I should be the first to admit that her manner to others was, upon occasion, displeasing. Had I been some of those others, I should have clocked Dorothy, as the saying goes, more times than I care to count.'

Daniel looked around the dentist's room as if there were something which might save him: at the pagoda-like lamp shades, colour of gum-drops from a plum-tree, with plum-coloured bobbles; the glossy television set, with drink cabinets built upon either side; the statuette, porcelain, of a meagrely-clad girl in a big hat leading a borzoi; the convex looking glass, rounded with barbola work, plum and blue and gold.

'What about Querini?' The cry burst from him so unexpectedly that he failed to catch the sound of it, but only the echo which beat like a budgerigar all round the stippled walls.

'Reverting,' said Cosmo, 'to Dorothy. I have not taken offence. You may accept that from me. Therefore – '

The telephone rang.

Daniel answered it, and received a passionate plea for an appointment from a Madame Sustermans whose filling had fallen out. 'So sorry,' he replied, as one chatting to a friend, 'poor old Khnopff can't be with us for a day or so. Call again –' and rang off.

'Therefore,' Cosmo went on, crossing and uncrossing his puny legs, 'let us leave Dorothy out of it. I accept the apology you would like to make without obliging you to make it. Anyway, between ourselves, serve her right. No: the question is Querini. I know about his negotiations for a Wouters, whoever Wouters may be: you have told me. And now he has told me. But, Skipton, I cannot lend him the equivalent of twenty-five pounds because I have only just enough money left to get me to The Hague. And so, as I know you have such a sum yourself – which you have also told me – I strongly advise you to lend it to our Italian friend for the down-payment. Otherwise, I shrewdly suspect that he will go cold on the deal.'

The way Cosmo said 'I shrewdly suspect' was a clue to the man's whole character. He would not pride himself upon honour, charity, magnanimity or intellect: shrewdness was his pride, the very word adorable, whether uttered with the delicious advance of tongue to gums, or written with the revelatory juxtaposition, secretive and narrow, of 'sh' to 'r', 'w' to 'd'. Daniel was so engrossed in this discovery that he failed, for a second to realise what Cosmo had suggested. When he did so it was with a jolt like the descent of an express lift.

'*I* lend it him?'

'Why certainly,' Cosmo cast a complimentary glance about the room in which he sat. 'It could scarcely hurt you. And Querini, you see, has a kind of babyish passion for the fine arts. If he can get a thing at once, he wants it: if he is frustrated he throws a fit of the sulks and lets it go. I am a business man myself; I cannot suppose that there is no profit for you in this transaction.'

Daniel did not deny it. He was struggling to order his thoughts which, like pin-brained sheep out of the shepherd's control, were attempting to wander away over all manner of irrelevant hillsides. Suppose he did lend the money, and the sale was not then completed? Wouvermans would have to pay him the half of it in commission, which would mean a total profit of only seventeen fifty instead of the three thousand five hundred on which he had been banking. But if there were no sale at all? He stood to lose the lot.

'From what he says,' Cosmo observed, reaching out his hand at last to take an Egyptian cigarette from the box, 'our friend is as rich as Croesus, but dependent upon his father. And one cannot distrust a man with his obvious talents and equally obvious antecedents, now can one? I admit I was at one time wrong about both. But in the circumstances –'

Dead-eyed, he displayed to Daniel a row of false teeth perfect as examples of the craft that went to their creation, but not perfect in their power of deluding the spectator. They were a beautiful colour, neither too yellow nor too blue, they had a snaggle of exquisite skill built into the upper set, but they were sunken into a rose-pink substance as far removed from human flesh as wax from the flesh of flowers.

'I can't afford it.'

Cosmo got up, with a sigh, from the pneumatic cushion of his chair.

'My dear chap, that is your business, not mine. I can only advise. In any case, I am an entirely disinterested spectator. Do as you please.'

'It must be easier for you to raise – ' Daniel began.

'My dear Skipton! Have you the slightest idea of how far the English allowance takes one? As it is I have calculated – and I am not joking – that I must take a packed meal with

178

me on the train tomorrow, as the restaurant car would throw me so hopelessly out that I should be unable to pay my hotel bill at The Hague.'

He sauntered out into the hall, Daniel behind him.

'Think about it, Skipton, consider it. You have about two minutes to consider it in, because Querini is just coming over the bridge. As to Dorothy' – suddenly he seized Daniel's hand and pressed it gently like a flower in an album between his own – 'don't give it another thought. She asked for it, she honestly did, you know. And though I could scarcely say that I applauded you – No, I couldn't say that. But I bore it without strain, Skipton, without strain. Look me up in London; you know, Cork Street, next to the hatter's. Bless you, take care of yourself. Write another book!'

'Write another book!' he shouted, making his exit just as Querini set foot on the quay. He skipped and waved, and skipped: the sun skipped on his silver-gilt hair, flushed his ruddy cheeks with a deeper colour, between flamingo and orange.

'Write another book!' he shouted again, and went on waving till he was out of sight.

Twenty-six

Querini rushed in, breathless, carrying a square valise.

'Skip! You will lend me the money? Oh, please do! I cannot bear to lose my picture now. I shall be back in Venice on May 18th and I will repay you at once. Please, do not let me down, I am so afraid the old man will sell, and it is twenty past two right now. Look, I 'ave my case 'ere to carry it in.'

Daniel had taken his decision. Ordering the Count to stay where he was, in the hall, not bothering this time to assume proprietorship of the dentist's flat, he raced upstairs and fetched the money from a tin box which he kept under a loose floorboard. When he returned however, the Count was in the sitting-room, making out an IOU on the dentist's writing paper. He appended his address in Bruges (he was, in fact, lodging with Mrs Geertgen, who kept a clean, comely little *pension* within a hundred yards of the station and whose nephew was the coke-washer who performed at Mimi's) and his address, Palazzo Querini, in Venice.

'You are a good friend,' he said, giving Daniel a hug, 'you are not a meezer or a pie-face. Listen, 'ave you 'ad luncheon? Because I 'ave not. Let us go at once to get our picture, then we 'ave celebration at the Duc de Bourgogne, I 'ave enough spare cash for that. Shall I ring them up and book a table? I think we will not be too late.'

Daniel accepted with relief. Once the money was in Wouvermans' keeping he could eat with good appetite.

Querini seized the telephone. 'I want the 'ead waiter... Conte Querini speaking. My friend Mr Skipton and I, we want to 'ave luncheon... Yes, we know we are late... No, not later than a quarter to three, we will be there. Listen, we want the corner table in the window – you know which I mean... People there now? Then turn them out, they 'ave 'ogged it long enough…Conte Querini, yes, Q-U-E-R-I- — Yes. You remember my friends, Mr 'Ines, Mr Moss and Mr Pryar... Yes, that is the table we want. Good. We will be with you. No, just for two.'

Turning to Daniel, he hugged him again. 'Now we really run. You want your 'at, no? Please do not fetch your 'at, it is all wasting time.'

They were out of the house, running along the Verwersdijk, across the bridge, along the Quai Vert, the bright leaves straining after them as the wind blew, the water rippling their way. Daniel began to feel sick with the speed they were making. He begged the Count to slow down. A few minutes could make no difference.

'No difference? Look, it is now 'alf past two' – the bells were clanging out the half hour, the light ones and the big boomer – 'and we promise we will be there by then. If that dealer from Brussels should come back, the old man will think we are not coming, and will sell. Please, Skip, do 'urry!'

They had come up to the Quai du Rosaire, where the bells were jangling in the depths of the olive-green water and the swans had clustered into a ring like a Victoria Regia lily.

Querini glanced desperately about him, desperately at Daniel.

'I know,' he said. 'Come.' Grabbing his arm he ran him across the bridge, into the tiny square behind it, and into the foyer of the restaurant.

'You stay 'ere, 'ave a drink. I will run on, rush back.'

The head waiter came to them.

'I am Conte Querini. You 'ave my table booked? Good. Which? – That's right. Now you give Mr Skipton an aperitif, and I will be back, and you are *not* to let our table go. Skip, you sit at our table, do not let it be taken whatever 'appens.'

Daniel felt too exhausted to get even so far as that, not for the moment. He collapsed on to a sofa, panting for breath.

'Give 'im an aperitif,' Querini shouted, 'at once! You 'urry. 'E needs it.'

Daniel opened his eyes and saw the Italian was giving him a brotherly look, gentle, and compassionate.

'You will be OK,' he said, and bolted for the quays.

After five minutes or so, Daniel felt restored. He went into the lavatory, spruced himself, made his tie into a neater bow and went to take possession of the corner table by the window. The restaurant was packed with people finishing luncheon, or smoking over the remains of it. The air was veiled with the sapphire of cigars and cigarettes, hanging like some gauzy pavilion of Arabia just below the ceiling.

For a second the spectacle of this gorging squeezed his heart. Each one of these people, in an hour and a half, would eat enough food to keep a pauper for a fortnight. He hoped they would discover, after death, that Dante was not a symbolist visionary but a naturalist, a naturalist as factual and as uncompromising as Zola or Theodore Dreiser. He hoped they would actually find themselves wallowing in muck, drenched by interminable rain and mauled about by the beastly muzzle of Cerberus.

Yet his desire for their punishment did not last. Before his eyes was the most enchanting scene in the entire city: the small quay, roped with shining creepers; across it the square of houses, more Swiss or Germanic than Flemish to his eye, approached through an archway from the Wollestraat. Scarlet geraniums sparkled at a high window. On the rim of the parapet, at the place where Daniel had seen Querini the night he dined with Hines and the others, a young American steadied his Leica to catch the flowering swans. The whole of the quay quivered under the rain of bells, scattered like largesse by a rider in the sky. Jan van Eyck. Jan van Eyck. All glory!

But he had to face facts. It was possible that Querini would fail to repay him. Rich he might be; and a gentleman; and an artist; but artists, however rich, however well-bred, were not infrequently distracted by the claims of their art from the claims of their creditors. If he did not pay up, Daniel would lose twelve pounds ten. Well, it had to be faced. It was a chance that must be taken.

At that moment a soft American voice sounded in his ear. 'I don't want to make a fool of myself, but haven't I the honour of addressing Mr Daniel Skipton?'

Daniel looked up into a soft, round, reverential face with glasses and pearly jaws, a thirty-year-old face, perhaps, eager, well-fed, diffident.

He rose and bowed.

'I thought so! I remembered you from the dustcover. Do you know, sir' – the American had slipped into a vacant seat,– '*The Damask and the Blood* was one of the formative influences of my life? When I was majoring in English literature at Northwestern, I – let me introduce myself, Harvey Foulkes, now of Trenton, New Jersey–'

Daniel bowed again, his heart swelling up like a plum. 'I

happened to hit on your novel, and it did something for me. And then when I looked across the room and saw you sitting there I thought, "I've got to speak to this man even if he bawls me out". Sir, when I remember first reading that passage about Ravaillac's thoughts on his way to execution... I shall always remember it; it was after a fraternity dance on a very hot night, I was staying with a friend and I wanted something to read... I can almost remember how it went. "He could not imagine pain except in terms of shape and colour, the lip-like shape of a tear in the flesh, the holy colour of blood—" '

'Ah,' said Daniel eagerly, for this was up his street as nothing upon earth, 'but do you remember the next paragraph?' He quoted: ' "Their eyes shone in upon him like stars through a grating, though not, like stars, impersonal: they were shining with the most atrocious of human emotions –" '

' "That fusion of comradely compassion and the pleasurable anticipation of cruelty, experienced in the bowels, for which there is no name," ' Harvey Foulkes chimed in, radiant with success.

He seemed to know the book almost by heart, as Daniel himself did: except that there was no 'almost' where Daniel was concerned.

'To think,' cried Foulkes ecstatically, 'that this great work, this *seminal* work, is practically unknown, except to the perceptive few! It makes me so mad, I tell you –'

What he told Daniel was so enticing that time was lost. Lost until the head waiter coughed at his elbow and asked when the Count was likely to return, whether he still wanted the table kept.

Daniel had been so enthralled by Harvey Foulkes that he had somehow failed to hear the chiming of the hour. What now rang in his ears, like the bells that rang for Ravaillac, was the chiming of three-fifteen.

Where was Querini? He leaped to his feet, art forgotten.

The waiter presented a chit for the aperitif. 'Damn your

eyes –' said Daniel. 'My privilege,' said Harvey Foulkes.

But he was not even thanked. There was no time to thank him. Daniel was out and away, running along the Dyver, across the bridge, down Sinte Katelinjestraat, down the shady canyon of step-gables to Wouvermans' shop.

All shut. All dark.

He pounded at the panels, shouted, kicked. 'Wouvermans! *Vervloekte dief! Wat zyt u verduiveld aan het doen?* Wouvermans!'

Steps across the shop floor, padded steps, fuddled and slow. Grumbling.

The door opened an inch. 'Now what is it?'

'Where's Querini? Where's my commission?'

'How do I know where he is? I haven't set eyes on your precious friend.'

'But he was coming straight to you –'

'Well, he didn't. And now leave me alone. Go away! Go away, meneer, I'm having my beauty sleep.'

'But –'

'Go away.'

The door slammed shut. Bolts ground across it from within.

'God in heaven,' cried Daniel, and pressed his fingers into his cheeks.

Then he was off again, in search of Mrs Geertgen.

He did not greet her. 'Where's Count Querini?'

'Well, fancy seeing you!' she said. She was a large, slow woman, with a stomach-growth which made her seem perpetually pregnant. 'It's a long time since I set eyes on you, Mr Skipton. How are you? All going well?'

'Where's Querini?'

'He left this morning,' she said. 'He paid up, took his little case and off he went. He's gone off to England.'

Weak, trembling, he left her. He had no more breath for running. He stumbled back through the endless streets to the Grand' Place, his head throbbing, his mouth dry as blotting-paper. He dared not think, he dared not consider total loss.

At the Memling Palace he asked for Cosmo Hines.

The desk clerk was sorry: Mr Hines had checked out about half an hour ago. He was off to Holland; he had gone, he thought, to the airport.

Daniel sat down.

'Are you Mr Skipton?' said the clerk. He was new to Bruges: he did not know people yet. 'If you are, there's a letter for you.'

Daniel took it, and tore it open. His heart froze.

'My dear Skipton,
'I have a strong feeling that by the time you get this Querini will have made an abrupt departure from this agreeable town. I hope for your sake that this is not so, but I fear it.

'Having a lively respect for the laws of slander I could not, of course, tell you what I happened to learn from the Marchese Guardini after the recital you so kindly arranged for us at the van Haecht's; but you will admit that I tried, however obliquely, to give you a word in season. My words were (I practised them beforehand, so I remember): "From what he says, our friend Querini is as rich as Croesus" – the operative words being, "From what he says". And I continued: "One cannot distrust a man with his obvious talents and antecedents, now can one?" – the operative words in this case being, "Now can one?". They should have given you pause, Skipton, they should indeed.

'The facts, according to Guardini, are as follows: our friend is the throw-out of a wealthy litter, more or less disowned by his father, who is not interested in living for art. Papa buys his clothes and makes him a small allowance; he also sees he is paid a salary to act as curator of the Palazzo Querini, which still houses the family collection of paintings, though it is the property of the Municipality of Venice. Papa does not care for singers, and regards Flavio in the good, old-fashioned light of a rogue and vagabond. One may not approve of the attitude, but it is often so, I am sorry to say. To put not too fine a point upon it, Querini lives by a now diminishing talent (he is no green youth, being nearly fifty-two) and by his wits.

'I do hope, my dear Skipton, that you have not been stung. But if you have, you may at least have the satisfaction of knowing that your money will be devoted to one purpose only, to the service of art. I hope that will be a consolation for you.

'With sincere regards,

'Ever yours,

'C R L Hines.'

'PS. It comes to my mind that I have heard you, in England, referred to as the "unspeakable Skipton"; let me assure you, however, that I consider this a misnomer. I myself find you eminently speakable, and have indeed spoken of you with my wife. After all, Skipton, Dorothy is my wife. And I am sure you will admit that you were, let us put it at its mildest, on the raw side.'

Daniel tore this letter into pieces so tiny that a wedding might have taken place in the hall of the Memling Palace.

The clerk protested.

'Sweep it up!' Daniel cried violently. 'Sweep it up! Haven't you slaves? Haven't you helots?'

He broke away into the wild brightness of the square, was held up by a rehearsal of the *Pucelles de Bruges*, trotting along with their pink mouths piping the *Veni Creator Spiritus*, their white hats and blue mantles flapping in the wind with a noise like tearing sheets. He burst through them, out of the harsh sun and into the cold spring shadow.

Why the devil was he running?

There was nothing left to run for. He had all the time in the world.

Querini.

Querini he thought, as he fell into the slow, aimless lope of a solitary man upon a desert island.

Singer.

Nobleman.

Pauper.

And twister.

There was always something one could do, however: go to sleep.

Twenty-seven

When he went to bed that night he was so sure he would not get up next day that he did something he had never done before: laboriously, for he felt like a piece of clockwork running down, he washed out both pairs of his hygienic socks and hung them out to dry upon the piece of string stretched on drawing-pins over a corner of the room.

'Aren't you well?' Lotte had asked him earlier, when she brought up his supper and his monthly parcel of English books, one regional novel, one rural fantasy and a historical romance about Mary Queen of Scots, for reviewing which he would receive a hundred and fifty francs. 'You ought to get yourself a tonic.'

He had not known whether he was well or ill. He simply felt empty, with that emptiness in which absolute clarity of thought is possible, since only one thought can exist in it at a time. He knew his financial position, saw it written out neatly on the slate of his mind, in his own graceful figures with the sevens crossed.

Left over from frs. 100 donated by Mrs Jones	26.75
To come from reviewing, when possible	
to collect from office.	<u>150.00</u>
	176.75

One hundred and seventy-six francs, seventy-five centimes. It was all he had, was to have, was ever again to expect in this world. He had never been a man for long-term thinking; but now he let the antennae of his thoughts protract a little further than was usual; and when they touched desert sand they shrivelled and retreated. He lay back in the soiled sheets, thinking what a slut Madame la Botte was, to let Lotte change them so seldom. Dante should have had a region, above the gluttons, perhaps, but below the lechers, for the physically unclean; or a worse one for the la Bottes who, spotless in themselves, forced uncleanliness upon others. He despised Dante, a little, for his lack of enterprise in leaving so many of the less-advertised sins unaccounted for. He saw his landlady in Malebolge, lying for eternity on mattresses of foul straw, with pillows of dung, her nails too sealed with filth to pick from the fat creases of her body the undying louse: yet somehow, the picture did not give him the satisfaction he had expected, and when he tried to consign Hines and Dorothy, Matthew Pryar, Duncan and Querini to appropriate hells his imagination refused to work. He had a sensation too fleeting to be recorded in full consciousness; a sensation of friends departed. A sensation of *missing*. It was not so much a question of missing anyone or anything in particular – he could hardly have missed the people who had insulted and cheated him – but of feeling that something was lost out of the city, that it was no longer a living thing but a parasite of stone drawing sustenance only from the past, the past alone holding brick upon brick, stopping the waters from subsidence into mere dykes of mud and slime. A hollow man, in his hollow room, in the hollow city, he gazed around the walls and saw nothing but plaster.

He slept.

He was in a great concert hall, a member of the audience or the orchestra, he did not know which. They were playing Beethoven, perhaps the *Emperor*: He thought he recognised 'Milk and water, milk and water, milk and water', then '-and water, – and water'; but it was not that at all, it was one of the last quartettes. The conductor was using a baton with a point of red light on the tip, like a burning cigarette-end. Leaning over, he touched it to Daniel's flesh, two inches below the nipple on the left side. 'The C Major of this life, Mr Skipton! The C Major of this life!' Daniel could not find C Major, he did not know on which instrument he was expected to play it. The conductor's face swelled up like a pig's bladder into his own. His voice rang hollow in the echo-chamber of the dream. 'The C Major of this life, Mr Skipton! Don't you know what it is?'

He awoke to find the glowing tip still there, transfixing him with pain. He tried to seize upon the baton, but his hands gripped only the sheets.

He sat up in the dawn, which had flushed the opposite wall with rose-quartz and the thin green of Solomon's seal. The sweat poured off him, gumming his vest to his spine. He sat motionless, sweating, panting, gripping his hands around his knees, till the sting of burning had died away.

Three hours till the entry of Lotte with the tray: but he had never longed for Lotte, and he did not intend to long for her now. He lay down again, and inside him the little man took shape in his image, cupped tulip hands to his head and made the slow and awful somersault. But this time it was not the mere terror of the absolute disturbance of vital organs, of heart, lungs, liver and bowels: there was pain with it, too, not acute pain but a slow exploratory turning of the winch. Three hours to go, and he was alone. He had never minded being alone, and he would not mind it. He refused to mind it.

When the pain moderated, he remembered his dream. The last quartettes of Beethoven. And it seemed to him, in an uprush of bliss and of certitude, that thus he had brought his work to a climax: that nothing he had ever done his whole life through had been designed for any purpose but to serve that work: and that the work itself justified his every action, each action was a humble stone in the erection of the final edifice, a stone of no value if he left to be kicked around on the seashore, but in its proper place a jewel of inestimable value.

He woke for the second time at eight o'clock with a passionate desire to look in the glass. It was his habit to keep a small pocket-mirror on the chair by the bed, so he could spruce himself for Lotte before she knocked, for he hated to appear before anyone at a physical disadvantage. At the sight of his yellow face, the hairy flesh scooped out below the cheekbones, the nose jutting preposterously between the glaring eyes, he flung the glass down and lay on his side upon the pillow. If he were going to be ill they should not know it, they should not batten upon his weakness. They should not peer pop-eyed upon him, lay their sausage fingers upon his pulse, quack about doctors. His body was, as it had always been, his own affair. He had loved only through his eyes. He had never allowed his flesh to be polluted either by human affection or human concern. He pulled the smelly sheets to the bridge of his nose, drew his knees up into his stomach.

Far away, over the toffeefied, fudgy crumbling of the rooftops, over the green still hair-oil of the waters, the bells were ringing. He knew, from the volume of their noise, which way the wind was: it was gone from the east: it had veered to the south-west. And the room had grown warmer, the air was sweetly stuffy upon such portions of his face as it could reach. All promised fair for the Feast of the Blood, the day after tomorrow, for the sacred flow that was to purify cobbles drenched by the unholy blood of the centuries: there would flow the blood of Cain, the blood of Isaac, hitherto unshed, the blood wrung from the panchromatic coat of Joseph, the blood of Christ borne in the mystic bowl by Nicodemus and Joseph of Arimathea. All red, all cleansing: a fountain filled with it.

If I cough, Daniel thought, I shall spit the blood of my heart, of my creative triumph, I shall write in blood the C Major of this life. He swallowed and lay still, so intent upon stillness that he did not hear the knock at the door.

The silence was rent by whoops of Lotte's luxuriant laughter, her own unique mirth, bursting out like oil from a well in Texas.

Daniel shot up out of bed.

'Oh I never saw twenty before,' Lotte moaned, on such

190

gusts of breath as she could draw, 'I've seen ten little toes, but never twenty!'

Simple as mud, her pig-face scarlet with hilarity and bulging like a windsock, she pointed to the pendant washing. 'I never saw twenty, oh, Mr Skipton, you'll be the death of me one day, I know you will!'

Dumping the tray down upon the table, she rolled towards the chair and sat in it heavily, face in her hands, her shoulders heaving.

'Damn you,' said Daniel, 'I am going to die!'

'Not twenty, oh, I can't bear to see twenty, not even when I knitted them with my own hands!'

'Did you hear what I said?'

'We all have to die some time or other,' she said upon a sob and a hiccough, showing thereby that his words had at least penetrated some wretched subway of her brain. 'Oh, meneer, if you knew what they looked like, if you knew –'

She looked up then, and seeing him, sobered upon a rasp. Her big breast heaved, her diaphragm contracted.

'I say, it's high time you did get a tonic, you're as yellow as a guinea.'

Death was written all over his face like graffiti on a wall: he knew it: and this fool could not read.

'You eat your breakfast,' said Lotte, 'it'll do you good. And then I'll pop round and ask Dr Joos…' Despite herself, she could not keep her eyes from travelling upwards. 'Oh, it's no use, I can't – I can't – ' Mirth swamped her again, so much a pleasure as an agony, shortening her breath, and perhaps, in the last analysis, her own days. 'Twenty little black toes,' she let out on her upper register, the last one operable for coherent speech, 'do take a look, meneer, twenty!'

He slid down on to the pillow. Somehow she managed to haul herself up, to grasp the tray, to dump it on his scissored legs.

Tears were streaming down her cheeks, pearls on pink satin.

'Damn you,' said Daniel.

'And you've got a letter.' She pushed it between his fingers and went reeling out of the room. 'Twenty little toes, I never saw the like, ten was funny enough, but twenty...'

He squinted at the writing. His sight was blurred now, and the burning tip of the baton, once more recalling him to the note that he must play, promising him that if he could not remember it the tip would turn into a red-hot O, and the O to a furnace that would consume his helpless body, made concentration difficult. He grasped that it was from Flabby Anne, and for one half-hearted second he attempted to slit the flap. Then he dropped it upon the bedside chair, clasped his hands together over his stomach and, still balancing the breakfast tray, so that the coffee should not topple over and make an even filthier mess of the sheets, lay in waiting.

It seemed to him that whatever she might have to say, Flabby Anne, his last of kin, *rentier*, hypocrite, barnstormer, it could not matter to him any more.

PRION HUMOUR CLASSICS

HOW STEEPLE SINDERBY WANDERERS WON THE FA CUP
J L Carr
introduced by D J Taylor
"a wonderful book" *The Observer*
1-85375-363-7

DIARY OF A PROVINCIAL LADY *
E M Delafield
introduced by Jilly Cooper
"an incredibly funny social satire… the natural predecessor to
Bridget Jones" *The Times*
1-85375-368-8

THE PAPERS OF A J WENTWORTH, BA
H F Ellis
introduced by Miles Kington
"a gloriously funny account of the day-to-day life
of an earnest, humourless and largely ineffective
school master" *The Daily Mail*
1-85375-398-X

A MELON FOR ECSTASY
John Fortune and John Wells
with a new introdution by John Fortune
1-85375-470 6

SQUIRE HAGGARD'S JOURNAL
Michael Green
introduced by the author
"marvellously funny spoof of the 18th-century
diarists" *The Times*
1-85375-399-8

THE DIARY OF A NOBODY
George and Weedon Grossmith
introduced by William Trevor
"a kind of Victorian Victor Meldrew" *The Guardian*
1-85375-364-5

THREE MEN IN A BOAT
Jerome K Jerome
introduced by Nigel Williams
"the only book I've fallen off a chair laughing at"
Vic Reeves
1-85375-371-8

MRS CAUDLE'S CURTAIN LECTURES
Douglas Jerrold
introduced by Peter Ackroyd
"one of the funniest books in the language"
Anthony Burgess
1-85375-400-5

HERE'S LUCK
Lennie Lower
"Australia's funniest book" Cyril Pearl
1-85375-428-5

THE AUTOBIOGRAPHY OF A CAD
A G Macdonell
introduced by Simon Hoggart
"wonderfully sharp, clever, funny and cutting"
Simon Hoggart
1-85375-414-5

THE WORLD OF S J PERELMAN *
S J Perelman
introduced by Woody Allen
"the funniest writer in America" Gore Vidal
1-85375-384-X

THE EDUCATION OF HYMAN KAPLAN *
Leo Rosten
introduced by Howard Jacobson
"the funniest, sweetest and most ingenious book ever written"
Mail on Sunday
1-85375-382-3

THE RETURN OF HYMAN KAPLAN *
Leo Rosten
introduced by Howard Jacobson
"exquisitely funny" Evelyn Waugh
1-85375-391-2

THE UNREST-CURE AND OTHER BEASTLY TALES
Saki
introduced by Will Self
"they dazzle and delight" Graham Greene
1-85375-370-X

THE ENGLISH GENTLEMAN
Douglas Sutherland
"extremely funny" Jilly Cooper
1-85375-418-8

MY LIFE AND HARD TIMES *
James Thurber
introduced by Clifton Fadiman
"just about the best thing I ever read" Ogden Nash
1-85375-397-1

A TOUCH OF DANIEL
Peter Tinniswood
introduced by David Nobbs
"the funniest writer of his generation"
The Times
1-85375-463-3

CANNIBALISM IN THE CARS – THE BEST OF TWAIN'S HUMOROUS
SKETCHES
Mark Twain
introduced by Roy Blount Jr
"as funny now as when it was written in 1868"
The Independent
1-85375-369-6

* for copyright reasons these titles are not available in the USA or
Canada in the Prion edition.